XANADU 2

XANADU 2

Selected and
Edited by
JANE YOLEN

TOR

A TOM DOHERTY ASSOCIATES BOOK • NEW YORK

For the Pre-Joycean Fellowship

—with love

XANADU 2

Copyright © 1994 by Jane Yolen and Martin H. Greenberg

This book is printed on acid-free paper.

A Tor Book
Published by Tom Doherty Associates, Inc.
175 Fifth Avenue
New York, N.Y. 10010

Tor® is a registered trademark of Tom Doherty Associates, Inc.

Library of Congress Cataloging-in-Publication Data

Xanadu 2 / edited by Jane Yolen.
    p.   cm.
    "A Tom Doherty Associates book."
    ISBN 0-312-85368-8   BT 19.95/10.85 - 2/94
    1. Fantastic literature, American. 2. American literature—20th century. I. Yolen, Jane. II. Title: Xanadu two.
    PS509.F3X36 1994
    810.8'015—dc20   93-33498
                                         CIP

First edition: January 1994

Printed in the United States of America

0 9 8 7 6 5 4 3 2 1

Contents

8 CONTENTS

Xanadu—After You

"In the summer of the year 1797 . . . [i]n consequence of a slight indisposition, an anodyne had been prescribed, from the effects of which he fell asleep . . . ," Coleridge wrote of himself. Actually he had been taking two grains of opium to check dysentery and the results were the poem "Kubla Khan," in which the fantasy world of Xanadu was first created. We have no idea whether the dysentery was affected by either the drug or the poem.

Or perhaps it was all set off—dream, dysentery, and drug reaction alike—by the lines in *Purchas's Pilgrimage* Coleridge was reading at the time: "Here the Khan Kubla commanded a palace to be built, and a stately garden thereunto. And thus ten miles of fertile ground were inclosed with a wall."

Ho hum. Out of such mundane and ordinary things great poetry and grand stories arise.

So, too, in this collection, it might interest you to

know that Richard Kearns's "Raven" is the result of a lifelong fascination with Native American stories, or that Tappan King's "A Most Obedient Cat" is very autobiographical. Well, at least somewhat autobiographical. Or that my poem "Orkney Lament" arose after a trip to the island where I devoured a biography of Orkney's Saint Magnus, by George Mackay Brown.

Then again it might make as little difference to your reading of the stories and poems herein as knowing that Coleridge by his own account was "a *dreamer*—[who] acquired an indisposition to all bodily activity—and . . . was fretful, and inordinately passionate, and . . . could not play at any thing, and was slothful . . . despised and hated by the boys. . . ." In other words he was an early couch potato.

As for his famous poem, to some it is a masterpiece, to others hogwash and hot air. Coleridge often provoked that response in people. It is said that he could talk ceaselessly without intermission and that one time he had gone on about two hours, with Wordsworth listening attentively, nodding every now and then as if in assent. Afterward, Samuel Rogers, who had been there as well, cornered Wordsworth.

"For my own part," Rogers said, "I could not make head or tail of Coleridge's oration. Did you understand it?"

Wordsworth replied, "Not one syllable of it."

For my own part, I can't stand Wordsworth. And *that's* what makes horse races, folks.

—Jane Yolen

The Fifth Squashed Cat

Megan Lindholm

"That's the fourth squashed cat we've passed today," Cheryl observed as the left front wheel bumped gently. I didn't trust myself to reply. I was trying to remember why driving cross-country to New Mexico with Cheryl had seemed like a good idea. Had working at Ernie's Trucker Inn really been that bad? The grease. The noise. The rude customers. Ernie's flatulence. The peepholes poked through the wall from the men's room to the ladies' room that Ernie would "repair" by poking full of wet paper towels. The witty way Cheryl would shout, "Hey, Sheila! Drop another order of chicken tits in the fryer. This guy's no leg man." Watching her turn back and simper at some infatuated trucker while I tried to fix six orders at once. All of that had added up to make me believe there must be a better job somewhere.

Chicken tits. I pulled irritably at my seat belt. Resettled, I focused my eyes down the endless stretch of rainy afternoon freeway. So I had quit my job, to drive to New

11

Mexico, where it was warmer and maybe there would be better work. That much made sense. But why had I chosen to take someone who thought "chicken tits" the epitome of humor? Why hadn't I realized that the same person would find counting squashed cats an exercise in higher mathematics?

"Hey, where are the Chee-Tos? I know we had nearly a full bag back here somewhere. You eat them while I was asleep?"

"No, Cheryl, I didn't eat your Chee-Tos." Nor your Ding-Dongs, Nerds, Twinkies, not even your Jalapeño And Sour Cream Flavored Pork Rinds. God only knew how I had resisted them, but I had.

She had twisted around and was hanging into the backseat, rummaging for food. I glanced over at her and saw only a pair of blue-jeaned cheeks. She continued to rustle papers and toss unwanted items to the floor. Reminded me of a black bear ransacking a garbage can.

"You sure you didn't eat my Chee-Tos?" she asked again, a small whine slinking into her voice. " 'Cause remember, when we bought them, you said you didn't like them, and I said, 'Okay, I'll eat them, then,' and you said okay. Remember? 'Cause I don't think it's fair if you ate them like that, after you said you didn't like them. If you'd said you'd liked them, I woulda bought two bags and then there would have been enough for both of us. But you said you didn't . . ."

"Cheryl," I said in a level, reasonable voice. "I didn't eat your crummy Chee-Tos."

"Well, jeez, don't get all pushed out of shape about it." She dove deeper into the wreckage in the backseat. "I just wanted to, you know, ask . . ." Her rear end pressed against the ceiling of the car. I wondered what passing motorists thought she was doing.

It was then that I saw the hitchhiker. He was carrying a backpack with a green sleeping bag strapped to the bottom of it, and his worn felt hat was dripping water off the brim. He wore old green fatigue pants and a red-checked wool jacket and high-laced hiking boots. The hair that stuck out from under his hat was grey. He was hoofing along the side of the road, his querying thumb stuck out almost like an afterthought. I like that, when hitchhikers are walking while they hitch. I never pick up the ones that just stand there with their thumbs stuck out. They're too much like beggars. I like the ones that look like they're determined to get somewhere, whether you help or not. I hit the turn signal and tapped the brakes to get a station wagon off my bumper before I swerved to the shoulder of the road. Cheryl gave a squeal of distress.

"What are you doing?" she demanded, plopping back into her seat.

"Giving a guy a lift," I muttered.

A big grin was splitting his weathered old face as he jogged toward us. I was impressed. The guy had to be at least seventy. Gutty old man, hitching his way somewhere at that age.

"Well, you didn't even ask me! I don't think that's a good idea, I mean, all that stuff you read in the paper, he might have a knife or be an escaped convict or anything. Sheila, pull out quick before he gets here. I never pick up hitchhikers."

I ignored Cheryl, something I was getting better and better at doing. She folded her arms across her chest and started that huffy breathing she always did when she was pissed. Used to drive the truckers crazy, big boobs bobbling up and down like corks in a swell. Didn't bother me at all. By this time the hitchhiker was stand-

ing outside her door, but she wasn't moving. He grinned
at me and tried the back door on her side of the car. It
was locked, and she didn't move to unlock it. I unlocked
the one on my side. He came around right away, and
opened the door and pushed Cheryl's junk over to make
room for himself. He squished in with his backpack on
his lap. As soon as he slammed the door, I pulled back
onto the freeway. I glanced in the mirror but all I could
see was backpack and hat.

"So where you headed?" I asked. Cheryl was still
huffing.

"Where you going?" he asked in return.

"New Mexico," I said, swerving slightly to miss
some bloody fur on the road.

"Sounds good to me," he said.

Cheryl muttered, "That's the fifth squashed cat we've
passed today."

"Actually, that looked more like a coon to me, missy.
Didn't ya see that ratty kind of tail it had? More likely
a coon. Dead cat, its tail don't look like that lessen it's
been rained on a lot, and it hasn't rained all that much
yet today. Besides, that one looked near fresh. Cat's tail
don't look like that until it's been out there, oh, two,
three days. Probably a coon. Dumb old thing. Nothing
dumber than a roadkill."

About then I was thinking there were at least two
things dumber than a roadkill. Possibly three, if you
counted the person responsible for getting both of them
into the same car.

"You see any Chee-Tos back there?" Cheryl asked
him, her voice brightening. Nothing like shared interests for bringing people together. I heard the sounds of
dedicated rummaging, and Cheryl turned, presenting

cheeks once more. Great. Well, maybe they'd occupy each other and leave me alone.

"Here they are!" announced the old man, and handed her the bag after helping himself to a generous handful. Cheryl flopped back into her seat again and thrust the bag into my face.

"Here, Sheila, you want some?"

"No." I pushed her hand away and she sat back. The crackle of cellophane and the rhythmic grinding of teeth filled the car. "Why are you going to New Mexico?" I asked the old man. Anything to cover Cheryl's feeding sounds.

"Me? I thought *you* were going to New Mexico."

"Well, yeah, we are, but when you got in, I thought you said you were going to New Mexico, too."

"No." The old man had a cheerful, hearty voice. Nothing old about the way he sounded. "No, I don't think I said that at all. I think I said, 'Sounds good to me.' That's what I said. And it does. New Mexico. 'Bout time those Mexicans got a fresh start somewhere. Maybe in New Mexico they'll do things a little better. Their biggest mistake, I always thought, was in having Mexico so close to Texas. Bound to be a bad influence. Glad they got a new place now."

I forced a chuckle at his humor and then glanced at the rearview mirror. His eyes were blue and calm as a summer sky. Not joking. I couldn't think of anything else to say.

"Hey. Hey, missy. Did you say that was the fifth dead cat you passed today?"

"Yeah. Only if that's a coon like you say, then it's only the fourth." Cheryl sounded disappointed.

"Yeah?" The old man sounded incredibly pleased. "Well, that's good, really, actually, that's good. Fifth dead cat you see is always the lucky one. When we get to number five, now, you just pull over and I'll show you a thing or two about a number five squashed cat. Thing most of you young folk don't know nothing about.''

I really wished the radio was working. Maybe I'd check the fuse box at the next gas stop. Maybe it was only a blown fuse and there was an alternative to listening to a dialogue about dead cats.

''Why's it got to be a number five dead cat?'' Cheryl was asking earnestly.

''Well, it just does, that's all. You can work it out any way you like. Crystals, pyramids, channeling, or tarot. No matter how you compute it, it always comes out to a number five dead cat. And if you don't believe me, just have your aura checked. Number five, every time.'' The old man chuckled happily. ''Guess I'm just lucky, throwing in with you and having you folks be on cat number four already. Know how long it usually takes me to pass five dead cats on foot? Days, sometimes. Days! And an old man like me, it's hard for me to go days between number five squashed cats. Gimme a few more of them Chee-Tos things, missy.''

Cheryl obligingly passed the bag back to him.

''Only fifty-two more miles to the California border,'' I observed brightly as my contribution to the conversation.

''There's some Kool-Aid Koolers back there in little boxes, if you want,'' Cheryl offered. ''Would you pass me one, too?''

The Chee-Tos bag and a little waxed box of Kool-Aid was passed forward. Sensitive as I am, I realized they were ignoring me. Childish as I am, I felt piqued by it. ''Wait a minute,'' I interrupted loudly. ''How do you know which cat is the fifth one? Doesn't it all depend on when you start counting?''

"It sure does!" The old man was delighted. "And I'm real glad you saw it right off, like that. Only the fifth dead cat will work, and it all depends on when you decide to start counting them. Ain't that real Zen, now?''

I didn't think it was Zen any more than I thought it was tapioca pudding, but I didn't say so. The conversation lagged.

Cheryl jabbed her straw into the grape box, took a long gurgling sip, and suddenly choked. "Omigod!" she exclaimed, pointing down the road. "What's that?''

"Something dead," I muttered, changing lanes.

The old man craned his head forward. "Cat for sure! Look's like a calico, but it might be a Persian with real good tire tracks. Hit the brakes, kid, this here's pay dirt!''

"You've got to be kidding," I said, not even easing up on the gas.

"Please. You've got to!" The old man's hand closed on my shoulder and squeezed like a vise as Cheryl began bouncing up and down on the seat, squealing, "Please! Please, Sheila! Please stop! I wanna see it. It'll only take a second. Come on, Sheila, be a sport!''

So I pulled off on the shoulder, more out of concern for my car's shocks than for any curiosity. Besides, it was the only way to get the old man's grip off my shoulder. I hate being touched by strangers. And the old man was definitely a stranger, and getting stranger all the time. Maybe if I stopped, I could leave him with his dead cat. I wished I could leave Cheryl, too, but she was paying half the gas and it was her cousin in New Mexico

we were going to stay with until we got jobs. So I pulled
my old Chevette over, and cut the engine.

Cheryl and the old man were out before I got the car
into park. I leaned back in my seat. I wasn't getting out.
I'd seen dead cats before. Their little mouths are always
open, fangs bare, neat pink tongues curled, as if making
a final snarl at death. I like animals. Seeing dead ones
always gives me a sense of loss, of waste. Tiny little
lives, flame bright and candle brief, snuffed out. Probably been someone's pet.

I glanced in the rearview mirror and nearly gagged.
The old man had found a piece of cardboard by the
roadside and had coaxed most of the cat's body onto it.
The hindquarters were dangling. Obviously everything
in the cat's middle was crushed. He was using a stick to
poke the rest of it onto his improvised stretcher. Cheryl
trotted back to the car and jerked open a back door. Her
eyes were wide, her face pink.

"Get in," I said softly. "And let's get the hell out of
here. Just push his stuff out the door."

She reached in and grabbed his backpack and un-
strapped the top flap. She dug into it, pulling out a
single-burner hiker's stove, and then an aluminum pot.

"What are you doing?" I demanded. "Just drag the
whole thing out."

"What? No. This is all we need. Oh, and Dougie says
it would look better if you got out and acted like you
were changing the tire or looking under the hood.
Okay?"

She didn't wait for an answer, but stepped away from
the car, and nestled the stove down into the gravel of the
ditch, and set the pot on top of it. The car blocked the
casual glances of passing motorists. "Cheryl!" I hissed,
but she crouched down by the pot, not hearing me.

I opened my door just as a semi whooshed past. A gust of damp air sucked at me and a horn blared aggressively. I staggered out in the wake, slamming the door behind me, and hurried around the car.

"What is going on?" I demanded, but I had a sick feeling I knew. Dougie was sliding the cat off the cardboard and into the pot. It didn't quite fit, so he bent it in half and tamped it down with the stick.

"Now we need the canteen of water," he announced, and they both looked up at me like I was supposed to bring it.

"This is sick," I told them. "And I'm leaving."

"Sheila!" Cheryl whiningly protested, even as Dougie asked her, "Well, what's the matter with her?"

I got back in the car and slammed the door. Cheryl opened the door and leaned in. "You can climb in and go with me," I told her. "Or you can pull your stuff out and stay here. But I'm leaving."

"Sheila, why? What's the matter with you?" She looked genuinely perplexed.

"Look. I'm not sticking around while you two barbecue a roadkill. It's disgusting."

"Oh, Sheila!" Cheryl started laughing. She reached over the seat and fished a canteen out of the old man's pack. "We aren't barbecuing anything, silly."

"Then what are you doing?"

"Just boiling it down," she said reasonably. "Dougie says we boil it down to the bones. Then there's this one certain bone, and you put it under your tongue and . . ."

"Oh, gross!"

"It confers perfect health and vitality upon you. Dougie says that's all he does anymore. He used to work for a living, go after that old paycheck, slave away for somebody, just to keep body and soul together. But no more. All he has to do now is hike along the road until he gets to a fifth squashed cat, boil it down, and put the bone under his tongue. Easy. And his life is his own.''

Her cheeks were flushed with more than the wind that was blowing her hair across her face. Her blue eyes sparked through the net of her hair. Oh, you True Believer, you.

''That's stupid,'' I told her bluntly.

''Oh, Sheila, don't you ever try anything new? Look, it's only going to take a minute or two. Come on. Have an open mind.''

I looked at her, unable to believe what I was hearing.

''In the interests of science,'' she added, as a finishing touch. She spun away from the car, leaving the door open. As I leaned across the seat to reach the handle, I saw her dumping water onto the cat in the pot. Yes. It had been a Persian with good tire tracks. Gotta give it to the man, he sure knew his roadkills. Dougie dug in his jacket pocket and came out with one of those camp knives that unfold a spoon at one end and a fork at the other. He prized the spoon out and began poking the cat down into the pot with it. That did it.

''Cheryl. I'm leaving. Either get in or get your stuff out of my car. You, too, Dougie.''

They glanced over at me, then back at their cat. It was gently steaming now, and the smell of simmering cat blended with the smell of rainy freeway. Dougie spoke, but not to me. ''For me, it's the fifth neckbone down from the headbone. Now, I don't know what one it's gonna be for you. Too bad you never had your aura done with a crystal, so's you'd know. But what we can do, Miss Cheryl, is just try the bones one at a time, keeping track of which one is which, until we get the right one. Okay?''

I slammed the door on it. Damn, I was mad. Furious. Because they knew, both of them, that my threats were empty. They weren't even worried. I am not the kind of person that can drive off and leave two people stranded on a freeway, even if they're sautéing a dead Persian. Because I'm a sucker. A wimp. I closed my eyes and worked on my anger. Remember the time I asked Cheryl to quit calling back orders for chicken tits? Remember how she smiled at the trucker and said that it was the girls with little tits who got offended about tit jokes, because they didn't have anything to laugh about? Remember the night her drunk boyfriend threw up all over the men's room and I had to clean it up because she had to drive him home and none of the guys would touch it and Ernie was coming in any second? Remember that I am almost sure she's the one who snitched all my tips out of the coffee mug I was keeping them in?

Remember that she's the one who has a cousin in New Mexico for me to stay with while I job-hunt?

So I heaved out a big sigh and lolled my head back on the headrest and looked at the ceiling. I have always been a spineless wimp. And I think I give off some signal that attracts people who prey on spineless wimps. I despised myself. And I despised those assholes out there boiling their cat. Cretins. But then, I thought, Oh, well, what the hell, and slid to the passenger seat and watched. It couldn't be any worse than what I was imagining.

It was raining in a misty, invisible way. Damp made a sheen on Dougie's wool jacket and jeweled Cheryl's hair. They were hunkered down beside the pot in cheerfully primeval companionship. The cat had softened

and sunk into the pot. Maybe it had been dead longer
than I thought. Dougie kept poking at it with his spoon
and nodding approvingly. He noticed me watching
them, and waved the spoon at me and said something.
Cheryl laughed. A few minutes later she got up and
came back to the car. She opened the door, letting in
rain and cat steam.

"Dougie says he's not offended or anything. Come on
over and he'll figure out which cat bone is right for
you."

Like Mommy tapping at your bedroom door and saying, "Okay, you can come down to dinner now if you
promise to behave and not call your brother 'snotnose'
anymore." Same answer to both.

"No. Thanks."

"Suit yourself, then." She turned and went back to
her stewpot, leaving the door open. She whispered to
Dougie and he shrugged elaborately. They ignored me
assiduously.

She'd make someone a great mommy someday. Now,
Priscilla, don't sulk in your room. Come down to the
family room and suck on your kitty bone like a good
girl. What a crock!

I slid out of the car to stretch my legs. The afternoon
was fading. We could have been in California by now.
Unremarkable stretch of freeway. Pavement, gravel
shoulder, chain-link fence, nondescript woods beyond
it. Cretins stewing a cat.

"There now! See how that's falling apart. I think
she's ready. Now, you hold that cardboard steady."

I turned involuntarily as they fished out the cat.
Soggy, steaming fur slipping off grey boiled meat that
was sliding off bones. Dougie burned his fingers as he

arranged it on the cardboard. It was falling apart, legs going different ways, the trailing guts swollen shiny.

"Usually I ain't so careful," Dougie explained as he laid his patient out. "Usually I just count down from the headbone. But we gotta be careful until we find out what bone is right for you. And for your friend there." He tipped his head at me, but his eyes never left the stewed kitty. I folded my arms and watched from a distance.

"Hope you don't mind I go first, Missy Cheryl. I'm an old man, and it's been two days since my last fifth cat. My Vital Essences need recharging bad." The blade of his camp knife lifted the cat's neck and spine free of the clinging meat. I stepped closer to watch. He counted and coaxed free one tiny spinal bone. A gobbet of cord dangled from it when he picked it up in his thick fingers. He popped it into his mouth.

He closed his eyes, rocked back on his heels, and glowed. Glowed like a jack-o'-lantern with a candle inside it. The light limned out the bones of his skull, glowing redly through his nose and eye sockets, showing his teeth against his cheeks. Cheryl gazed at him raptly. I stumbled back until I felt the chain-link highway fence cold against my back.

The glow faded as slowly as embers being masked by ash. Dougie smiled and opened his eyes. He looked more like forty than seventy. My heart was hammering in my chest and the skin of my face went hot with blood. But I wasn't scared, or even awestruck. I was furious.

See, I'd never respected people who hung crystals from their rearview mirrors and suspended pyramids over their beds and read their horoscopes every day. I laughed at their ignorant hope that they could get through life that way. I respected people who knew the world was real and lumpy, and that you had to make your own way in it, not look for some mystical shortcut. Practical, realistic people who worked hard and bettered themselves with education and saved money for the future. People like me.

I was angry at the monstrous unfairness of it. It worked. It was real. But the whole thing was too damn easy. It wasn't fair for anything in life to be that easy, for anyone. I didn't want it to be real, and I was pissed off that it was. It's tough to find out you're wrong about something as basic as that.

Cheryl's eyes were wide. "What happened to the bone?"

"Gone," he told her, and opened his mouth wide to show her. She craned her head to peer into his mouth.

"So it is!" she exclaimed delightedly. "Okay. Now me. How do I start?"

"Well, let's just start with the tip of the tail and work forward from there. May take us a while, Missy Cheryl. These cats gotta lotta bones, specially when you get down to all their little toesie bones and such. Let's hope it ain't the headbone. Be awful hard to get that under your tongue."

They laughed together over their feline box social. The mesh fence was cold against my fingers. I let go of it, crept closer. Dougie was neatly laying the tail open, lifting the thread of bones out skillfully. He set it carefully on the grubby piece of cardboard. The tip of his knife blade freed the end one. "Here ya go," he said, picking it up. "Number one tailbone. Now we gotta keep track, unless you wanna try every bone in every number five cat you ever use. So pay attention. Just pop this under your tongue. If it takes, you'll know. If not, just pass it on to your friend there. Maybe it'll be the right one for her."

"Well, come on, Sheila, don't just stand there! This is gonna be fun!" Cheryl waved me over excitedly, then opened her mouth to receive the first bone from Dougie's grubby fingers.

I swallowed as I watched her take it like she was receiving communion. She shut her eyes and rocked back on her heels. After a few seconds she opened them. "Nothing," she said matter-of-factly, and reached fingers into her mouth to fish out the bone. "Here, Sheila." She held it out to me.

"No." I crossed my arms on my chest.

"Yes," she said simply. "You have to believe it. It works. You saw it. You'd be crazy not to try it."

"It's not that." My skepticism was hanging in tatters. No hiding behind that. "It's sick. The whole idea of spending your life that way. What are you going to do, Cheryl? Go hiking down freeways forever, sucking on the tailbones of every fifth squashed cat? Is that what life is going to be for you?"

"You're making it out a bit bare, missy," Dougie interceded. "It ain't all asphalt and exhaust, it ain't even all freeways. A lot of time it's backcountry roads, with the birches turning gold along the shoulders, or bare white stretches of snowy highway in Utah, or the hilly streets of San Francisco. I mean, squashed cats are everywhere. Criss-crossed this country ten or more times; seen a lot of Canada and Mexico, too. I've had blue-sky days and thunderstorm nights; I've waited out hailstorms under overpasses, and slept in deep sweet-smelling hayfields under harvest moons. My time belongs to me. I get lonely, I hitch a little. Sure, I get a little cold, I get a little wet. But as long as I get my number five cat bone, I don't get old. Don't get tired, don't get sick. It may not be a fancy-dancy way to live. But it ain't a bad life, and you got no right to go scaring Missy Cheryl away from it.''

Cheryl's chin had come up. She looked me straight in the eye and spoke with a dignity I'd never known she possessed. ''No one's scaring me away from this. You and me, Sheila, we worked a few months together. You think you know all about me. But it's me who knows about you. I seen how you are. You're looking. You believe you're gonna end up doing something better. Being something better than I'll ever be. Well, maybe you will. But I won't. I know that. I've seen myself in every truck stop we passed. All those old waitresses, swollen ankles and big behinds. Still getting pinched by the truckers, still putting out cups of coffee for guys who don't tip. That's as good as it's ever going to get for me. And frankly, this looks better.''

She set the rejected bone down on the dusty cardboard and took the next one from Dougie's fingers.

A curious embarrassment overtook me. I'd always known I was smarter than Cheryl. No. Smarter's not the right word for it. But the world's a different place for me. I've known hundreds of girls like her. Guys, too. High school was full of them, and all the seedy little jobs I'd taken since screwing up my college had put me right alongside them. The biggest dream the guys ever have is, like, rebuilding the '66 Thunderbird that's rusting behind Uncle Joe's shed. For the girls, it's always something to do with a guy. A handsomer guy, a richer guy, a sexier guy. The biggest change they ever make is going on a diet or dyeing their hair. I had plans and dreams they didn't understand. I'd always felt both pity and scorn for them. What I'd never realized was that Cheryl had known, all this time, that my future was brighter than hers, that the things that would work for me would crumble to pieces in her hands. She had always known it, and lived with my secret scorn for her shopworn hopes and generic dreams.

What Cheryl was doing right now, placing the second bone under her tongue, took a sort of grubby courage. She was reaching for something a little better than she believed she was entitled to. And I, who had always believed that when my chance came, I would boldly seize it, I was hugging myself with cold hands, shivering in the gliding caress of the raindrops sliding down my arms.

Wimp out.

So I stepped into their magic circle and picked up the bone that Cheryl had discarded. It was warm from the pot and slick with her saliva, but I slipped it under my tongue and waited. Nothing. I set it aside and reached for the next one. Nothing. Now she was waiting for me, and I took the bone she fished out from under her tongue and put it under my own. Nothing. But there was an excitement building, an electrical current jumping and sparking from Dougie to Cheryl to me and yes, to the dead cat, and around again. A mystic togetherness that was warm and friendly. We three would soon be free of the world's bonds. Another bone. Nothing. We would walk with our heads bare under the bright blue skies of autumn, the scent of falling leaves blowing past us. Another bone. Spring would sprout about our feet. We'd see the Grand Canyon, hike across Death Valley. Nothing. Another bone. The snows of winter might chill us, but the ways of man, of jobs and money and petty rules, would no longer bind us. Nothing. True freedom to see the world with eyes uncluttered by schedules and obligations. Like the old gods, like fey folk. Another bone.

We were about halfway through the cat, going down

the ribs, when Cheryl lit up. Twice as bright as Dougie, like a blast furnace. I felt the warmth radiate from her body before I even turned my head to see her transfig-urement. She had a halo like a Catechism saint. The brassy blondness burned out of her hair, and it went a rich mahogany. Her complexion cleared as if her body were casting off all impurities. I stared at her as the glow gradually faded. I crouched long moments in the rain, blinking the drops from my lashes, waiting for the last light to fade from her face before I realized it wasn't going to. That new light would stay, a vitality burning inside her, giving off the same aura of health and deter-mination that had made me stop and pick Dougie up. She smiled, and it was like someone pulling up the blinds to let in a sunny day. I felt blessed.

"Well, go on," she told me, and it took an instant for me to realize what she was talking about.

"That there was the sixth rib on the left side, Missy Cheryl. You're going to want to remember that now."

Cheryl smiled her beatific smile and gestured toward me. Dougie passed me the next bone. We worked slowly through the rest of the ribs. I felt a shiver of excitement as we started down the left front leg. Soon. Only the legbones left. Cheryl and I exchanged a smile as I started on the right front leg. Soon now. She was watching me closely, waiting for it. She reminded me of a lover I had who always tried to look at my face during orgasm. It seemed a very personal thing, but I wasn't bothered by it. Cheryl and Dougie and I would soon share a very unique bond. I didn't mind her witnessing my initia-tion.

The left hind leg. Dougie was handing me the bones more slowly now, and I held each under my tongue a few seconds longer, just to be sure. As I took the first bone of the right hind leg under my tongue, my heart began hammering against my ribs. I felt heat rise in my face. For a moment I thought this was it, but it was only my building excitement. "Come on, come on!" Cheryl was chanting as I continued down the legbones, the fine thin bones of the leg, and then the smaller, knuckly bones of the foot and toes, and then . . .

There were no more bones.

I stared in disbelief as Dougie dropped the last remnant of boneless cat onto the heap of discarded fur, meat, and entrails. It still steamed faintly in the fading afternoon light.

"What happened?" I asked groggily. I felt as if I were just coming to after a faint. The blackened burner of the camp stove, the scorched pot, the slithered-flat cat remnants, the mounded bones on the road-dusty cardboard. It was like a videocassette tape snapping, or sex suddenly interrupted. I couldn't grasp what had happened. Dougie looked like a man who had suddenly lost his erection just before his partner climaxed. "What happened?" I demanded again. "What went wrong?"

"Ain't gonna work for her," Dougie announced, and turned away.

"What do you mean?" I cried out, and Cheryl asked, "How come?"

Dougie jerked open the car door and started dragging his stuff out. "Look at her," he said gruffly. "She's not like us. I shoulda seen it. Bones don't work for someone like her."

I swung my gaze to Cheryl. I tried to meet her eyes, but her look roved over me, summing me up. "I see," she said slowly.

I looked back to Dougie. I felt like the family pet at the moment when the car door swings open on the country road and Bubby pushes you firmly out. Dumped. Cheryl stood up, took the kettle, and emptied out the liqueur of cat.

"Wait a minute," I said as she handed Dougie the empty kettle. "I probably just missed a bone. Just missed it, that's all." I grabbed one at random, slipped it under my tongue. Nothing. Go on to the next one.

"Nope." Dougie's voice was final as he picked up the camp stove. "Don't work for people like you. And you knowed it all along."

"No!" I wailed around a mouthful of ribs. I spat them out, grabbed another handful of tiny bones, and shoved them into my mouth. "Wait," I choked as I struggled to get my tongue over them. "Eweul see."

"What'd she say?" Cheryl asked Dougie.

"I don't know. Who cares? Now look, missy, you can't take all this stuff. You got like a pack or something?"

"I got a pillowcase," Cheryl said brightly. She dug through the back of the car, came up with her pillow. "And a sleeping bag."

"Well, good. Now that's real good. Dump out the pillow, 'cause you ain't gonna need that. Keep the sleeping bag. Now, in the pillowcase, you put a change of clothes, a comb, that sort of thing. Nothing much, 'cause you ain't gonna need much no more. No, forget makeup, you're prettier without it. Sure, take the Chee-Tos. Not that we'll be hungry, but snacking's fun as we walk along. Now let me tie it up for you."

The bones were wet with rain, and grit from the cardboard clung to them. I calmed myself, forced myself to do one bone at a time. They'd see. Any minute now, they'd see. As I watched them hike away, I thought how I'd jump and shout and they'd look back to see me glowing like a torch, brighter than either of them, burning like a bonfire. I'd show them. The rain pelted down faster. It grew harder to see them through the dusk and falling water. It didn't matter. I had the car, I'd catch up with them. I picked up the next bone.

I don't know how many times I went through the bones. I stopped when blue and white lights started flashing before my eyes, wondering if I'd hit it. A blaze of white light hit my face and blinded me, and a cop asked, "You okay, miss? I saw your dome light on and stopped. You sick or something?"

He took his flashlight beam off my face as I staggered upright and leaned against my car. I'd never closed the door, and the dome light inside was still burning. Cheryl's stuff was spilled half out of the car. I told him something about the stuff in my backseat falling over so I stopped to rearrange it. He couldn't have believed it, not with my clothes soaked to my body and my hair dripping down my back. He played his light over the deboned cat while I stuffed everything back into the car. Probably decided he didn't want to know what was going on. He stayed behind me while I got my car started again, and watched me pull out onto the freeway before he spun off the gravel shoulder and passed me in a flicker of headlights.

I drove on, not going anywhere special now, just counting the cats. I never saw Dougie or Cheryl again, but I did once find another stewed cat by the side of the road. I gathered up what was left of it and took it to a motel that night. I tried every bone. Probably two or three times. Nothing.

I never got to New Mexico either. I stopped off in San Rafael, to live between my car and the women's shelter there until I found a computer firm that would hire me.

They're paying me to go to night school now, and I
know that things are getting better for me. If I study hard
and pay attention to my job and get along with my
coworkers, I'll get ahead. If I work at it.

There are still times when I think about it. Sometimes, when I'm lying in bed, semi-awake after a rest-
less night, waiting for my alarm clock to go off,
sometimes I think of them, rising from a peaceful night
in some dewy field, glowing with health, to start their
daily trek down the highways and byways of America.
No clocks to punch. No classes to study for. Nothing to
do but hike down the road in the fresh morning air,
looking for that fifth squashed cat. That's what works
for them. And what works for me is getting up at five to
leave the house at six so I can fight traffic and get to
work by eight. Who's to say which way is better? Who's
to say who has the better life? But sometimes, on those
mornings when I wonder, I step out of my door early, at
five-thirty, into the fresh morning air. I look at the wide
blue sky, at the sun just opening the day. And I get into
my car and drive slowly and carefully to work.

I wouldn't want to hit someone's cat by accident.

Just Another Dragon-Slaying

Vivian Vande Velde

Bad enough, Lylene thought, having the kind of dragon which demands young virgins at regular intervals: after all, only a small percent of the community is directly affected, commerce continues more or less as usual, and those most personally involved are prohibited by age and sex from sitting at council where policy is determined. It's quite another matter when a dragon goes on a general rampage, laying waste to valuable farmland on which all depend, devastating trade, scattering tax records and recorders alike.

Lylene thought about economic exigencies and evaluated the blackened fields, the scorched and/or flattened cottages, and decided she had seen worse. The citizens of Cheldenholme would not be relieved to hear that. They were no doubt in a state approaching panic despite the fact that, uncharacteristically, the most serious damage was to the outlying areas.

Lucky townspeople, Lylene thought.

Lylene didn't believe in luck.

Approaching the center of the town, she snapped the reins to get the draft horses moving faster and nudged Weiland with her foot. Then she glanced at him, slouched next to her, with his arms folded across his chest, and she saw that he was awake after all, and making his own silent appraisals.

They were used to getting more of a reaction. The expensive destriers tethered to the back of the wagon were unusual enough, as was her waist-length copper-colored hair. But then there was Weiland's hair—blond and shoulder-length, evidence of a Viking heritage—more noticeable even than his weapons, the swords and knives and daggers he wore ostentatiously tucked into belt and harness.

She slowed to avoid a barefooted child's gaggle of geese, then pulled the horses to a stop in front of the wealthiest-looking house: the one made of stone. Here, finally, was attention: a score of townspeople clustered, their faces pinched in disapproval.

Weiland looked at her with raised eyebrows.

Lylene scrambled from the wagon. Though she barely came to Weiland's shoulder, she was as tall as most of the men they faced—too tall, her mother had always complained. Weiland insisted her height was an advantage. She tried to bear this in mind as she addressed an elderly man in the forefront, a merchant by his dress, who was flanked by another merchant and a clergyman. "You sent for us?"

The man's eyes flicked from Weiland to Lylene back to Weiland. "You're the wizard?" he asked, as though unsure whether that should be a source of relief or concern.

"Yes," said Lylene, and nothing more until he faced her again and not Weiland. "I am the wizard."

The priest made the sign of the cross while the crowd muttered warily.

"You?" the second merchant sputtered. "But you . . . you're . . . you're . . ."

"You're a *woman*," the first finally got out, in a tone which could, conceivably, have been surprise.

"Yes," she said.

The three drew in, to confer in frantic whispers. The rest of the crowd, eager to voice their opinions also, swallowed them up.

Lylene played at nonchalance. She wasn't used to doing the talking; normally Weiland set things up. But their constant bickering of the last few weeks had escalated into a full-fledged argument that morning, an argument she had ended by declaring that, after all, *she* was the wizard and therefore *she* was in charge.

"You want me to leave?" he had asked.

"No!" That was instinctive—and came out sounding panicked. Then, "No," she'd said, "damn you. We're in this together. We agreed. The advance is spent, and you're not backing out now and leaving me to do this all by myself."

He'd said nothing, sitting beside her in the wagon, distractingly close.

"The dragon first. Then you can suit yourself. I don't care."

"All right." Weiland had been, as always, impenetrably cool.

And now he offered no help at all, but only watched with his infuriating bland but superior expression.

Annoyed all over again, she forced her attention to the countryside. Cheldenholme was situated next to a small lake, dominated by a mountain which had a vast stretch of level ground almost at the top. Dragon country. It didn't take an expert to see that.

Weiland, she could tell, was focused in closer, gauging the townspeople.

"Our agents," the elder merchant said, breaking away from the priest—who, by his fluttery hands and sour expression, hadn't had all his say—"our agents were supposed to hire a wizard."

He was going to demand back the advance fee, she could tell.

"May I be so bold as to ask what sort of magic you specialize in?" the second merchant cut in.

"Multiplications," she said. "And divisions."

"I beg your pardon?"

Beside her, Weiland shifted position. Had it been anyone else, Lylene would have thought it idle fidgeting. But she knew Weiland never made idle moves, and the townspeople seemed to guess that too. Several backed away a pace or so.

She hoped nobody noticed her face flush with annoyed embarrassment at his unsolicited aid. "I will collect the balance of my fee when the dragon is gone," she said.

The elder glanced around for support, found it wasn't coming, and nodded.

"We will need a room—clean and well lit, either an inn or someone's home."

In a tone indicating his worst presumptions had been confirmed, the priest said, "One room?"

The two merchants tried to unobtrusively shoulder him back, into the anonymity of the crowd.

But she only said, "Yes." Let them think what they would: despite any disagreements, she and Weiland always closed ranks in times of danger. And this, she was convinced—despite the plain peasant faces and the innocuous words—surely qualified.

Evening. The door to the room—neither clean nor well lit—flew open, banging into the wall, and she jumped. But it was only Weiland, come back from scouting out the town. He unbuckled his sword belt and tossed it onto the bed beside her, then started removing his knives one by one.

"Well," said Lylene, as though he hadn't left fully six hours earlier, "so what do the townspeople have to say?"

"They wonder why a wizard needs a bodyguard."

Bodyguard. Lylene shrugged. Whatever Weiland was, he wasn't her bodyguard.

He rested his foot on the bed to take the long thin blade from his boot. "We're in the barony of Sir Tirrell de Montgrise."

She fought to pay attention. She had been startled, not only by the suddenness of his entrance but by the fact that he had returned at all. On the best of days, there was always the possibility that he would not. And this had certainly not been the best of days. She prepared herself for the inevitable by repeating each time they separated that this was the time, and that it made no difference. It never got easier.

If Weiland noticed her tendency to jump whenever he entered a room, he never mentioned it.

"So what has this Sir Tirrell of Montgrise done to try to kill the dragon?"

"Ah. Well." He glanced up and flashed his cold smile. "Nothing."

"Nothing?" She thought back to the man who had

contracted them. What had originally seemed innocently vague now seemed dangerously elusive. "Who's
paying us—Tirrell or the town?"

"Town." Weiland unfastened the leather harness that
housed most of his weapons—or at least most of the
ones he wanted seen.

"But that doesn't make any sense."

"No. It doesn't."

Angry with herself for being so desperate for companionship, she finally observed, "You were gone a long
time."

It was his turn to shrug. He nodded toward her papers,
papers she had bought, along with a certain package,
from a Saracen trader just back from the Orient. "Figure
out how to use that magic powder?"

"As a matter of fact, yes. Figure out how to use that
bent sword?" If he thought she had thrown their money
away buying the powder without a demonstration, she
didn't see what he wanted with yet another weapon,
particularly such an awkward-looking one.

"Curved," he corrected. "Scimitar. Someday." He
pulled his shirt over his head, and she glanced away,
unwilling to admit to the fluttery things he did to her
resolve, even when she was angry. "Do you get the
bed," he asked a bit too smoothly, "being the wizard,
and in charge and all?"

She pulled out the old Phoenician coin they kept for
such decisions. "King or god?" she asked, tossing it
into the air. They had bedded together, she and Weiland, those nights it had been too cold to think of anything else, and that time he'd held her throughout the
night when she'd been convulsed with fever, an arrow-
head in her shoulder. But sex was one complication she
knew they didn't need, and perhaps Weiland knew it

too, for it was one of the few things about which he
didn't give her an argument.

"King," he said as she caught the coin against her
thigh.

Lylene checked, then dumped her things onto the
floor. Normally she'd say something like, "I hope the
bedding has fleas," but tonight that seemed to be pushing too far. "I'll take first watch," she said instead.

Wrapped in the spare blanket, watching the flickering
shadows the undoused candle made on the rough plastered walls, she listened for the low rumble of talk and
laughter and song which normally comes from an inn's
common room, and heard none of it.

Dawn was hot and humid.

The two of them passed close enough to the abbey,
halfway up the mountain, to hear the bells ring for the
sunrise prayers of Prime. A little farther on, they rested,
and that was when they saw the dragon. It circled the
mountain summit lazily, and when its enormous
shadow touched her skin, Lylene shivered. It was big.
Much bigger than the townspeople had indicated. This
was Lylene's third dragon, and they were always bigger
than the townspeople indicated. But if she and Weiland
worked fast enough, they'd be gone before it returned
from its foraging.

By the time the brothers at the abbey would be singing
Tierce, she and Weiland had reached the broad, flat
expanse visible from the town of Cheldenholme below.

It was as though the peak had been split vertically,
and one half removed. The level rock on which they
stood was scored with grooves, which Lylene thought
were probably from the dragon's talons, and spattered
with dark stains that didn't bear thinking on at all. The

remaining half of the peak was hollowed out, forming a huge cave.

Between them and that cave was a knight, sitting on horseback, watching them.

He lowered his lance, with the soft metal whisper of chain mail, and said: "I respectfully request you to leave."

Lylene's horse snorted, pawing at the hard ground. She patted its neck and told the knight, "Listen, it's all right. You don't understand. I'm a wizard. There's nothing to worry about. I—"

"I respectfully request you to leave," he repeated.

For a moment she felt light-headed. Nothing seemed to fit, and she had to start fresh. "Are you here to fight the dragon?"

He hesitated a moment too long before answering, "Yes."

"One of Baron Tirrell's men?"

He inclined his head.

"I see."

Despite the heat, he was wearing a helmet, and the noseguard gave his face the distorted, anonymous look of any other knight, in any other place. His chain-mail tunic sparkled in the sunlight, though the eastern half of the sky was filling with dark thunderclouds. Did dragons mind rain? On top of everything else, did she have to worry that the creature was even now heading back here? "We could stay," Lylene suggested, "in case—"

"No."

It was more than knightly arrogance could account for. Lylene believed the part about Baron Tirrell, but not that the man was here to fight the dragon. Which left that Tirrell wanted to stop them. But why? Why would anybody want to protect a dragon?

"Please get out of the way," she said. Then, when the man made no move, she said to Weiland: "Get rid of him."

She meant, *Scare him off,* but when she turned to him, she saw that he had been sitting with his hands crossed over the reins. And Lylene knew there was a small throwing knife hidden in the leather bracer that bound his left wrist, the wrist on which his right hand was resting.

Before either of them had time to do anything—Weiland to extract the knife or Lylene to protest (which she would have done, she assured herself)—Baron Tirrell's knight let drop the lance which gave him such an advantage and drew a sword. This he raised before his face, commending his soul to God.

"I am Sir Sherard, son of Volney," he declared, formality which startled them, "and I normally do not fight unarmored men, sir. But if you persist, I must challenge you for the right to be here. Should I win, you must depart, with no further questions; should you win, you shall, of course, do as you please."

"Chivalry," Weiland said, almost a purr, "how nice." His hand dropped from his wrist and went for his own sword.

Lylene fought back her horse, which—battle-trained—wanted to join the coming fracas. She dragged on the reins, but that only pulled him into a tight circle just as Weiland and the knight Sherard came at each other. She missed seeing the first blow, but whoever struck it, the other parried successfully.

In fact, in almost no time Lylene saw that the fight was just about evenly matched, certainly more even than Weiland was used to.

"Back!" she snapped at her horse. She thought to use

sorcery to help Weiland, but realized she couldn't bring herself to it, and that was a surprise, to find at this stage of her life that there were some things, after all, which were beneath her.

Sherard moved in to parry what turned out to be a feint, left himself overextended and unbalanced as Weiland began the real slash. He tried to wheel about, but Weiland's mount kicked his on the shin, and horse and knight both went down. He hit the ground and rolled, just missed getting his head caved in as his horse struggled to regain its feet.

Weiland leapt off his horse to close in and finish the fight before the other could regain his orientation. But the knight was not so badly rattled as it had seemed he must be: his foot lashed out, hooking behind Weiland's leg, and Weiland came down hard, sitting, his sword skittering across the rocky ground. It was over that quickly.

Sherard, who had somehow held onto his own weapon, was already back on his feet, holding that weapon against the base of Weiland's throat.

"No!" Lylene cried, though logic said that had Sherard intended, Weiland would have been skewered already.

Weiland remained motionless, his arms extended behind for balance.

Without moving the sword, Sherard included her with an upward nod of the head. "I have successfully overcome you on the field of combat. Agree you to depart?"

"Yes," Lylene said even as he was still speaking.

The knight hesitated.

"Yes," Weiland said.

Sherard sheathed his sword and removed his helmet,

revealing a chubby, well-scrubbed face. "It was a well-fought fight." He extended his hand to help his opponent to his feet.

Weiland winced, as though more than his pride had been hurt. Sherard took him by the arm, supporting his weight. Weiland let him do all the work, then drove his elbow into the side of the knight's head.

Sherard dropped, probably without knowing what had hit him.

Weiland rubbed his elbow and looked down at him. "Jackass," he said.

His action, Lylene complained as he bound and gagged Sir Sherard, had been unfair and reprehensible.

Weiland, never loud, let his voice drop practically to a whisper. "If you feel that bad about it, we could still do what he asked, and leave."

She turned her back on him. In the end, that was the only argument with which she was left: that she *had* no argument, but that at least she didn't like it. She turned her back on him and left him. There wasn't much time. The sky was ominously dark for the hour, and the papers she had purchased from the Saracen indicated the spell wouldn't work in the wet. There was also the danger that the threat of rain could bring the dragon back to its den.

She knelt before the cave. With her hands around, but not touching, the package for which she had paid the entire fee from their last job, she closed her eyes against the glare that always formed. A second package pressed against her hands, forcing them farther apart. Again she concentrated. Two more packages materialized; then those also doubled.

When they grew again to sixteen, she stacked the

packages so that they would be less bulky. She was aware of Weiland, crouched just off to one side, watching with his usual dispassionate interest.

"Isn't that enough?" he asked. "How many do you need?"

"Better too much than too little."

Finally satisfied, she saved the original package for future use, since her duplicates had a tendency to fade after several hours, and were always gone within a day. She tied that one behind her saddle, then went to help Weiland arrange the others inside the cave.

Baron Tirrell's man, Sherard, had come to, and was watching with eyes grown large. Lylene glanced at the still-darkening sky and considered ordering him to help; but while she would have trusted him had Weiland won fairly, trust under these circumstances seemed risky.

Finished, Weiland stretched, pressing against the small of his back. "Use him, why don't you?" he suggested, with a nod toward Sherard.

She shook her head.

"I mean for your magic."

"I know what you mean," she snapped, angry with herself because she hadn't known, not for sure, and the clarification, by its very nature, chilled her. She looked away, shook her head again. "Get Sherard mounted, then I'll need you."

Weiland approached, gingerly as always, and now angry as well. She put a hand on either side of his shoulders and closed her eyes. This was her one advantage, the only thing no one could touch. In her darkest moods, she didn't care. She put less energy into this than she had with the powder, for she wanted a mere fetch, an image, not an exact duplicate which would have a life and feelings of its own. The first time she had used her sorcery like this, she had felt the death of the creature she had made, had felt it *know* its death, an anguish inside her head from which she had thought she would never recover. But, of course, she had.

She stepped back, unable to look this duplicate Weiland in the eye. "Go into the cave," she said. "When the dragon returns, let it see you."

The fetch nodded, expressionless. There was no telling at this point how much it knew or felt.

Weiland had never looked at it, was single-mindedly attending to his horse. They had discussed once whether she might be all unwittingly chipping away at his life, at his very soul: a double murder. Weiland insisted he felt nothing more than squeamishness at the sight of his own form on someone, something, else. Would he know?

No danger, the one who had given her the power had said, but that had been no friend—hers or Weiland's. She would have used Sherard, could she be certain his fetch would do what she commanded.

They took the same path down as they had used to come up, though Sherard's presence indicated there were others. They rode where they could, walked when necessary. During a rocky, narrow stretch that was easier on foot, she removed Sherard's gag, warning, "One wrong word, and it'll go right back on." She had seen the way his pale face had stolen glances at her, but still she waited for him to nod before unfastening the cloth.

"The hands stay tied," Weiland growled, tethering Sherard's mount to his own.

And Lylene, for the third or fourth time, said, "We're not going to harm you."

Again Sherard nodded, obviously forcing himself to believe.

The black clouds closed in, smelling of imminent rain, and she rubbed her chilled arms. "Now. What's going on with this dragon? Why doesn't Tirrell want it destroyed?"

Weiland, never interested in motivations, walked ahead, guiding the two horses.

Lylene held onto her own reins and fell in next to Sherard. "Why?" she repeated.

Sherard moistened his lips. "Money."

"How do you mean?"

"The Baron sold some land and rights to the towns-people, which he now regrets. He stands to get them back at a good price should the people be desperate enough."

"If the land is temporarily unusable," Lylene mused. Then, another thought: "Or the people dead."

Sir Sherard, the honorable knight, shrugged.

Up ahead, Weiland suddenly swore. A living black shadow swooped down to the heights they had just left. Even from this distance, she could feel the whoosh of air from its passing.

They all instinctively pressed against the side of the mountain, though if the dragon had looked their way, it would have seen them; and if it had seen them, they were beyond help already.

In the lead, Weiland picked up the pace.

Sherard held his hands out to her. "If you unbound my wrists, I could move faster."

Lylene stopped, but Weiland, without turning back, called: "No."

She hesitated, watching him broaden the distance between them. Sherard waited. "Come on," she told him, avoiding his eyes.

The path, a narrow shelf on the outside edge of the mountain, narrowed yet more so that Lylene and Sherard had to go single file, her horse between them. "Tirrell thinks he can control *that?*" she called back to him. No doubt but that he'd follow: protecting an absent dragon is one thing, going back to warn it is another.

"Now what?" he panted.

"Hopefully the dragon will become enraged when it sees what looks like a human challenger in its cave."

"It'll incinerate him."

"Yes." She was glad he couldn't see her face.

"Those packages you were making—what was in them?"

"Magic powder from Cathay, east of the Holy Land."

"Poison?"

"No. It—"

Above them, at the mountain's almost-summit, Weiland's fetch died.

Lylene fought for air. The repercussions of her creation's never-vocalized scream threatened to shatter her skull. She pressed her hands to her ears, shuddering convulsively, and sank to her knees even though she knew she was inches from the edge.

The top of the mountain blew off, and the ground beneath them shook.

Over the incredible crashing noise, she was aware of Weiland shouting her name, unable to get around the suddenly frantic horses which separated them. Her own horse shied and reared, missed trampling her by chance alone.

They were spattered by falling stones, and a huge

boulder hit the shelf to which they clung, shattering the section they had crossed seconds earlier.

A loud *crack!* and an entire section of the mountain behind them seemed to just crumble away.

Sherard was trying to calm her horse which separated them, and Weiland was leaving, going on without them after all, pulling the two other horses with him.

"Look out!" Sherard cried, and Lylene pressed herself tighter against the mountain as another boulder bounced down the steep slope. It skipped over her, hit the shelf just beyond her knees, splintering it even narrower. Her horse made an almost human scream, then was gone in a flurry of sliding debris.

Lylene put her hands on the unsteady rock wall behind and grappled herself to her feet. Sherard ducked a smaller flying rock, was suddenly beside her, once more holding his bound wrists to her. "Cut the rope!"

She reached for the knife Weiland insisted she wear, and the mountain shuddered again.

Sherard, unable to fling his arms out for balance, tipped precariously. Then slowly, so slowly that it seemed Lylene had all of time to grab for him, he slid over the edge, and her hands closed on empty air.

She reached too far, teetered out of control, saw the ground tip up to catch her.

Then straighten again. At a safe distance again. Weiland was holding onto the back of her shirt, pulling her from the crumbling edge. "Sherard," she said, but he wasn't interested. He guided her, dragging her when she stumbled, to where the path widened—to where he had been able to maneuver his way around the horses.

"Overhang," he shouted over the noise, pointing. "Do we take our chances out here, or risk getting trapped?"

Nothing, she figured, could be worse than this. They crawled into the tight space, coughing from the dust of crushed rock, and huddled with their arms around each other, silently praying that it wouldn't collapse on them. Or at least Lylene prayed: there was never any telling with Weiland.

Eventually the ground stopped quaking. Their overhang had stood firm. They crawled out into a new landscape, a landscape where even the birds had been shocked into silence, and the mountain had taken on a new shape entirely.

Somehow Weiland had wrenched a knee. (She assumed he had wrenched it. The alternative—having to do with the dead fetch, with the progression of dead fetches—was too awful to consider.) He was able to walk, but only by leaning on her. Lylene kept waiting for him to say, "I told you that was enough powder," but he didn't, which was even worse.

For her part, she kept thinking that if she had untied Sherard's hands when he first asked, he would still be alive.

The surviving horses, Weiland's and Sherard's, they found grazing peacefully by the abbey. The avalanche had swept away at least one of the annex buildings and damaged several others, including the granary. The monks were scurrying about trying to get the scattered wheat and barley under cover, out of the light drizzle which had started. They gave Lylene and Weiland baleful stares, but said nothing.

Silently, the two of them mounted the horses and continued toward Cheldenholme. Her horse, carrying the magical powder which had cost so much, was gone without a trace.

The drizzle turned to a fierce rain, and they were

soaked by the time they reached the town. A good section of the town wall was crushed under a new arm of the mountain, which had moved on to flatten the adjoining houses.

Townspeople peered out of windows. Not a word was spoken. At the inn, their belongings had been removed from their room and placed in their wagon, which was standing, hitched to the workhorses, all unprotected in the rain.

Lylene clenched her teeth, and didn't look at Weiland.

They rode on to the house in front of which they had stopped the day before. Now there was nobody there, friendly or not, to greet them.

"Yo! Townsman!" Weiland called. When there was no answer, he dismounted stiffly and banged on the door. He sighed, then kicked in the door.

Lylene followed him in. She caught a glimpse of a badly aged twenty-year-old who clutched several children by the unlit hearth and who watched Weiland drip rainwater on her well-scrubbed floor. The older of the merchants to whom she had spoken the day before approached, brandishing a wooden stave. But Weiland stood there, with his arms crossed over his chest as though daring him, and the man let the weapon drop.

"We got rid of the dragon," Weiland said cooly.

The merchant tried twice before he got his voice to work. "It destroyed an entire warehouse this morning before you got around to it," he finally answered, angry enough to transcend his fear, "and *you*: you took down half the town wall, scattered rocks over two-thirds of the few fields the dragon had left us, destroyed seven shops—including my brother-in-law's—killed five people, injured a score more, caved in the public well, and pelted the whole community with barrel-sized pieces of roast dragon.''

''Well,'' said Weiland, ''those things happen.''

Lylene stepped forward. ''I'm sorry. The magic I used was stronger than I had thought. We'll settle for half the balance of the agreed-upon fee. The rest can go to the affected families.''

''Half?'' the merchant squeaked. ''*If* that would pay for the damages—which it would not—''

Weiland grabbed him by the front of his shirt.

''We don't have it,'' the merchant whispered.

''You don't have what?''

''The rest of the fee.''

Weiland turned to her, still holding onto the merchant. ''Shall we burn down the town?''

''What do you mean, you don't have the fee?'' Lylene asked. ''What trickery is this?''

''No. No trickery. We *had* the money. But the town alderman . . .''

''What?'' Weiland shook him.

''Made off with it. We're still looking for him.''

''All this since morning?''

The man squirmed. ''Two weeks ago.''

''Let's burn the town down,'' Weiland repeated.

Lylene turned and pushed past him. She walked out of the house, past Sherard's horse, past the inn with their wagon parked in front, past the rubbled wall. She kept walking, through fields ruined that day and before, until she slipped in the wet and landed on her knees in the mud, with the rain beating down on her bowed back.

Eventually she heard the rattle of the wagon coming up behind her. She didn't look up, even when Weiland came round to stand before her. Absently, she noticed that his limp had gotten worse. "Did you burn down Cheldenholme?" she asked.

"It *is* raining," he pointed out, which she hoped, in a detached sort of way, meant no.

"I've been thinking about leaving." She finally looked at him. "This isn't working, you know, you and me together."

He stooped down in front of her, wincing at the movement, close enough to touch.

But never touching.

"Sometimes," she said, "sometimes your conduct is despicable."

"Mine?" he asked, his blue eyes wide with innocence and amazement that she could say such a thing. But she remembered too many things, and knew better. He flashed a smile. "Ah, but you've known that from the beginning."

She nodded, wouldn't look at him anymore.

"So you want to divide up the things, then? Go our separate ways?"

"I don't know what I want." She rested her face in her hands. "I'm too tired to think. You decide, Weiland."

When he didn't answer, she looked up. He shook his head, refusing the responsibility; and the cold rain continued to pelt them. Finally he reached forward, took her money purse.

At first she thought it was to count the money for dividing, but he took only the old Phoenician coin. With a questioning look, he held it in front of her. "King, we stay together; god, we separate," he suggested.

She nodded, thinking she was too tired to care, much less to make the decision. But by the time the coin reached the top of its arc, she found herself wishing which face would land up.

Which was a good thing, because that's the one that did.

Laurel, Again

Carol Jane Bangs

As a girl I dangled
my hand in the spring,
watched my face dissolve in ripples,
then gather together, so fat, so smooth,
the skin of my cheeks like ripe fruit,
my bright hair pinioned with leaves.
When the young shepherds chased
over hillock and valley
I was always a step out of reach,
my white feet slender
and light on the clover,
my bare arms gleaming in sunlight,
in the blue shadows under the trees.
When we reached the woodland
those boys always lost me,
beat wildly at dappled ferns and brambles,
saw without seeing the silver-barked trunk
into whose cracks I poured my laughter,
clinging tightly, my face in my hands.

Not every transformation comes early.
Men grow old before trees and
young men age fastest of all.
Two axes it took, and many awls, to shape
the wood for my husband's coffin
and the coffins of his sons.
Many years since this stubborn body
could wear a tree's thin shadow,
yet still I lift my dancing arms
toward the faint light sifting through branches,
my mouth remembers the language of stones,
and my silver hair rises in long coils,
scatters into a thousand leaves
that shake and twist in autumn breeze.

In the Drought

Ursula K. Le Guin

Sarah was watering the tomato plants, letting the water flow from the hose along the runnel between the big droopy messy bushes promiscuously mingling their green and red and yellow and little pearshaped and middlesized plumshaped and big tomatoshaped tomatoes so that she couldn't tell which one grew on which of the six plants. She ate a little yellow pearshaped one. It was like tart honey in her mouth. The marvelous bitter smell of the leaves was on her hands now. She thought it was time to get a basket and pick some of the reddest and yellowest ones, but only after she finished watering; there were still the two old roses needing a drink, and the youngest azalea looked very thirsty. Late afternoon light struck through the air at a long angle, making the water from the hose seem reddish. She looked again; there must be rust coming through the pipes. The flow from the end of the hose was reddish-brown, and increasingly opaque. She held up the hose and let the stream arch out so she could watch it. The color deepened fast to crimson. Striking the earth it made puddles of that intense and somber color on the dirt, slow to soak in. She had not touched the faucet, but the flow had increased. The red stream shooting from the end of the hose looked thick, almost solid. She did not want to touch it.

She set the hose down in the runnel and went to the standpipe to turn it off. It seemed wrong to water plants with water that looked like that. Puzzled and uneasy, she went up the two back stairs and into the kitchen, hooking the screen door shut behind her with a practised foot. Belle was standing at the sink. "There's something funny," Sarah began, but Belle looked at her and said, "Look."

From the arched steel faucet ran a red stream, spattering on the white enamel of the sink and pooling in the strainer before it ran down the drain.

"It must be the hot-water heater," Belle said.

"The garden hose is doing it too," Sarah said.

After a while Belle said, "It must be the drought. Something in the reservoirs. Mud from the bottom of the lakes, or something."

"Turn it off," Sarah said.

Belle turned off the hot tap. Then slowly, as if compelled, she turned on the cold tap. The red, thick flow spurted out, spattering heavily. Belle put her finger into the stream. "Don't!" Sarah said.

"It's hot," Belle said. "Almost hot." She turned it off.

They watched the red drops and splatters slide sluggishly towards the drain.

"Should we call the plumber," Belle said—"no, I guess not—but the city water thing, water department, bureau? Do you think? But I suppose it's happening to everybody, everybody would be calling at once, wouldn't they? Like earthquakes."

Sarah went into the front room and looked out the picture window, over the brown grass and across the street. The lawn sprinkler on the Mortensons' lawn was still going. Sunday evening was one of the two days a week watering was permitted under the drought restrictions. You were supposed to water only by hand and only shrubs and vegetable gardens, but Mr. Mortenson turned on his little lawn sprinkler and nobody said anything or reported him. He was a big man with two big teenage sons who rode motorbikes. He never spoke to Belle and Sarah and never looked at them. The sons never spoke, but sometimes they looked, staring while they talked with their friends who came in pickups and on motorbikes. Mr. Mortenson was in his carport cutting firewood, the whine of the power saw rising to a scream, stopping abruptly, starting again. Mrs. Mortenson had gone by an hour ago on her way to church; she went morning and evening on Sundays. She always looked away from Belle and Sarah's house when she passed it.

The telephone rang, and Sarah answered it to shut it up. It was Neenie. "Sarah! The darnedest thing! You won't believe! I went to pee and I looked in the toilet, you know, I just noticed, and it was all *red* and I thought oh, my heavens, I've got my period, and then I thought, but I'm sixty-*six!* and I had a hysterectomy, didn't I? and so I thought oh, oh no, it's my kidneys, I'm going to die, but I went to wash my hands, and the water came out of the *faucets* all red. So it isn't me, it has to be the city water, isn't that the strangest thing? Maybe some kind of fraternity joke thing? Eleanor thinks it's mud, because the water up in the watershed is so low, from the drought, but I called the city and they said nobody had reported any abnormalities. I don't suppose your water's coming funny, is it?"

"Yes," Sarah said, standing watching the low sunlight strike through the crystal showers from Mr. Mortenson's sprinkler. "Listen, Neenie, I'll call you back, I have to make a call now. Don't worry about it. Okay?"

"No, no I won't worry, it just seems so strange, goodbye," Neenie said hurriedly. "Love to Belle!"

Sarah called Andrew and got his recorded voice: "Hullo! Sorry, Tom and I aren't doing the telephone just now; but we'll get back to you soon." She waited for the beep and said, "Andrew, this is Sarah," and paused, and said, "Is there something funny with—" and Andrew came on the line: "Hullo, Sarah! I was monitoring. Tom says I mustn't feel guilty about monitoring."

"Andrew, this is weird, but is your water okay? your tap water?"

"Should I look?"

"Yes, would you?"

While Sarah waited, Belle came into the room. She straightened the afghan on the sofa and stood looking out across the street.

"Their water looks all right," she said.

Sarah nodded.

"Rainbows," Belle said.

Andrew came back on the line after a considerable time. "Hello, Sarah. Did you taste it?"

"No," she said, seeing again the thick, strong, bright red rush of it from the hose.

"I did," he said, and paused. "I asked Mrs. Simpson in the apartment downstairs. They have water. Not— what we have."

"What should we do?" Sarah said.

"Call the city," he said vigorously. "We pay for our water. They can't let this happen!"

"*Let* it happen?"

After a little while Andrew said, "Well, then, *we* can't let it happen."

"I'll call around," Sarah said.

"Do that. I'll call Sandy at the paper. We can't just . . ."

"No," she said. "We can't. Call me back if you find out anything. Or decide anything."

"You too. Okay? Talk to you soon. Chin up, not the end of the world!" He hung up; Sarah hung up and turned to Belle. "We'll get something going," she said. "There's a good network."

Belle went back to the kitchen, and Sarah followed her. Belle turned both taps full on. The red rush from the faucet spattered and coiled on the enamel. "Don't, don't," Sarah whispered, but Belle put her hands in the stream, turning and rubbing them together, washing them. "There are songs about this," she said. "But they're not my songs." She turned off the taps and deliberately wiped her hands on the white and yellow dish towel, leaving great smears and clots that would soon stiffen and turn brown. "I don't like city water," she said. "Never did. Or small-town water. It tastes funny. Tastes like sweat. Up in the mountains, you could drink from little creeks that run right out of the glaciers, out of the snowmelt. Like drinking air. Drinking sky. Bubbles without the champagne. I want to go back up to the mountains, Sarah."

"We'll go," Sarah said. "We'll go soon." They held each other for a while, close, silent.

"What *are* we going to drink?" Sarah whispered. Her voice shook.

Belle loosened her hold and leaned back a bit; she stroked Sarah's hair back from her face. "Milk," she said. "We'll drink milk, love."

Young Woman in a Garden

Delia Sherman

Beauvoisin (1839–1898)

Edouard Beauvoisin was expected to follow in the footsteps of his father, a provincial doctor. However, when he demonstrated a talent for drawing, his mother saw to it that he was provided with formal training. In 1856, Beauvoisin went to Paris, where he worked at the Académie Suisse and associated with the young artists disputing romanticism and classicism at the Brasserie des Martyrs. In 1868, he married the artist Céleste Rohan. He exhibited in the Salon des Refusés in 1863, and was a member of the 1874 Salon of Impressionists. In 1876 he moved to Brittany where he lived and painted until his death in 1898. He is best known for the figure-studies *Young Woman in a Garden* and *Reclining Nude*.

Impressions of the Impressionists
(Oxford University Press, 1970)

M. Henri Tanguy
Director
Musée La Roseraie
Portrieux, Brittany
France

January 6, 1994

Monsieur:

I write to you at the suggestion of M. Rouart of the Musée d'Orsay to request permission to visit the house of M. Edouard Beauvoisin and to consult those of his personal papers that are kept there.

In pursuit of a Ph.D. degree in the History of Art, I am preparing a thesis on the life and work of M. Beauvoisin, who, in my opinion, has been unfairly neglected in the history of Impressionism.

Enclosed is a letter of introduction from my adviser, Professor Boodman of the Department of Art History at the University of Massachusetts. She has advised me to tell you that I also have a personal interest in M. Beauvoisin's life, for his brother was my great-great-grandfather.

I expect to be in France from May 1 of this year, and to stay for at least two months. My visit to La Roseraie may be scheduled according to your convenience. Awaiting your answer, I have the honor to be

Your servant, Theresa Stanton

When Theresa finally found La Roseraie at the end of an unpaved, narrow road, she was tired and dusty and on the verge of being annoyed. Edouard Beauvoisin had been an Impressionist, even if only a minor Impressionist, and his house was a museum, open by appointment to the public. At home in Massachusetts, that would mean signs, postcards in the nearest village, certainly a brochure in the local tourist office with color pictures of the garden and the master's studio and a good clear map showing how to get there.

France wasn't Massachusetts, not by a long shot.

M. Tanguy hadn't met her at the Portrieux station as he had promised, the local tourist office had been sketchy in its directions, and the driver of the local bus had been depressingly uncertain about where to let her off. Her feet were sore, her backpack heavy, and even after asking at the last two farmhouses she'd passed, Theresa still wasn't sure she'd found the right place. The house didn't look like a museum: gray stone, low-browed and secretive, its front door unequivocally barred, its low windows blinded with heavy white lace curtains. The gate was stiff and loud with rust. Still, there was a neat stone path leading around to the back of the house and a white sign with the word *"jardin"* printed on it and a faded black hand pointing down the path. Under the scent of dust and greenery, there was a clean, sharp scent of salt water. Theresa hitched up her backpack, heaved open the gate, and followed the hand's gesture.

"Monet" was her first thought when she saw the garden, and then, more accurately, "Beauvoisin." Impressionist, certainly—an incandescent, carefully balanced dazzle of yellow light, clear green grass, and carmine flowers against a celestial background. Enchanted, Theresa unslung her camera and captured a couple of faintly familiar views of flower beds and sequined water before turning to the house itself.

The back door was marginally more welcoming than

the front, for at least it boasted a visible bellpull and an aged, hand-lettered sign directing the visitor to *"sonnez,"* which Theresa did, once hopefully, once impatiently, and once again for luck. She was just thinking that she'd have to walk back to Portrieux and call M. Tanguy when the heavy door opened inward, revealing a Goyaesque old woman. Against the flat shadows of a stone passage, she was a study in black and white: long wool skirt and linen blouse, sharp eyes and finely crinkled skin.

The woman looked Theresa up and down, then made as if to shut the door in her face.

"Wait," cried Theresa, putting her hand on the warm planks. *"Arretez. S'il vous plait. Un moment.* Please!"

The woman's gaze travelled to Theresa's face. Theresa smiled charmingly.

"Eh, bien?" asked the woman impatiently.

Pulling her French around her, Theresa explained that she was making researches into the life and work of the famous M. Beauvoisin, that she had written in the winter for permission to see the museum, that seeing it was of the first importance to completing her work. She had received a letter from M. le Directeur, setting an appointment for today.

The woman raised her chin suspiciously. Her smile growing rigid, Theresa juggled camera and bag, dug out the letter, and handed it over. The woman examined it front and back, then returned it with an eloquent gesture of shoulders, head, and neck that conveyed her utter indifference to Theresa's work, her interest in Edouard Beauvoisin, and her charm.

"Fermé," she said, and suited the action to the word.

"Parent," said Theresa rather desperately. *"Je suis de la famille de M. Beauvoisin."*

From the far end of the shadowy passage, a soft, deep voice spoke in accented English. "Of course you are, my dear. A great-grandniece, I believe. Luna," she shifted to French, "surely you remember the letter from M. le Directeur about our little American relative?" And in English again. "Please to come through. I am Mme Beauvoisin."

In 1874, Céleste's mother died, leaving La Roseraie to her only child. There was some talk of selling the house to satisfy the couple's immediate financial embarrassments, but the elder Mme Beauvoisin came to the rescue once again with a gift of 20,000 francs. After paying off his debts, Beauvoisin decided that Paris was just too expensive, and moved with Céleste to Portrieux in the spring of 1875.

"I have taken some of my mother's gift and put it toward transforming the ancient dairy of La Roseraie into a studio," he wrote Manet. "Ah, solitude! You cannot imagine how I crave it, after the constant sociability of Paris. I realize now that the cafés affected me like absinthe: stimulating and full of visions, but death to the body and damnation to the soul."

In the early years of what his letters to Manet humorously refer to as his "exile," Beauvoisin travelled often to Paris, and begged his old friends to come and stay with him. After 1879, however, he became something of a recluse, terminating his trips to Paris and discouraging visits, even from the Manets. He spent the last twenty years of his life a virtual hermit, painting the subjects that were dearest to him: the sea, his garden, the fleets of fishing-boats that sailed daily out and back from the harbor of Portrieux.

The argument has been made that Beauvoisin had

never been as clannish as others among the Impressionists, Renoir and Monet, for example, who regularly set up their easels and painted the same scene side by side. Certainly Beauvoisin seemed unusually reluctant to paint his friends and family. His single portrait of his wife, executed not long after their marriage, is one of his poorest canvases: stiff, awkwardly posed, and uncharacteristically muddy in color. "Mme Beauvoisin takes exception to my treatment of her dress," he complained in a letter to Manet, "or the shadow of the chair, or the balance of the composition. God save me from the notions of women who think themselves artists!"

In 1877, the Beauvoisins took a holiday in Spain, and there met a young woman named Luz Gascó, who became Edouard's favorite—indeed his only—model. The several nude studies of her, together with the affectionate intimacy of *Young Woman in a Garden*, leave little doubt as to the nature of their relationship, even in the absence of documentary evidence. Luz came to live with the Beauvoisins at La Roseraie in 1878, and remained there even after Beauvoisin's death in 1898. She inherited the house and land from Mme Beauvoisin and died in 1914, just after the outbreak of the First World War.

> Lydia Chopin, *"Lives Lived in Shadow:*
> *Edouard and Céleste Beauvoisin,"*
> *Apollo,* Winter, 1989

The garden of La Roseraie extended through a series of terraced beds down to the water's edge and up into the house itself by way of a bank of uncurtained French doors in the parlor. When Theresa first followed her

hostess into the room, her impression was of blinding
light and color and of flowers everywhere—scattered on
the chairs and sofas, strewn underfoot, heaped on every
flat surface, vining across the walls. The air was somno-
lent with peonies and roses and bee-song.

"A lovely room."

"It has been kept just as it was in the time of
Beauvoisin, though I fear the fabrics have faded sadly.
You may recognize the sofa from *Young Woman Reading*
and *Reclining Nude,* also the view down the terrace."

The flowers on the sofa were pillows, printed or nee-
dlepointed with huge, blowsy, ambiguous blooms.
Those pillows had formed a textural contrast to the
model's flat-black gown in *Young Woman Reading* and
sounded a sensual, almost erotic note in *Reclining Nude.*
As Theresa touched one almost reverently—it had sup-
ported the model's head—the unquiet colors of the room
settled in place around it, and she saw that there were
indeed flowers everywhere. Real petals had blown in
from the terrace to brighten the faded woven flowers of
the carpet, and the walls and chairs were covered in
competing chintzes to provide a background for the
plain burgundy velvet sofa, the wooden easel, and the
portrait over the mantel of a child dressed in white.

"Céleste," said Mme Beauvoisin. "Céleste Yvonne
Léna Rohan, painted at the age of six by some Academi-
cian—I cannot at the moment recollect his name, although M. Rohan was as proud of securing his services
as if he'd been Ingres himself. She hated it."

"How could you possibly . . ." Theresa's question
trailed off at the amusement in Mme Beauvoisin's face.

"Family legend. The portrait is certainly very stiff and
finished, and Céleste grew to be a disciple of Morisot

and Manet. Taste in aesthetic matters develops very young, do you not agree?"

"I do," said Theresa. "At any rate, I've loved the Impressionists since I was a child. I wouldn't blame her for hating the portrait. It's technically accomplished, yes, but it says nothing about its subject except that she was blonde and played the violin."

"That violin!" Mme Beauvoisin shook her head, ruefully amused. "Mme Rohan's castle in Spain. The very sight of it was a torture to Céleste. And her hair darkened as she grew older, so you see the portrait tells you nothing. This, on the other hand, tells all."

She led Theresa to a small painting hung by the door. "Luz Gascó," she said. "Painted in 1879."

Liquid, animal eyes gleamed at Theresa from the canvas, their gaze at once inviting and promising, intimate as a kiss. Theresa glanced aside at Mme Beauvoisin, who was studying the portrait, her head tilted to one side, her wrinkled lips smoothed by a slight smile. Feeling unaccountably embarrassed, Theresa frowned at the painting with self-conscious professionalism. It was, she thought, an oil study of the model's head for Beauvoisin's most famous painting, *Young Woman in a Garden*. The face was tilted up to the observer and partially shadowed. The brushwork was loose and free, the boundaries between the model's hair and the background blurred, the molding of her features suggested rather than represented.

"A remarkable portrait," Theresa said. "She seems very . . . alive."

"Indeed," said Mme Beauvoisin. "And very beautiful." She turned abruptly and, gesturing Theresa to a chair, arranged herself on the sofa opposite. The afternoon light fell across her shoulder, highlighting her white hair, the pale rose pinned in the bosom of her high-necked dress, her hands folded on her lap. Her fingers were knotted and swollen with arthritis. Theresa wondered how old she was and why M. Tanguy had said nothing of a caretaker in his letter to her.

"Your work?" prompted Mme Beauvoisin gently.

Theresa pulled herself up and launched into what she thought of as her dissertation spiel: neglected artist, brilliant technique, relatively small ouvre, social isolation, mysterious ménage. "What I keep coming back to," she said, "is his isolation. He hardly ever went to Paris after 1879, and even before that he didn't go on those group painting trips the other Impressionists loved so much. He never shared a studio even though he was so short of money, or let anyone watch him paint. And yet his letters to Manet suggest that he wasn't a natural recluse—anything but."

"Thus Luz Gascó?" asked Mme Beauvoisin.

"I'm sorry?"

"Luz Gascó. Perhaps you think she was the cause of Beauvoisin's—how shall I say?—Beauvoisin's retreat from society?"

Theresa gave a little bounce in her chair. "That's just it, you see. No one really knows. There are a lot of assumptions, especially by *male* historians, but no one really knows. What I'm looking for is evidence one way or the other. At first I thought she couldn't have been . . ." She hesitated, suddenly self-conscious.

"Yes?" The low voice was blandly polite, yet Theresa felt herself teased, or perhaps tested. It annoyed her, and her answer came a little more sharply than necessary.

"Beauvoisin's mistress." Mme Beauvoisin raised her brows and Theresa shrugged apologetically. "There's not much known about Céleste, but nothing suggests that she was particularly meek or downtrodden. I don't think she'd have allowed Luz to live here all those years, much less left the house to her, if she knew Luz was . . . involved with her husband."

"Perhaps she knew and did not concern herself." Mme Beauvoisin offered this consideringly.

"I hadn't thought of that," said Theresa. "I'd need proof, though. I'm not interested in speculation, theory, or even in a juicy story. I'm interested in the truth."

Mme Beauvoisin's smile said that she found Theresa very young, very charming. "Yes," she said slowly. "I believe you are." Her voice grew brisker. "Beauvoisin's papers are in some disorder, you understand. Your search may take you some weeks, and Portrieux is far to travel twice a day. It would please me if you would accept the hospitality of La Roseraie."

Theresa closed her eyes. It was a graduate student's dream come true, to be invited into her subject's home, to touch and use his things, to live his life. Mme Beauvoisin, misinterpreting the gesture, said, "Please stay. This project—Beauvoisin's papers—it is of great importance to us, to Luna and to me. We feel that you are well suited to the task."

To emphasize her words, she laid her twisted hand on Theresa's arm. The gesture brought her face into the sun, which leached her eyes and skin to transparency and made a glory of her silvered hair. Theresa stared at her, entranced.

"Thank you," she said. "I would be honored."

Young Woman in a Garden (Luz at La Roseraie), 1879
   Edouard Beauvoisin's artistic reputation rests on this portrait of his Spanish mistress, Luz Gascó, seated in the garden of La Roseraie. As in *Reclining*

Nude, the composition is arranged around a figure that seems to be the painting's source of light as well as its visual focus. Luz sits with her face and body in shade and her feet and hands in bright sunlight. Yet the precision with which her shadowy figure is rendered, the delicate modeling of the face, and the suggestion of light shining down through the leaves onto the dark hair draw the viewer's eye up and away from the brightly-lit foreground. The brushwork of the white blouse is especially masterly, the coarse texture of the linen suggested with a scumble of pale pink, violet, and gray.

"The Unknown Impressionists,"
exhibition catalogue,
Museum of Fine Arts, Boston, Mass.

"This is the studio."

Mme Beauvoisin laid her hand on the blue-painted door, hesitated, then stepped aside. "Please," she said, and gave Theresa a courteous nod.

Heart tripping over itself with excitement, Theresa pushed open the door and stepped into Beauvoisin's studio. The room was shuttered, black as midnight; she knocked over a chair, which fell with an echoing clatter.

"I fear the trustees have hardly troubled themselves to unlock the door since they came into possession of the property," said Mme Beauvoisin apologetically. "And Luna and I have little occasion to come here." Theresa heard her shoe heels tapping across the flagstone floor. A creak, a bang, and weak sunlight struggled over a clutter of easels, canvases, trunks and boxes, chairs, stools, and small tables disposed around a round stove and a shabby sofa. *The French sure are peculiar,* Theresa thought. *What a way to run a museum!*

Mme Beauvoisin had taken up a brush and was standing before one of the easels in the attitude of a painter interrupted at work. For a moment, Theresa thought she saw a canvas on the easel, an oil sketch of a seated figure. An unknown Beauvoisin? As she stepped forward to look, an ancient swag of cobweb broke and showered her head with flies and powdery dust. She sneezed convulsively.

"God bless you," said Mme Beauvoisin, laying the brush on the empty easel. "Luna brings a broom. Pah! What filth! Beauvoisin must quiver in his tomb, such an orderly man as he was!"

Soon, the old woman arrived with the promised broom, a pail of water, and a settled expression of grim disapproval. She poked at the cobwebs with the broom, glared at Theresa, then began to sweep with concentrated ferocity, raising little puffs of dust as she went and muttering to herself, witch-like.

"So young," she said. "Too young. Too full of ideas. Too much like Edouard, *enfin.*"

Theresa bit her lip, caught between curiosity and irritation. Curiosity won. "How am I like him, Luna?" she asked. "And how can you know? He's been dead almost a hundred years."

The old woman straightened and turned, her face creased deep with fury. "Luna!" she snarled. "Who has given you the right to call me Luna? I am not a servant, to be addressed without respect."

"You're not? I mean, of course not. I beg your pardon, Mlle . . . ?" And Theresa looked a wild appeal to Mme Beauvoisin, who said, "The fault is entirely mine, Mlle

Stanton, for not introducing you sooner. Mlle Gascó is
my companion."

Theresa laughed nervously, as at an incomprehensi-
ble joke. "You're kidding," she said. "Mlle Gascó? But
that was the model's name, Luz's name. I don't understand. Who are you, anyway?"

Mme Beauvoisin shrugged dismissively. "There is
nothing to understand. We are Beauvoisin's heirs. And
the contents of this studio are our inheritance, which is
now yours also. Come and look." With a theatrical
flourish, she indicated a cabinet built along the back
wall. "Open it," she said. "The doors are beyond my
strength."

Theresa looked from Mme Beauvoisin to Mlle Gascó
and back again. Every scholar knows that coincidences
happen, that people leave things to their relatives, that
reality is sometimes unbelievably strange. And this was
what she had come for, after all, to open the cabinet, to
recover all the mysteries and illuminate the shadows of
Beauvoisin's life. Perhaps this Mlle Gascó was his il-
legitimate granddaughter. Perhaps both women were
playing some elaborate and obscure game. In any case,
it was none of her business. Her business was with the
cabinet and its contents.

The door was warped, and Theresa had to struggle
with it for a good while before it creaked stiffly open on
a cold stench of mildew and the shadowy forms of dispatch boxes neatly arranged on long shelves. Theresa
sighed happily. Here they were, Beauvoisin's papers, a
scholar's treasure trove, her ticket to a degree, a career,
a profession. And they were all hers. She reached out
both hands and gathered in the nearest box. As the
damp cardboard yielded to her fingers, she felt a sudden
panic that the papers would be mildewed into illegibil-

ity. But inside the box the papers were wrapped in oil-cloth and perfectly dry.

Reverently, Theresa lifted out a packet of letters, tied with black tape. The top one was folded so that some of the text showed. Having just spent a month working with Beauvoisin's letters to Manet at the Bibliothèque National, she immediately recognized his hand, tiny and angular and blessedly legible. Theresa slipped the letter free from the packet and opened it. *I have met,* she read, *a dozen other young artists in the identical state of fearful ecstasy as I, feeling great things about Art and Beauty which we are half-shy of expressing, yet must express or die.*

"Thérèse." Mme Beauvoisin sounded amused. "First we must clean this place. Then you may read Beauvoisin's words with more comfort and less danger of covering them with smuts."

Theresa became aware that she was holding the precious letter in an unforgivably dirty hand. "Oh," she said, chagrined. "I'm so sorry. I *know* better than this."

"It is the excitement of discovery." Mme Beauvoisin took the letter from her and rubbed lightly at the corner with her apron. "See, it comes clean, all save a little shadow that may easily be overlooked." She folded the letter, slipped it back into the packet, returned it to the box, and tucked the oilcloth over it.

"Today, the preparation of the canvas," she said. "Tomorrow, you may begin the sketch."

Edouard Beauvoisin had indeed been an orderly man. The letters were parcelled up by year, in order of receipt, and labelled. Turning over Manet's half of their long correspondence, Theresa briefly regretted her choice of research topic. Manet's was a magic name, a name to conjure up publishers and job offers, fame and what passed for fortune among art historians. She'd certainly get a paper or two out of those letters, maybe petition for permission to edit them, but she didn't want a reputation as a Manet scholar. Manet, documented, described, and analyzed by every art historian worth a pince-nez, could never be hers. Beauvoisin was hers.

Theresa sorted out all the business papers, the bills for paint and canvas, the notes from obscure friends. What was left was the good stuff: a handful of love notes written by Céleste Rohan over the two years Beauvoisin had courted her, three boxes of letters from his mother, and two boxes of his answers, which must have been returned to him at her death.

It took Theresa a week to work through the letters, a week of long hours reading in the studio and short, awkward meals eaten in the kitchen with Mme Beauvoisin and Luna. It was odd. In the house and garden, the two old women were everywhere, present as the sea smell, forever on the way to some domestic task or other, yet never too busy to inquire politely and extensively after her progress. Or at least Mme Beauvoisin was never too busy. Luna mostly glared at her, hoped she wasn't wasting her time, warned her not to go picking the flowers or walking on the grass. It didn't take long for Theresa to decide that she didn't like Luna.

She did, however, discover that she liked Edouard Beauvoisin. In the studio, Theresa could lose herself in Beauvoisin's world of artists and models. The letters to his mother from his early years in Paris painted an intriguing portrait of an intelligent, naïve young man whose most profound desire was to capture and define Beauty in charcoal and oils. He wrote of poses and technical problems and what his teacher M. Couture had said about his life studies, reaffirming in each letter his intention *to draw and draw and draw until every line breathes the essence of the thing itself.* A little over a year later, he was speaking less of line and more of color; the name Couture disappeared from his letters, to be replaced by Manet, Degas, Duranty, and the brothers Goncourt. By 1860, he had quit the Ecole des Beaux Arts and registered to copy the Old Masters at the Louvre. A year later, he met Céleste Rohan at the house of Berthe Morisot's sister Edma Pontillon:

> *She is like a Raphael Madonna, tall and slender and pale, and divinely unconscious of her own beauty. She said very little at dinner, but afterwards in the garden with Morisot conversed with me an hour or more. I learned then that she is thoughtful and full of spirit, loves Art and Nature, and is herself something of an artist, with a number of watercolors and oil sketches to her credit that, according to Morisot, show considerable promise.*

Three months later, he announced to his mother that Mlle Rohan had accepted his offer of hand and heart. Mme Beauvoisin the elder said everything that was proper, although a note of worry did creep through in her final lines:

> *I am a little concerned about her painting. To be sure, painting is an amiable accomplishment in a young girl, but you must be careful, in your joy at finding a soul-mate, not to foster useless ambitions in her breast. I'm sure you both agree that a wife must have no other profession than seeing to the comfort of her husband, particularly when her husband is an artist and entirely unable to see to his own.*

When she read this, Theresa snorted. Perhaps her mother-in-law was why Céleste, like Edma Morisot and dozens of other lady artists, had laid down her brush when she married. Judging from her few surviving canvases, she'd been a talented painter, if too indebted to the style of Berthe Morisot. Now, if Céleste had just written to her future husband about painting or ambition or women's role in marriage, Theresa would have an easy chapter on the repression of women artists in nineteenth-century France.

It was with high hopes, therefore, that Theresa opened the small bundle of Céleste's correspondence. She soon discovered that however full of wit and spirit Céleste may have been in conversation, on paper she was terse and dull. Her letters were limited to a few scrawled lines of family news, expressions of gratitude for books her fiancé had recommended, and a few, shy declarations of maidenly affection. The only signs of her personality were the occasional vivid sketches with which she illustrated her notes: a seal pup sunning itself on the rocks at the mouth of the bay; a cow peering thoughtfully in through the dairy window.

Theresa folded Céleste's letters away, tied the tape neatly around them, and sighed. She was beginning to feel discouraged. No wonder there'd been so little written on Edouard Beauvoisin. No wonder his studio was neglected, his museum unmarked, his only curators an eccentric pair of elderly women. There had been dozens of competent but uninspired followers of the Impressionists who once or twice in the course of their lives had managed to paint great pictures. The only thing that set Edouard Beauvoisin apart from them was the mystery of Luz Gascó, and as Theresa read his dutiful letters to his mother, she found that she just could not believe that the man who had written them could bring his mistress to live with his wife. More importantly, she found herself disbelieving that he could ever have painted *Young Woman in a Garden*. Yet there it incontrovertibly was, hanging in the Museum of Fine Arts, signed "Edouard Beauvoisin, 1879," clear as print and authenticated five ways from Sunday.

A breeze stirred the papers scattered across the worktable. Under the ever-present tang of the sea, Theresa smelled lilies of the valley. She propped her chin on her hands and looked out into the garden. A pretty day, she thought, and a pretty view. It might make a picture, were there anything to balance the window frame and the mass of the linden tree in the left foreground. Oh, there was the rose bed, but it wasn't enough. A figure stepped into the scene, bent to the roses, clipped a bloom, laid it in the basket dangling from her elbow: Gascó, a red shawl tied Spaniard-wise across her white morning gown, her wild black hair escaping from its pins and springing around her face as she stooped. Her presence focussed the composition, turned it into an interesting statement of light and tension.

Don't move, Theresa thought. For God's sake, Gascó, don't move. Squinting at the scene, she opened a drawer with a practiced jerk and felt for the sketchbook, which was not on top where it should be, where it always was. Irritated, she tore her eyes from Gascó to look for it. Lying in the back of the drawer was a child's *cahier,* marbled black and white, with a plain white label pasted on its cover and marked "May-June 1898" in a tiny, angular, blessedly legible hand.

"Out of place," she murmured angrily, then, "This is *it,"* without any clear idea of what she meant by either statement.

Theresa swallowed, aware that something unimaginably significant had happened, was happening, that she was trembling and sweating with painful excitement. Carefully, she wiped her hands on her jeans, lifted the *cahier* from its wooden tomb, opened it to its last entry: June 5, 1898. The hand was scratchier, more sprawled than in his letters, the effect, perhaps, of the wasting disease that would kill him in July.

The Arrangement. A pity my death must void it. How well it has served us over the years, and how happily! At least, C. has seemed happy; for L.'s discontents, there has never been any answer, except to leave and make other arrangements of her own. Twenty years of flying into rages, sinking into sulks, refusing to stand thus and so or to hold a pose not to her liking, hating Brittany, the cold, the damp, the gray sea. And still she stays. Is it the Arrangement that binds her, or her beloved garden? Young Woman in a Garden: Luz at La Roseraie. *If I have a fear of dying, it is that I must be remembered for that painting. God's judgment on our Arrangement, Maman would have said, had she known of it. When I come to make my last Confession, soon, oh, very soon now, I will beg forgiveness for deceiving her. It is my only regret.*

By dusk, Theresa had read the notebook through and begun to search for its fellows. That there had to be more notebooks was as clear as Monet's palette: the first entry began in midsentence, for one thing, and no man talks to himself so fluently without years of practice. They wouldn't be hidden, Beauvoisin hadn't been a secretive man. Tidy-minded. Self-contained. Conservative. He stored them somewhere, Theresa thought. Somewhere here. She looked around the darkening studio. Maybe it would be clearer to her in the morning. It would certainly be lighter.

Out in the garden, Theresa felt the depression of the past days release her like a hand opening. *A discovery! A real discovery!* What difference did it make whether Beauvoisin had painted two good paintings or a dozen? There was a mystery about him, and she, Theresa Stanton, was on the verge of uncovering it. She wanted to babble and sing and go out drinking to celebrate. But her friends were three thousand miles away, and all she had was Mme Beauvoisin. And Luna. Always Luna.

Theresa's quick steps slowed. What was her hurry, after all? Her news would keep, and the garden was so lovely in the failing light, with the white pebble path luminous under her feet, the evening air blue and warm and scented with lilies.

In the parlor, an oil lamp laid its golden hand upon the two women sitting companionably on the velvet sofa, their heads bent to their invisible tasks. The soft play of light and shadow varnished their hair and skin with youth. Theresa struggled with a momentary and inexplicable sense of déjà vu, then, suddenly embarrassed, cleared her throat. "I found a notebook today," she announced into the silence. "Beauvoisin's private journal."

Luna's head came up, startled and alert. Theresa caught a liquid flash as she glanced at her, then at Mme Beauvoisin.

"A journal?" asked Mme Beauvoisin blandly. "Ah. I might have guessed he would have kept a journal. You must be very pleased—such documents are important to scholars. Come. Pour yourself a brandy to celebrate—the bottle is on the sideboard—and sit and tell us of your great discovery."

As Theresa obediently crossed the room and unstoppered the decanter, she heard a furious whisper. *"Mierda!"*

"Hush, Luna." Mme Beauvoisin's tone was happy, almost gleeful. "We agreed. Whatever she finds, she may use. It is her right."

"I withdraw my agreement. I know nothing of these journals. Who can tell what he may have written?"

A deep and affectionate sigh. "Oh, Luna. Still so suspicious?"

"Not suspicious. Wise. The little American, she is of Edouard's blood and also Edouard's soul. I have seen him in her eyes."

Theresa set down the decanter and came back into the lamplight. "Wait a minute. I don't understand. Of course I have the right to use the journals. M. Tanguy promised me full access to all Beauvoisin's papers. And he didn't say anything about you or needing your permission."

Mme Beauvoisin's dark, faded eyes held hers for a moment. "Please, do not discommode yourself," she said. "Sit and tell us what you have found."

Hesitant under Luna's hot and disapproving gaze, Theresa perched herself on the edge of a chair and did as she was told.

"I'd no idea he was so passionate," Theresa said at last. "In his letters, although he speaks of passion, he's always so moderate about expressing it."

"Moderate!" Luna's laugh was a scornful snort. "Hear the girl! *Madre de Dios!*"

"Hush, Luna. Please continue."

"That's all. I didn't really learn much, except that he knew in June that he was dying. One interesting thing was his references to an Arrangement—that's with a capital *A*—and how he'd never told his *maman* about

it.'' Excitement rose in her again. ''I have to find the rest
of the journals!''

Mme Beauvoisin smiled at her. ''Tomorrow. You will
find them, I'm sure of it.''

''Céleste,'' said Luna warningly.

''Hush, my dear.''

Theresa retired, as always, before her elderly companions. As polite as Mme Beauvoisin was to her, she always felt uncomfortable in the parlor, as if her presence
there were an intrusion, a threat, a necessary evil.
Which, she told herself firmly, in a way, it was. The two
women had been living here alone for heaven only
knew how long. It was only natural that they'd feel put
out by her being there. It was silly of her to resent her
exclusion from their charmed circle. And yet, tonight
especially, she did.

Theresa curled up in a chair by the window, tucked
the duvet around her legs, and considered the problem
of Edouard's notebooks. A full moon washed the pale
roses and the white paths with silver. In her mind, she
followed Edouard down one of those luminous paths to
the studio, where he sat at his desk, pulled his current
notebook from the right-hand drawer, and reread his
last entry only to discover that he'd barely one page left.
He shook his head, rose, went to the cabinet, opened
one of the long drawers where he kept his paints and
pigments neatly arranged in shallow wooden trays.
Carefully, he lifted one tray, slipped a new marbled
cahier from under it, returned to his desk, and began to
write.

When Theresa opened her eyes, the garden was cool
in a pale golden dawn. Her neck was in agony, her legs
hopelessly cramped, but she was elated. The notebooks

were in the cabinet under the paint trays—they just had to be!

Twenty minutes later, she was in the studio herself, with the paint trays stacked on the floor, gloating over layers of black-and-white-marbled *cahiers*.

There were more than a hundred of them, she discovered, distributed over four drawers and forty-two years, from Beauvoisin's first trip to Paris in 1856 to his death in 1898. Theresa took out five or six of them at random and paged through them as she had paged through books as a child, stopping to read passages that caught her eye. Not entirely professional, perhaps. But thoroughly satisfying.

April 20, 1875

Paris is so full of bad paintings, I can't begin to describe them. I know C.'s would enjoy some modest success, but she will not agree. One of Mlle Morisot's canvases has sold for a thousand francs—a seascape not so half as pretty as the one C. painted at La Roseraie last month. I compliment her often on her work, and am somewhat distressed that she does not return the courtesy, from love of the artist if not from admiration of his work. But then C. has never understood my theory of light and evanescence, and will not agree with my principles of composition.

Theresa closed the notebook with a snap, unreasonably disappointed with Beauvoisin for his blindness to the structures of his society. Surely he must have known, as Céleste obviously knew, that men were professionals and women were amateurs, unless they were honorary men like Berthe Morisot and Mary Cassatt. Poor Céleste, Theresa thought, and poor Edouard. What had they seen in one another?

Over the next few days, Theresa chased the answer to that question through the pages of Edouard's journals, skipping from one capital *C.* to the next, composing a sketch-portrait of a very strange marriage. That Beauvoisin had loved Céleste was clear. That he had loved her as a wife was less so. He spoke of her as a travelling companion, a hostess, a housekeeper. A sister, Theresa thought suddenly, reading how Céleste had arranged the details of their trip to Spain in the winter of 1877. She's like the maiden sister keeping house for her brilliant brother. And Edouard, he was a man who saved all his passion for his art, at any rate until he went to Spain and met Luz Gascó.

I have made some sketches of a woman we met in the Prado—a respectable woman and tolerably educated, although fallen on evil times. She has quite the most beautiful skin I have seen—white as new cream and so fine that she seems to glow of her own light, like a lamp draped with heavy silk. Such bones! And her hair and eyes, like black marble polished and by some miracle brought to life and made supple. C. saw her first, and effected an introduction. She is a joy to paint, and not expensive. . . .

Eagerly, Theresa skimmed through the next months for further references to the beautiful *señorita*. Had Edouard fallen in love at last? He certainly wrote as if he had—long, poetic descriptions of her skin, her hair, her form, her luminous, living presence. At the same time, he spoke fearfully of her temper, her unaccountable moods, her uncontrollable "gypsy nature." In the end, however, simple painterly covetousness resolved his dilemma and he invited Gascó to spend the summer at La Roseraie.

May 6, 1878

Luz Gascó expected tomorrow. C., having vacated the blue chamber for her, complains of having nowhere to paint. Perhaps I'll build an extension to my studio. Gascó is a great deal to ask of a wife, after all, even though C. knows better than any other how unlikely my admiration is to overstep propriety. As a model, Gascó is perfection. As a woman, she is like a wild cat, ready to hiss and scratch for no reason. Yet that skin! Those eyes! I despair of capturing them and ache to make the attempt.

Fishing Boats *not going well. The boats are wooden and the water also. I shall try Gascó in the foreground to unbalance the composition. . . .*

How violently the presence of Luz Gascó had unbalanced the nicely calculated composition of Edouard Beauvoisin's life became clearer to Theresa the more she read. She hardly felt excluded now from her hostesses' circle, eager as she was to get back to the studio and to Edouard, for whom she was feeling more and more sympathy. Pre-Gascó, his days had unfolded methodically: work, walks with Céleste, drives to the village, letter-writing, notebook-keeping, sketching—each allotted its proper time and space, regular as mealtimes. *G. rises at noon,* he mourned a week into her visit. *She breaks pose because she has seen a bird in the garden or wants to smell a flower. She is utterly impossible. Yet she transforms the world around her.*

Imperceptibly, the summer visit extended into autumn and the autumn into winter as Beauvoisin planned and painted canvas after canvas, experimenting with composition, technique, pigment. By the spring of 1879, there was talk of Gascó's staying. By summer, she was a fixture, and Beauvoisin was beside himself with huge, indefinite emotions and ambitions, all of them arranged, like his canvases, around the dynamic figure of Luz Gascó. Then came July, and a page blank save for one line:

July 6, 1879
  Luz in the parlor. Ah, Céleste!

A puzzling entry, marked as if for easy reference with a scrap of cheap paper folded in four. Theresa picked it up and carefully smoothed it open—not carefully enough, however, to keep the brittle paper from tearing along its creases. She saw dark lines—a charcoal sketch—and her heart went cold in panic. What have I done? she thought. What have I destroyed?

With a trembling hand, she arranged the four pieces on the table. The image was a reclining woman, her face turned away under an upflung arm, her bodice unbuttoned to the waist and her chemise loosened and folded open. A scarf of dark curls draped her throat and breast, veiling and exposing her nakedness. The sketch was intimate, more tender than erotic, a lover's mirror.

Theresa put her hands over her eyes. She'd torn the sketch; she didn't need to cry over it too. Spilt milk, she told herself severely. M. Rouart would know how to restore it. And she should be happy she'd found it, overjoyed to have such dramatic proof of Beauvoisin's carnal passion for his Spanish model. So why did she feel regretful, sad, disappointed, and so terribly, overwhelmingly angry?

A shadow fell across the page. A gnarled, nail-bitten forefinger traced the charcoal line of the subject's hair.

"Ah," said Luna softly. "I wondered what had become of this."

Theresa clenched her own hands in her lap, appalled by the emotion that rose in her at the sound of that hoarse, slightly lisping voice. Luna was certainly irritating. But this was not irritation Theresa felt. It was rage.

"A beautiful piece, is it not?" The four torn pieces were not perfectly aligned: the woman seemed broken at the waist; her left arm, lying across her hips, was dismembered at the elbow. Luna coaxed her back together with delicate touches. "A pity that my own beauty may not be so easily repaired."

Surprised, Theresa looked up at Luna's aged turtle face. She'd never imagined Luna young, let alone beautiful. Yet now she saw that her bones were finely turned under her leathery skin and her eyes were unfaded and bright black as a mouse's. A vaguely familiar face, and an interesting one, now that Theresa came to study it. Something might be made of it, against a background of flowers, or the garden wall.

Luna straightened, regarding Theresa with profound disgust. "You're his to the bone," she said. "You see what you need to see, not what is there. I told her a stranger would have been better."

Theresa's fury had subsided, leaving only bewilderment behind. She rubbed her eyes wearily. "I'm sorry," she said. "I don't understand. Do you know something about this sketch?"

The old woman's mouth quirked angrily. "What I know of this sketch," she spat, "is that it was not meant for your eyes." And with a haughty lift of her chin, she turned and left the studio.

Was Mlle Gascó crazy, or senile, or just incredibly mean? Theresa wondered, watching her hobble across the bright prospect of the garden like an arthritic crow. Surely she couldn't actually know anything about that sketch—why, it had been hidden for over a hundred years. For a moment, the garden dimmed, as though a cloud had come over the sun, and then Theresa's eyes strayed to the notebook open before her. A sunbeam dazzled the single sentence to blankness. She moved the notebook out of the glare and turned the page.

The next entry was dated July 14 and spoke of Bastille Day celebrations in Lorient and a family outing with Céleste and Gascó, all very ordinary except that Beauvoisin's prose was less colorful than usual. Something was going on. But Theresa had already known that. Beauvoisin had grown immensely as a painter over the summer of 1879, and had cut himself off from the men who had been his closest friends. She was already familiar with the sharp note he'd written Manet denying that he had grown reclusive, only very hard at work and somewhat distracted, he hinted, by domestic tension: "For two women to reside under one roof is far from restful," he had written, and "Céleste and I have both begun paintings of Gascó—not, alas, the same pose."

Theresa flipped back to July 6. *Luz in the parlor. Ah, Céleste!* Such melodrama was not like Beauvoisin, nor was a week's silence, nor the brief, lifeless chronicles of daily events that occupied him during the month of August. Theresa sighed. Real life is often melodramatic, and extreme emotion mute. Something had happened on July 6, something that had changed Beauvoisin's life and art.

In any case, late in 1879 Beauvoisin had begun to develop a new style, a lighter, more brilliant palette, a more painterly technique that broke definitively from the line-obsessed training of his youth. Reading the entries for the fall of '79 and the winter of '80, Theresa learned that he had developed his prose style as well, in

long disquisitions on light and composition, life and art.
He gave up all accounts of ordinary events in favor of
long essays on the beauty of the ephemeral: a young girl,
a budding flower, a spring morning, a perfect understanding between man and woman. He became ob-
sessed with a need to capture even the most abstract of
emotions on canvas: betrayal, joy, contentment, es-
trangement.

> *I have set G. a pose I flatter myself expresses most perfectly
> that moment of suspension between betrayal and remorse.
> She is to the left of the central plane, a little higher than is
> comfortable, crowded into a box defined by the straight back
> of her chair and the arm of the sofa. Her body twists left, her
> face is without expression, her eyes are fixed on the viewer.
> The conceit pleases G. more than C., of course, G. being the
> greater cynic. But C. agrees that the composition is out of the
> ordinary way and we all have great hopes of it at the next
> Impressionist's Show. Our Arrangement will answer very
> well, I think.*

Reading such entries—which often ran to ten or fifteen closely written pages—Theresa began to wonder
when Beauvoisin found time to paint the pictures he had
so lovingly and thoughtfully planned. It was no wonder,
she thought, that *Interior* and *Woman at a Window* seemed
so theoretical, so contrived. She was not surprised to
read that they had not brought as much as *Young Woman
in a Garden* or *Reclining Nude*, painted two years later and
described briefly as *a figure study of G. on the parlor sofa,
oddly lighted. Pure whim, and not an idea anywhere in it. C.
likes it, though, and so does G.; have allowed myself to be
overborne.*

*   *   *

June had laid out its palette in days of Prussian blue, clear green, and yellow. In the early part of the month, when Theresa had been reading the letters, the clouds flooded the sky with a gray and white wash that suppressed shadow and compressed perspective like a Japanese print. After she found the notebooks, however, all the days seemed saturated with light and static as a still life.

Theresa spent her time reading Beauvoisin's journals, leaving the studio only to eat a silent meal alone in the kitchen, to wander through the garden, or, in the evenings, to go down to the seawall where she would watch the sun set in Turneresque glories of carmine and gold. Once, seeing the light, like Danaë's shower, spilling its golden seed into the sea, Theresa felt her hand twitch with the desire to paint the scene, to capture the evanescent moment in oils and make it immortal.

What am I thinking of? she wondered briefly. It must be Edouard rubbing off on me. Or the isolation. I need to get out of here for a couple days, go back to Paris, see M. Rouart about the sketch, maybe let him take me out to dinner, talk to someone real for a change. But the next day found her in the studio and the next evening by the seawall, weeping with the beauty of the light and her own inadequate abilities.

As June shaded into July, Theresa began to see pictures everywhere she looked and gave in at last to her growing desire to sketch them. Insensible of sacrilege, she took up Beauvoisin's pastel chalks and charcoal pencils and applied herself to the problem of reproducing her impressions of the way the flowers shimmered under the noonday sun and how the filtered light reflected from the studio's whitewashed walls.

At first, she'd look at the untrained scrawls and blotches

she'd produced and tear them to confetti in an ecstasy of disgust. But as the clear still days unfolded, she paid less and less attention to what she'd done, focussing only on the need of the moment, to balance shape and mass, light and shade. She hardly saw Mme Beauvoisin and Luna, though she was dimly aware that they were about—in the parlor, in the garden, walking arm in arm across her field of vision: figures in the landscape, motifs in the composition. Day bled into day with scarcely a signpost to mark the end of one or the beginning of the next, so that she sketched and read in a timeless, seamless present, without past, without future, without real purpose.

So it was with no clear sense of time or place that Theresa walked into the studio one day and realized that she had left her sketchbook in the parlor. Tiresome, she thought to herself. But there was that study she'd been working on, the one of the stone wall. She'd just have to go back to the house and get it.

The transition from hall to parlor was always blinding, particularly in the afternoon, when the sun slanted through the French doors straight into entering eyes. That is perhaps why Theresa thought at first that the room was empty, and then that someone had left a large canvas propped against the sofa, a painting of two women in an interior.

It was an interesting composition, the details blurred by the bright backlight, the white dress of the figure on the sofa glimmering against the deep burgundy cushions, the full black skirts of the figure curled on the floor beside her like a pool of ink spilled on the flowery carpet. Both figures were intent on a paper the woman on the sofa held on her up-drawn knees. Her companion's torso was turned into the sofa, her arms wreathed loosely around her waist.

What a lovely picture they make together, Theresa thought. I wonder I never thought of posing them so. It's a pity Céleste will not let me paint her.

Céleste laid the paper aside, took Gascó's hand, and carried it to her lips. Her gaze met Theresa's.

"Edouard," she said.

Theresa's cheeks heated; her heart began a slow, deep, painful beating that turned her dizzy. She put her hand on the doorframe to steady herself just as Gascó surged up from the floor and turned, magnificent in her rage and beauty, to confront the intruder. Her face shone from the thundercloud of her hair, its graceful planes sharpened and defined by the contemptuous curve of her red mouth, and the wide, proud defiance of her onyx eyes. Edouard released the door frame and helplessly reached out his hand to her.

"Be a man, Edouard!" Gascó all but spat. "Don't look like that. I knew this must come. It would have come sooner had you been less blind. No," as Edouard winced, "I beg your pardon. It was not necessary to say that. Or the other. But you must not weep."

Céleste had swung her legs to the floor and laid the sketch on the sofa-back on top of the piled cushions. She looked composed, if a little pale, and her voice was even when she said, "Sit down, Luna. He has no intention of weeping. No, get us some brandy. We must talk, and we'd all be the better for something to steady us."

"Talk?" said Edouard. "What is there for us to say to one another?"

Gascó swept to the sideboard, poured brandy into three snifters, and handed them around, meeting Edouard's eyes defiantly when she put his into his hand.

"Drink, Edouard," said Céleste gently. "And why don't you sit down?"

He shook his head, but took a careful sip of his brandy. The liquor burned his throat.

"Doubtless you want us to leave La Roseraie," said Céleste into a long silence.

"Oh, no, my heart," said Gascó. "I'll not run away like some criminal. This house is yours. If anyone is to leave, it must be Beauvoisin."

"In law," said Edouard mildly, "the house is mine. I will not leave it. Nor will you, Céleste. You are my wife." His voice faltered. "I don't want you to leave. I want things as they were before."

"With your model your wife's lover, and you as blind as a mole?"

Edouard set down his half-finished brandy and pinched the bridge of his nose. "That was not kind, Gascó. But then, I have always known that you are not kind."

"No. I am honest. And I see what is there to be seen. It is you who must leave, Edouard."

"And ruin us all?" Céleste sounded both annoyed and amused. "You cannot be thinking, my love. We must find some compromise, some way of saving Edouard's face and our reputations, some way of living together."

"Never!" said Gascó. "I will not. You cannot ask it of me."

"My Claire de Lune. My Luna." Céleste reached for Gascó's hand and pulled her down on the sofa. "You do love me, do you not? Then you will help me. Edouard loves me too: we all love one another, do we not? Edouard. Come sit with us."

Edouard set down his brandy snifter. Céleste was holding her hand to him, smiling affectionately. He stepped forward, took the hand, allowed it and the smile to draw him down beside her. At the edge of his vision, he saw the paper slide behind the cushions and turned to retrieve it. Céleste's grip tightened on his hand.

"Never mind, my dear," she said. "Now. Surely we can come to some agreement, some arrangement that will satisfy us all?"

The taste in Theresa's mouth said she'd been asleep. The tickle in her throat said the sofa was terribly dusty, and her nose said there had been mice in it, perhaps still were. The cushions were threadbare, the needlework pillows moth-eaten into woolen lace.

Without thinking what she was doing, Theresa scattered them broadcast and burrowed her hand down between sofa-back and seat, grimacing a bit as she thought of the mice, grinning triumphantly as she touched a piece of paper. Carefully, she drew it out, creased and mildewed as it was, and smoothed it on her knees.

A few scrawled lines of text with a sketch beneath them. The hand was not Edouard's. Nor was the sketch, though a dozen art historians would have staked their government grants that the style was his. The image was an early version of *Young Woman in a Garden,* a sketch of Gascó sitting against a tree with her hands around her knees, her pointed chin raised to display the long curve of her neck. Her hair was loose on her shoulders. Her blouse was open at the throat. She was laughing.

Trembling, Theresa read the note:

My Claire de Lune:
    How wicked I feel, how abandoned, writing you like this, where anyone could read how I love you, my *maja*. I want to write about your neck and breasts and

hair—oh, your hair like black silk across my body. But the only words that come to my mind are stale when they are not comic, and I'd not have you laugh at me. So here is my memory of yesterday afternoon, and your place in it, and in my heart always.

Céleste

Theresa closed her eyes, opened them again. The room she sat in was gloomy, musty, and falling into ruin, very different from the bright, comfortably shabby parlor she remembered. One of the French doors was ajar; afternoon sun spilled through it, reflecting from a thousand swirling dust motes, raising the ghosts of flowers from the faded carpet. Out in the garden, a bird whistled. Theresa went to the door, looked out over a wilderness of weedy paths and rosebushes grown into a thorny, woody tangle.

Céleste's letter to Luz Gascó crackled in her hand, reassuringly solid. There was clearly a lot of work to be done.

from **The Book of the Dead Man (#2)**

Marvin Bell

1. First Postscript: About the Dead Man

The dead man thinks he is alive when he hears
    his bones rattle.
Hearing his bones rattle, the dead man thinks he
    is alive.
He thinks himself alive because, what else would
    he think?
Now he can love and suffer, as in life, and live
    alone.
The dead man no longer hears the higher
    registers of the chandelier.
The dead man listens for pedal notes and
    thunder, tubas and bassoons.
He reads lips without telling anyone, but others
    know.
He can no longer scratch his back so he stands
    near walls.

To the dead man, substance and meaning are all
  one.
To the dead man, green and black are not
  estranged, nor blue and gray, nor here and
  there, nor now and then.
The dead man has separate sets of eyes for here
  and there.
In the dead man's world, all time and stories are
  abstract.
In a concrete house with real walls, he lies down
  with the news.
The screen's flickering pixels are to him eyelets
  through which the world each morning is laced
  up for the day.
The dead man rises from his bed at night with
  great effort.
He is a rolling map of veins, a hilly country built
  on flatland.
The map of the body is of no use to the dead
  man.
When the dead man turns his neck, it's
  something to see from a distance.

2. *Second Postscript: More About the Dead Man*

Asleep, the dead man sinks to the bottom like
  teeth in water.
Whatever came to be by love or entropy, all that
  sprouted and grew, all that rotted and
  dissolved, whatever he saw, heard, felt, tasted
  or smelled, every wave and breeze has its
  metabolic equivalent in his dreams.

He is the bones, teeth and pottery shards to be
   claimed eons hence.
He is the multifaceted flag of each deciduous
   tree, reenacting time.
The dead man will not go away, the dead man
   holds up everything with his elegant
   abstentions.
All his life he had something to say and a string
   on his finger.
The dead man will be moving to Florida or
   Maine, or sailing to California, or perhaps he
   is staying put.
He has only to say where he wishes to be, and it
   can be arranged.

Inside the dead man, there is still a mellow
   sparking of synapses.
Unsent messages pool on the wavery deck, hit
   tunes that would last forever, jokes that never
   staled.
The dead man is an amphitheater of dramatic
   performances, ethereal scripts now written in
   the air like used radio signals in space.
The dead man mistakes natural disasters for
   applause—erosion in Carolina, quakes in
   California.
The dead man's shoes are muddy from being
   constantly on stage.

The Little Tailor and the Elves

Barbara Hambly

For as long as anybody could remember, Levitsky's Tailor Shop had been in business in the basement of 113 West 34th Street. Solly Levitsky had opened the place in 1941, building it up from pressing pants and doing alterations; by the time his son, Irv, took over in the late sixties it had expanded into the main floor of the building and included a dry-cleaning establishment as well. Irv's work was excellent and everyone in the neighborhood thought very well of him.

Unlike his father, who was big for a Polish Jew—six feet one and built like a refrigerator—Irv, stocky and powerful, barely topped five three, though he wore built-up shoes and invariably claimed five five. Maybe his size had something to do with his temper, and his determination to be twice the tailor his father had been, no easy feat, considering his father's expertise. "It's great, it's great," the Italian businessmen would say, who'd been coming into the shop for years to have their suits made, standing in front of the big three-way mirrors under the fluorescent lighting that made even the dim back rooms of the basement as clear and flawless as day. And, in Irv's opinion, it *was* great: the perfect hang of the iron-gray wool, forty dollars a yard with a hand to it like silk, the precise shaping of the shoulders over just sufficient padding to smooth away the annoying little variations to which mortal flesh is heir—it was a suit you couldn't buy off the rack no matter how much you spent.

But always, as Irv was tucking the final payment check into the drawer of the electronic till which had replaced that old cast-iron clunker his father had kept in the shop till the day he retired, he'd overhear them as they went out the front door and up the half dozen chipped cement steps to where their limos were double-parked in traffic: "You think this is good, Vinnie? You should have seen the one his old man made me back in '58. Now, that was a suit that *sang.*"

And Irv would go upstairs in a bitter temper and slap his wife.

"She's a perfectly lovely girl, Irving." Iris Levitsky put her head down on the kitchen table again, trying to will away the familiar clammy sensation she got in the pit of her stomach at the sound of her mother-in-law's voice. "But would you just tell her what I said about newspapers being best for cleaning windows? Newspapers and ammonia, and never mind all this fancy-schmancy stuff they peddle over the TV. Newspapers and ammonia and good old-fashioned elbow grease." In the front hall the coat-cupboard door creaked; above the brimming kitchen sink, the tangerine and avocado cotton curtains shifted with the night wind and the sounds of *M*A*S*H* on the neighbors' TV set.

Iris closed her eyes with wretchedness, knowing what was coming next.

"Iris . . . !" She flinched at the singsong whine of anger in her husband's voice.

She raised her head. He was standing in the kitchen doorway in his shirtsleeves with his tie loosened, hands on his hips. People always said he was a short little man, but Iris was tinier yet—her head just cleared the top of his shoulder—and the angry bunch of those heavy black eyebrows filled her with panic.

"I got to tell you, Iris, you embarrassed the hell out of me tonight in front of my folks! What the hell you do around here all day, sit around eating bonbons?" He gestured furiously towards the avocado-green plates which couldn't fit into the sink lined up like a Manet painting on the harvest-gold Formica of the counter. "I mean, it's eight-thirty, for Chrissake, and them dishes are still dirty! It's not like you gotta go out and work or anything!"

Iris heartily wished she *could* go out and work or something. She'd been far happier when she'd only been the store's accountant instead of the owner's wife. But she could only whisper, "I'm sorry, honey."

"Yeah, well, I'm sorry, too!" His voice rose and Iris shrank further back against the table. The first time he'd struck her—the week after they'd come back from their honeymoon—he'd been miserably repentant for days, and it had been nearly six months before he'd slapped her again. Lately he'd quit going through the formality of saying *I don't know what got into me.* Whatever it was, it got into him fairly often in the seven years of their marriage so far.

"I'm sorry I'm the one who's gotta be at the store six days a week until seven o'clock at night making sure them *schwartze* girls upstairs ain't robbing the place blind and leaving spots on the customers' clothes, making enough money to have a nice house, a good car, a decent living for you and Melissa, and that I gotta come home after all that and find the dishes ain't done, the house is a pigsty, my daughter's running around with dirt on her face like some wop brat and you sittin' on your can reading a goddamn newspaper!"

He turned furiously away and got a beer from the refrigerator. "I'm gonna be watching TV. And for God's sake take some time out from whatever the hell you do all day and wash the goddamn windows! I can see the dirt from here!"

His words weren't necessary. Iris had already resolved to turn over a new leaf and wash the windows tomorrow—surely she'd have time between picking Melissa up from school and taking her to her dance lessons . . . But as she plunged her arms into the froth of suds, Iris recalled that she'd promised to take old Mrs. Callahan to the clinic tomorrow.

For a moment she wondered whether she ought to call the old lady and cancel, but Jessie Callahan was over eighty, still living alone in her own little house with her four dogs, and the bus ride to the clinic would be hard on her. A guilty glance at the clock showed Iris that it was nearly nine, and Melissa still to bathe and be told her story . . . Tears of frustration crept down her cheeks as she piled the silverware into the rack to dry. It would leave spots, but those could be wiped off before she put them away, if she had time. Mama Levitsky had also commented on the dirty grout in the bathroom tiles.

Well, maybe tomorrow there'd be time to wash a few windows before picking Melissa up . . .

She dashed a handful of cold water over her eyes, so that Melissa wouldn't see she'd been crying, as she went to get her daughter a bath.

At the clinic the next day, Jessie Callahan shook her head over Iris's shaky-voiced account of her own failings and her husband's justified anger. "I know I should be better," Iris admitted, looking straight ahead at the harassed Medicare staffers because she knew if she looked at her friend she'd burst into tears again. "I mean, Irv's mother keeps their house spotless and she's more than forty years older than I am. But with Melissa, and doing the accounts for the store, I just . . . I just *can't!*"

A small black child, who'd been there with her parents when Jessie and Iris had arrived nearly an hour and a half ago and still hadn't been seen, pelted noisily by. Iris fished in her purse for the package of butterscotch Lifesavers she always carried for Melissa, and gave the child one, guessing that the little girl hadn't had any lunch.

"Now, honey," said Jessie Callahan in her soft voice, "there are worse things in the world than a little dirt, and turning your brain into a mushroom and your soul into mold by spending the whole day cleaning property is one of them. Don't worry about it. These things all work out."

Queerly enough, when Iris got home—far later than she'd thought she would, for the clinic had been jammed and Jessie had had to wait nearly three hours to be seen—she found that she must have dried the silverware after all. The silverware basket and dish drainer were not only empty, but hung neatly on their hooks on the inside of the broom-closet door; the dishes were stacked, gleaming, in the cupboard, the silverware grinned brightly at her when she opened the drawer. Behind the tangerine-and-avocado-pattern curtains— and surely the curtains looked cleaner and crisper than Iris remembered them yesterday—the windows sparkled, too.

I must have been tireder than I thought, Iris reflected, *if I don't even remember putting the silverware and dishes away.* She had easily enough time to do the very small amount of laundry which needed doing, and iron Irv's shirts and the fresh tablecloth and napkins Irv always insisted upon, before it was time to put dinner on.

That was the first time it happened, and the last time Irv had genuine cause for complaint about her housekeeping.

It didn't happen with tremendous frequency after that, at first. But it happened often enough. After the fourth or fifth time that Iris found some particularly daunting piece of housework done—the kitchen floor stripped and rewaxed just before another of Mama Levitsky's unscheduled drop-in visits—Iris started keeping track. It troubled her; she began to wonder if she was developing multiple personalities or having housework blackouts, and she took to running time-and-motion studies on herself until it occurred to her that even if she *were* doing the housework unconscious, that was far preferable to being aware of each mind-numbing chore.

Mama Levitsky still picked holes, of course, and Irv still shouted and threatened, but it seemed to Iris that they had to look harder for faults to find. She continued to drive Jessie to the local Senior Center and the Adult Literacy Resource Center where they both did volunteer teaching, and, weirdly enough, the housework continued to get done.

It was only when Melissa spoke about seeing ''little men'' that Iris became truly worried, and spoke to Jessie about it.

''Ah, I thought that's what might be happening,'' the old lady smiled. ''It's the elves.''

''*What?*'' Iris stared at her. She'd gone over to cook Jessie some lunch and play cards with her—since Jessie's stroke in the spring of '77 the old lady could barely get around—and they were sitting together in Jessie's neat white kitchen.

Jessie raised her snowy brows. ''The elves,'' she said. ''They've been around me as long as I can remember. They did things for Mother, too—Mother cleaned houses out here in Long Island, and there were eleven of us back home, and only me to raise and look after the little ones. But Mother was never too tired to help out her friends, or take care of those in the neighborhood who couldn't take care of themselves. She'd always say that chores like this had a way of getting done. I first saw the elves when I wasn't much older than Melissa . . .''

She nodded towards the little girl, happily tossing a Wiffle ball for the dogs to chase across the neat handkerchief of lawn outside.

''Only glimpses of them I'd get, out the corners of my eyes, usually in the winter, when it got so early dark. It seemed to me then they were three or four little brown-faced men dressed in cobwebs, with long ears like dogs, but that might have been something I made up later, or something I read in a book.''

She sighed, and shook her head, and reached tremblingly for a spoon to eat the scrambled eggs Iris had made her, but seemed to find it too much effort, and put it down again. Iris worried that as she grew feebler, Jessie would be unable to keep the house at all, but so far it hadn't happened, and she dreaded the day when the old lady would be taken to some kind of state institution because she could no longer look after herself, as much for Jessie's sake as for how badly she'd miss the old lady's company.

"Mother used to say they weren't good folk," Jessie murmured, her arthritic fingers stirring at the spoon—a tiny coffee spoon, with a decorative cartouche at the top saying PERTH—WESTERN AUSTRALIA on it. "Neither good nor evil, she said, but rather like children that never had no mother: queer and selfish and cunning. But leave them out food, in the shop or in the house, and don't put no cold iron above the doors, and they'll be your friends. And that's what I used to do."

"Leave them food?" asked Iris, seeing Jessie's mind begin to drift. "Like some kids leave cookies for Santa on Christmas Eve?"

"Of course, for what's Santa Claus but the memory of some other helping spirit? But these . . . They aren't good folk, having no souls, but they see good in humans, and are drawn to it, like cold children to a flame. As they were drawn to Mother." All that complicated erosion-map of facial lines crumpled and changed with her smile.

"And do you know," she went on, "somehow all the dishes did get done at our house, and the food did get cooked, and none of my brothers and sisters ever went dirty, and Mother managed to keep those rich folks' houses spotless, too, be there ever so many of them. I never was afraid of the elves, and I'd bake cookies to leave out for them, but Mother never did let any of us alone in the dark if she could help it. I still leave them cookies, time to time. There's not much to do around this place, now I'm too old to mess it up much. I'm glad they've found somebody else to help. They don't like to be idle."

Iris wasn't sure just what to say to that. Jessie was very old, and her mind wandered, but the fact remained that things got done that Iris didn't remember doing, and Mama Levitsky had less and less cause to complain.

That didn't stop her from complaining, of course. In fact, she seemed to complain more. Even after Solly and his wife retired to Miami in 1978, Iris's husband continued to find fault with everything his wife did, or didn't do.

A number of things happened in 1978. A big, glossy tailoring and alterations establishment opened on West 35th Street, utilizing, Irv swore nightly in gusts of bourbon, cheap Vietnamese labor who'd work for fifty cents an hour up in the attics. Moreover, fewer businessmen were buying bespoke suits, preferring instead to frequent the high-end designer stores like Neiman-Marcus and I. Magnin. He found himself doing more alterations work and less tailoring as such, and most of the money came in from the dry-cleaning establishment upstairs.

That was the year Iris went back to work. In addition to doing the books—which she'd always done, having been hired for the purpose just out of high school—Irv put her in charge of the dry-cleaning side of the operation. "That way I can fire those stupid girls who can't do a decent job anyway," he groused, pacing around the kitchen, beer can in hand, while Iris and Melissa stood silent beside the sink where they'd been washing dishes when he'd come in. "Filthy broads, anyway, always off in the back combing their hair or drinking Cokes—

Cokes! I caught one of them actually leaving a wet ring on the counter, where customers' clothes go!''

"Did they get Coke on a garment?'' asked Iris, shocked. She'd been in the store and knew the girls were pretty conscientious about wiping up crumbs and spills from lunch. Surely they couldn't have deteriorated that much in a few weeks.

"That ain't the point, stupid!'' yelled Irv, losing his temper, and at the sound of his voice, Melissa edged a little closer to Iris's leg. Iris had told Melissa she'd gotten her current black eye from running into a door; she didn't know whether the little girl believed her or not. She always kept a close eye on Melissa and didn't think Irv had ever done more than yell at his daughter, but since business had been steadily worsening, Irv had taken to drinking more beers in front of the TV set evenings and weekends. He'd taken to coming home later in the evenings, too, and by the smell of his breath the hour or so in between he was spending in the Seventh Avenue Grill.

"The point is them stupid *nafkas* is careless around the customers' clothes! They eat their goddamn greasy hamburgers there, probably on the folding table if I know anything about *schwartzes!* No wonder the place got roaches!''

Iris knew better than to point out that any establishment in Manhattan had roaches, particularly one situated between a Mexican restaurant and a grocery store.

"I shoulda figured you wouldn't know the difference if the store was clean or dirty! God knows what's gonna happen to my reputation—to Dad's reputation—with *you* in charge there!''

"Melissa,'' said Iris gently, recognizing the signs of a

full-fledged storm brewing, "why don't you go upstairs and run your bath? I'll finish up here."

"The hell she will!" bellowed Irv in a gusty blast of Miller High Life. "You're teaching her to be just as crummy as you, running off and leaving her job half-done so you can go fix sandwiches and sit around and bullshit with that senile old Mick! My mother was right about you! Well, I'm not gonna have no lazy slob for a daughter, even though I got one for a wife! And if I see so much as one spot, one hair, one pin out of place, I'll teach you to be clean myself, God damn it! And that goes for you, too," he added, turning savagely to his silent daughter, "when your mother's away at work, you hear?"

Nevertheless, Melissa slipped away quietly halfway through Irv's ensuing tirade. Iris remained, taking the shouts and blows in head-bowed silence, reflecting that he did have a point. She was spending a good deal of time with Jessie, now that the old lady was practically helpless. Later she went up to Melissa's room, not turning on the light because she could feel her lip puffing up—she'd have to put ice on it before going into the shop tomorrow—and found the little girl sitting up in bed in the dark.

"Don't worry about Daddy, Mommy," said Melissa softly. "The little men will help me keep house, and then he won't be mad."

Iris hugged her, but reflected that it would take more than the elves' housekeeping to prevent Irv from working himself into the furies that seemed to be the only outlet for his frustration with the generally poor condition of the world, his business, and his life.

She wasn't sure at what point she came to accept the elves as a reality, and rely on them for their help as

matter-of-factly as Melissa did. Perhaps it was during
the year which followed, when it became obvious to her
that someone *was* helping Melissa with the housework—a seven-year-old girl couldn't *possibly* keep everything from the bathroom faucets to the outsides of the
upstairs windows gleaming like that. And thankfully,
Irv never complained about Melissa, or bawled her out
for leaving sandwich crumbs on the counter or imagined tasks undone.

This was more than could be said about his attitude
towards Iris's performance in the dry-cleaning shop.
Nothing was ever clean enough, ever organized enough,
ever quick enough, and when it was, it cost too much
and she was wasting money or not treating the customers right. He developed a positive mania about food
crumbs attracting roaches, and after every sighting of
even the smallest insect, he would comb the shop,
searching for crumbs and screaming curses at the top of
his lungs. Such performances were usually followed by
the dismissal of whatever counter help they had that
week, and a hideous shouting-at—if nothing worse—
for Iris. Most of these scenes, Iris noticed, came on the
days when Irv had been sitting downstairs with nothing
to do but watch his miniature television set, or when the
few customers that entered sang the praises of old
Solly's suits. At one time, early in her marriage, Iris had
thought she'd probably get used to Irv slapping her
around, but as the years went by she only grew more and
more afraid of him, until she passed each day in stom-
ach-clenched silence, terrified to arouse his wrath.

"It isn't your fault," she whispered one day to the
empty shop (that was after yet another girl had been
canned) after Irv had pasted her a few for leaving half
her sandwich on the desk, then went storming out to the

Seventh Avenue Grill. ''You keep the place spotless and so beautiful, and I'm grateful. Maybe not having anything really to complain about is what makes him mad.''

She reflected, a moment later as she tried to tidy her hair over the bruise he'd left on the side of her face, that she really must be going crazy, talking to imaginary fairies like that. And yet, out of the corner of her eye, she thought she glimpsed something or someone standing just behind her chair, a slip of bony cobweb-clad knee barely visible on the edge of the mirror, a rustly shadow among the whispering plastic ranks of hanging garments. It was November, and almost dark though it was only four o'clock. In the shadows between the alien metal form of the pants press and the cold gleam of the shelf of flatirons for delicate work—and God help her if Irv found so much as a water spot on their stainless-steel smoothness—she wondered if she only imagined the silvery gleam of eyes.

Not human eyes, Iris thought, laying her forehead down wearily upon her crossed wrists. Her mind wandered back to Jessie, during her last illness at the Shady Rest Home, that thread of a voice coming from the fallen pink face. ''Just leave them a little something—they don't need it exactly, but they like to be thanked,'' she'd said. ''And probably best you don't let Melissa be alone in the shop when it's getting dark . . .''

Her head on her hands in the darkening shop, Iris could see them now, reflected in the long mirror. Two thin shadows, like brown bones wrapped up in gray webs of rags. Between the glare of the lights outside upon the plastic garment bags, and the glint of the mirror itself, it was hard for her to tell what she was seeing, especially with her head at that angle. But she thought

the taller of the two—who wasn't even as tall as she, at
her four feet ten—crept stealthily towards the desk,
where the offending half-sandwich still lay a few inches
from her elbow. She had an impression of huge colorless eyes between straggling torrents of hair the color of
ash, eyes blinking down at her like opalescent glass,
behind which moved longings and needs foreign to anything she had ever known. A thin brown hand reached
out to touch the abandoned food; the smaller of the two
creatures clung and whispered . . .

Two, thought Iris cloudily. She had earlier had the
impression there were more of them. *Of course. One at
least is home helping Melissa with the housework . . .*

She thought of her daughter, finishing her household
chores and putting dinner on, while the dusk gathered
in the corners of the house and silver-opal eyes gleamed
out at her . . .

The terror of the thought jarred her back to wakeful-
ness, gasping with shock.

The shop, nearly dark, was quite empty. A stray, and
very small, cockroach scurried out of sight under the
baseboard on the grocery-store side. Hastily, Iris
removed her pink plastic wrap with ''Iris'' embroidered
on its breast, put on her coat, double-checked the regis-
ter and receipts, locked up all the doors and windows.
She knew she was supposed to sweep up and wipe down
the table, counters, pants press, and irons, but even with
the radio and all the lights in the place on, she felt the
darkness and the silence, and avoided going anywhere
near the whispery forest of plastic garment bags, or the
shadows which seemed to linger near the sinister bulk
of the press. There'd be time to clean up there in the
daylight.

At the moment, nothing in the world would induce

her to remain in the shop. When she returned the following morning she couldn't remember whether she'd thrown out the half-sandwich or not, but it certainly wasn't there. After that she began taking a few extra cookies in her lunch to leave out at closing time, something she'd half known Melissa had been doing at home for years.

It was the cookies that finally caused the trouble.

Over the years, as his drinking had increased and the profits of the shop had gone down, Irv's mania for cleanliness had increased. Or perhaps, Iris speculated, it was simply that he needed to believe that there was something causing his problems which could be corrected. In any case, he reached the point of forbidding her or any of the girls to eat or drink anything in the shop at all. Since with the cutbacks in the help as business declined she almost never got a chance to leave the building for lunch, she took to smuggling candy bars in her purse. After Irv started searching her purse, Iris would bring the candy bars, and cookies for the elves, wrapped tightly in tinfoil and plastic in her coat pockets. She did try very hard not to anger Irv and to keep the shop as clean as his mother once had. At one time— after he broke her ribs—she'd thought of leaving him. But with outmoded accounting skills—Irv never would have the books computerized—and a ten-year-old daughter to support, she knew it would be hard, even if Irv didn't track her down as he said he would.

Irv usually left far earlier than she, to have a few drinks at the Seventh Avenue Grill before taking the subway home, so Iris was able to leave cookies for the elves in the shop before she locked up for the night. She simply got used to the fact that there was never so much as a crumb left in the morning.

How long the situation would have gone on she didn't know. Maybe forever. But one evening in late October the telephone in the tailoring shop downstairs rang just as she was preparing to leave, and she ran down to get it—there hadn't been a job of tailoring in weeks. As she did so she heard the electronic bell on the cleaning-shop door beep, announcing a customer. So when she finished explaining to the caller that 846-3992 was the number of the Thunderhump Massage Parlor, not 846-3995, she ran upstairs once more, and found Irv, standing next to the folding table, staring down at the six oatmeal cookies there in an almost visible cloud of bourbon and rage.

"So what the hell is this, Iris?" He swung to face her, and instead of roaring as usual, his voice was a deadly whisper. The hand that held up the largest of the cookies was trembling. "You wanna tell me what the hell is this?"

Iris glanced automatically towards the door, but the counter blocked most of that side of the room, and where he stood by the table, Irv was between her and the opening through which she could get to the outside. The next second the cookie whizzed past her ear like a brown-sugar shuriken and splattered into crumbles against the wall, and Irv was screaming, "You filthy sow! Getting crumbs all over the customers' clothes! No wonder this place got roaches! No wonder we can't get no customers! No wonder . . . !" He lunged at her, caught her by the front of her pink coverall, and slammed her with vicious force back into the shelf containing the steam irons and bottles of benzine.

The shelf cut her back and took her breath away—

three irons hit the linoleum with a noise that made her scream. She screamed again as he raised his fist, backed into a corner in terror. "You touch me and I'm leaving you!"

It was the first time she'd ever said the words, and she wouldn't have, if she'd taken the time to think. His face turned so red it was almost purple, dark eyes bulging out in bloodshot webs of veins. "You don't leave me!" he roared. "You don't leave me, you lazy, filthy slut!" He caught up one of the big steam irons, ten pounds at least of tempered stainless steel in one heavy fist, and lunged at her . . .

It really was, Iris reflected, a terrible mess. Blind terror, panic, the inability to breathe or scream or think, the knowledge of murder she saw reflected in those bulging drunken eyes—and then this. She stood for a long time, a big steam iron in her tiny hand, looking down at her late husband's body on the floor at her feet.

There was blood everywhere. On the pants press, on the forest of plastic-wrapped clothes, on Mrs. Haberman's expensive silk charmeuse dress hanging by the counter . . . Quite a lot of blood on the floor.

The electronic doorbell tweeped. Iris looked up, more startled than anything else, and for a moment found herself staring into the eyes of a very young and flustered blond man in a gray suit who had just dropped an armful of sports jackets on the floor. He gasped, "Holy shit!" and exited.

Iris looked down at the iron in her hand. The iron was covered with blood. So was her hand. She had never realized what that quantity of blood smelled like.

Numbly, she set the iron down on the folding table next to the plate of cookies, wiped her hand on Mrs.

Haberman's dress—the charmeuse was ruined anyway—and carefully removed her pink plastic overwrap. Then she went downstairs to the bathroom and washed her hand and her face.

She wondered what they'd do to Melissa, while she was in jail. She might, she supposed, plead self-defense, but with the number of times Irv had beaten her up before, surely the judge would merely ask, "Why didn't you leave him?" The judge obviously hadn't lived with Irv.

She didn't feel bad about Irv at all. She knew, as surely as she knew her own name, that he would have killed her.

She wondered if she could make a little candy money in prison by cleaning up other prisoners' cells.

Upstairs, Iris heard the doorbell beep again. That, she knew, would be the police.

It was. Two blue-uniformed New York's Finest, with an extremely shaken-looking young businessman in a gray suit, stood in the gap between the counter and the rest of the shop, looking around them in the deepening shadows of the October evening.

"Are you Iris Levitsky?" asked one of the cops. "This man says there was a crime committed here."

The other cop reached across to the wall, and switched on the light.

As he did so, Iris realized that the smell of the blood was gone.

The bright fluorescent glow revealed, in the next moment, that this was because the blood itself was gone. Mrs. Haberman's dress hung beside the counter spotless, unwrinkled, clean as it had come out of the big fluff-dryer.

Irv's body was gone, leaving not so much as a stain on the green linoleum.

Every iron was back on the shelf, polished like a grinning row of steel teeth; Iris's pink plastic coverall depended neatly from its accustomed hanger; the young man's shirts and sports jackets lay neatly over the spotless counter; not so much as a fleck of blood sullied the garment bags, the pants press, the counter.

The cookies were gone, too.

Iris smiled.

NOTE: In 1991, after her missing husband was declared legally dead, Iris Levitsky sold Levitsky's Tailoring and Dry Cleaning to a Korean dry-cleaning chain, and used the money to put her daughter through college. Iris and Melissa now jointly own and manage the enormously successful Midnight Magic Housecleaning Service, investing the proceeds in a diversified stock portfolio and funding a small shelter for battered women on Long Island. Melissa has recently opened a shop selling homemade cookies.

Metamorphosis

Milbre Burch

Once in a kingdom surrounded by marshes, there lived a golden-eyed king who was proud of where he'd gotten to, considering where he'd started from, and his rather modern queen. Together they had three fine sons. The boys were only nine and eighteen months apart in age, and late one summer, it seemed as if all three reached manhood simultaneously.

"Children grow up so fast these days," remarked the queen, forgetting that she herself had been a bride at fifteen.

And so the king bade his sons to go out into the world and find themselves a suitable mate.

The eldest had a flair for cooking and gardening. He decided to join a gourmet club to meet prospective dates.

The middle son was an athlete with an artistic bent. Following his workout, he lay down on a rug he had woven and composed a personal ad.

The youngest prince had no expectations at all in the matter of finding a bride. An amateur biologist with a degree in literature, he knew from his reading that often it didn't matter what tack the youngest prince took: fate usually had something special in store for him.

He'd spent most of his years reading, or sitting in the marshes musing over the flora and fauna. He felt awkward around people in general, and females in particular. He wasn't sure what to do with himself, much less what to do with a companion, especially if he were expected to tolerate her for a lifetime. The fact of the matter was this: the youngest prince was more at home with amphibians and fish than with humans.

If he noticed either of his parents watching him out the window as he sat overlooking the garden fishpond with his lap full of papers, he'd shuffle them loudly, bite his pencil and murmur: "Youngest prince desires Pisces poetess . . ." But his parents weren't fooled; they knew he was describing the movements of the carp in the pool, or else writing poetry. Or both.

"He's a romantic," whispered the king over his wife's shoulder. "That's because of you."

"He's a water sign," she'd sigh into her husband's beard. "That's because of you."

The king made it a point not to pry into his children's affairs. However, the future of the kingdom was tied up in their success in this venture. And so when summer gave way to autumn, he decided that three months was grace period enough.

Besides, his two oldest boys definitely seemed preoccupied in a very pleasant sort of way. (The youngest son was always preoccupied.) So one morning at breakfast, he asked the princes if they were seeing anyone special. All three blushed simultaneously.

He took this to be a good sign. So, he suggested that they meet for a buffet dinner at the club and invite their steady dates. Their blushes deepened in color. The queen leaned over to look at them closely, and asked whether they thought they were coming down with something.

They shook their heads vigorously, and the eldest suggested that they have a simple afternoon tea at the castle the following day, and introduce their significant others, et cetera, at that time. Everyone agreed to this plan. But of the three, the youngest looked most doubtful.

The next noon, the youngest prince stood up to his knees in the marsh, collecting samples in a goblet etched with gold leaf. He was mesmerized by the dance of water bugs on an archipelago of algae. In the back of his mind, he cursed his two older brothers for finding companions through club memberships and the mail.

With one arm, he wiped the sweat from his forehead, and noticed that the sun looked like a golden ball hanging in the heavens. Suddenly, he wished there were someone with whom he could share that observation. He sighed into his goblet and wondered aloud if in fact there weren't more to the world than empirical data and poems on paper.

"Of course, there is," said a voice as he bent down to scoop up some algae in the goblet. The prince was so startled at hearing a voice without having first heard someone approach that he straightened up suddenly.

In doing so, he lost his balance and sat down with a splash, flinging the contents of the goblet over his right shoulder. Goblet in hand and marsh water up to his chest, he heard a soft chuckle.

"Where are you?" he asked without trying to get up.

"Right here," came the voice from a point level with his nose. He peered in amongst the reeds along the bank of the marsh, and saw a small green frog making goo-goo eyes at him.

"Why are you looking at me like that?" asked the prince. One of his boots had come off in his fall, and feeling around underwater, he could not find it. He struggled to his feet, dripping in every direction.

"Because," said the frog, "you're the biggest and strangest amphibian I've ever seen."

The prince stood up again. This time he was chuckling. "Oh, no, I'm not an amphibian. I'm a man."

The frog rolled her eyes and backed into the reeds to hide.

"You're not out gigging frogs, are you?" she asked from her hiding place.

"No, no," he said. "I'm unarmed—except for this." He held up the empty goblet. "I'm a scientist—sort of."

She did not answer.

"I study life forms—like frogs, or birds, or insects, or even marsh grass, anything that's living."

"And how do you study these life forms?" she asked.

"Well, I take samples, and . . . I . . . uh . . ." He grew quiet. "Actually, I just do this as a hobby . . . as a matter of fact, I'm a prince."

"A prince!" she said, hopping out of the reeds again. "Does that mean you're the best of your kind?"

Now he was silent.

So she spoke again. "I've heard stories about you creatures—not many of them flattering, mind you. I understand that some of you consider frog legs a delicacy." She shuddered. "Is that true?"

"Yes, but I've never seen them served in my father's house."

Silence again.

"I wish you no harm," he said. "In fact, I could use your help. I'm having a little trouble finding my boot." She looked at him blankly until he balanced on one foot, pulled the remaining boot off and showed it to her. "Can you help me?"

"Perhaps," she said, blinking her golden eyes. "Will you stay and talk with me awhile here? I would like to know more about your people. Our frog-lore on you creatures is a bit one-sided."

The prince was delighted to be asked, and said so. The frog dove under the water and surfaced again. "Your boot-thing is just below me here."

The prince reached into the water and felt the collar of his boot. It was stuck fast in the mud. He set his goblet to float in the water, and pinching the other boot under one arm, tugged with both hands until the mired boot came free. For the second time he toppled backward, and the splash sailed his sparkling goblet out into the deeper water behind him.

Watching over his shoulder, the prince saw the frog swim with strong strokes after the bobbing glassware. Corralling it, she turned and swam back, pushing the goblet ahead of her until he could reach it again. She treaded water by his side. "Thank you," he said. She blinked and looked away.

He stood up, streaming, and sloshed after her as she swam to shore. He threw his boots onto the bank beyond her and climbed out of the water. There he stripped off his shirt and began to wring it out. The frog watched him with interest. "How often do man-princes shed their skins?" she asked.

"A few times a day," he laughed. "These aren't skins; they're called clothes. Human cover them-

selves . . ." Suddenly he blushed and quickly unrolled
his shirt and put it back on. Since it was still very wet,
this took some doing. "We wear clothes to keep warm,"
he said, shivering, "and to decorate ourselves."

He stretched out on his back in hopes of drying off and
asked, "What did you mean earlier—when you first
answered me? What else is there in the world besides
data and poetry?"

"Well, for one thing," she said, "there's magic."

The prince was startled by this answer. Then he broke
into a sunny smile. "You are the most intriguing creature I've ever met."

It turned out that she was a story-singer, and they
amused one another for hours, swapping tales. He
thought the poetry of her culture was primitive and perfect; she marveled at the sonnets he could recite from
memory.

When the sun began to sink behind the castle, the
prince realized that he had missed afternoon tea with
his family. He prepared to take his leave of her, but first
secured her promise to appear at brunch at the castle the
next morning. When he had gone, she noticed that he'd
left the glinting goblet behind.

He reached the castle and went in the back way, passing a set of doors to the dining room. Since they were
open a crack, he could see his mother and father sitting
at the table alone. Across the table were place settings
for tea, and all but two of the dessert plates had crumbs
on them. He could hear his parents talking together.

The king cleared his throat. "I have to say our middle
son took me by surprise. When he and that young man,
the potter, came in, well, naturally I assumed . . ."

"Never assume anything, my darling," said the
queen, squeezing his hand. "Hadn't you noticed that

woven and porcelain wall-hanging above the fireplace? I'm not surprised to learn their artwork grows out of their love for one another.''

"But when I said to go out and find a life partner, I meant a woman . . .'' started the king.

"Really, my darling, you of all people ought to be tolerant of unexpected combinations. Ours has worked out very nicely.''

"Very nicely, indeed,'' said the king. "He does seem happy. And the potter is a likable enough chap.''

"Now, I admit I was taken aback to see our eldest holding hands with a woman my age,'' admitted the queen.

"I'm holding hands with a woman your age,'' said the king, leaning closer to kiss her fingers.

She smiled at him. "Well, her children have certainly taken to him. And she is a lovely human being.''

The youngest prince winced slightly at this remark, and started to tiptoe past the door. Halfway across, he let out a great sneeze, whereupon his mother called him in. He came toward the table, strewing little bits of dried mud and algae in his wake.

"We missed you at tea, dear heart,'' said his mother, turning to take his hand.

"And you missed an opportunity to meet your brothers' new friends,'' his father began.

He watched their eyes grow wide as they took in his appearance. "I'm sorry, I didn't mean to be so rude. You see, I fell into the marsh, and I met someone there, and our visit was so enchanting that I lost track of the time.''

Their faces brightened. "You've met someone?'' they asked together.

"Yes,'' said the prince, "and she's wonderful: smart and funny and sweet and . . .'' He faltered and then decided to go forward, ". . . and a beautiful shade of green."

"Green?" His parents' eyes widened again.

"Yes," said the prince. "Why, she's a frog, don't you see? With the loveliest voice and golden eyes. It's just like a fairy tale!" He noticed that his parents had gotten rather silent, and were looking at each other strangely. "I hope it's all right: I've asked her to join us for brunch tomorrow."

"Spp-splendid!" sputtered the king.

"Perfect!" erupted the queen, and then she grasped her husband's hand and started to giggle. When she did that, he began to guffaw.

"Are you laughing at me?" asked the prince.

"No, not at all," cried the queen, jumping up to embrace him amid puffs of mud dust.

"We're very happy at your news," said the king, coming to enclose them both in his embrace. "It just reminds us of something . . ."

They held their son until his embarrassment died away. Then, arm-in-arm, still chuckling, they went up the stairs to their suite.

Their bewildered son watched them go. Then he went into his study and gathered his collection of frogs, toads and fish, preserved in bottles of alcohol, several stuffed birds in glass cases, and a small box of pinned insects. He carried them outside to the rose garden, where he found his brothers and their guests.

His clothing was streaked and rumpled and his arms were full of free-floating fish, taxidermied birds and impaled invertebrates. He knew he was making quite a first impression. He begged their pardons for missing the tea and then explained rather urgently what he intended to do.

Then he knelt on the ground, removed the lid from each bottle and drained off the alcohol; lifted each bird from its false perch; and tenderly unpinned each beetle, bug and butterfly. He asked his eldest brother to bring him a shovel, and he dug several small holes among the flower bushes. Upon request, his middle brother brought him a stack of woven cloth pieces.

While they watched, he wrapped all the dear, dead creatures in the beautiful cloth, and buried them. That night, the prince fell asleep at his window, listening to the chug-chugging of the frogs in the marshes all around him.

Brunch the next noon was a riotous affair. The eldest prince and his ladyfriend, her two children, the middle prince and his potter, the king, the queen and their youngest son were all gathered 'round.

The long table was covered with homemade pastry, cheese and fresh fruit. And in the middle was a woven and porcelain centerpiece. The youngest prince was nursing a cold, but his spirits were high. On the table, close to his elbow, was a small covered dish of minced insects, sautéed in wine. Next to him was an empty chair, piled high with cushions. In the background, musicians played ''Water Music.''

The butler announced the frog's arrival, carrying her gingerly in one hand, and the gold-leaf goblet in the other. The prince, his brothers and the king rose as the butler set her carefully on the top cushion. Struggling to maintain his dignity, the butler turned to the youngest prince and said, ''Your guest, sir.''

The king sat down again and his wife whispered, ''Remember?'' He winked at her. Introductions went around the table, and the queen was quick to thank the frog for returning the glassware.

"It has sentimental value to us," she explained.

"We had them made especially for our wedding," said the king. "The gold comes from an old play-toy of your mother's."

"I never knew that," stammered the youngest prince. "Or I'd never have used it . . ."

"No matter," said the queen. "Your friend has brought it back to us." And she smiled her golden smile at their small green guest.

Brunch was very pleasant indeed, with a short concert after the meal had ended. Then the youngest prince and the frog excused themselves to go out to the garden and sit by the pond, filled with golden carp. All around them the leaves on the trees were turning orange and red.

"My mother likes you," the prince said, blowing his nose. "My father, too."

"It was thoughtful of them to have something fixed especially for me."

"Yes," said the prince. "Strange . . . but Mother called it an old family recipe."

"Your father seemed to enjoy it, too."

They sat for a while in the sun in silence, and then she spoke up saying, "I'll be going away soon."

"Why? Where to?" asked the prince.

"The weather is changing," she said. "My people go underground to sleep through the cold time."

"Oh, yes, hibernation, I should have thought of that," said the prince. "But you'll miss the winter, the snow, the flocks of geese passing by overhead."

"Ah," said the frog, "but we dream the winter, as you call it, while we sleep."

The prince looked at her for a long time, nodding, and taking it in. "But I'll miss you," he said at last.

She looked at him. "I will miss you too."

They were quiet together once more, until the prince said, "You can speak . . . you tell stories . . . surely you possess magic. Are you . . . could you be . . . an enchanted frog?"

She cast her pop eyes down as best her three lids would let her, and answered, "Yes."

The prince felt a flutter of excitement. "Do you mean that you have the power of transformation?" he asked.

"I do," she admitted.

"Then couldn't you . . . change into a woman, and stay with me?"

She looked at him a moment. "No, I could never do that."

"Oh!" said the prince. "I thought that you cared about me the way I care about you."

"I do," she said, hopping toward him, "but I can't make that kind of change."

"But you said you were enchanted," the prince said.

"I am. But the spell I am under gives me the power to change another, not myself."

"Into what?" asked the prince.

"Why, a frog, of course. What else would I want to change my beloved into?"

The prince could see her point. "Dear me," he sighed, "this does complicate things."

"How so?" she asked.

"Well," stammered the prince, "I guess I had imagined that we'd fall in love and then you'd change into a woman and we'd get married and live happily ever after."

The frog's green complexion seemed to redden. "I admit I had a similar fantasy, except that, in my mind, you were the one who would change."

"I see," said the prince. "Well, this gives me a lot to think about. When do you go underground?"

"In seven days," she said, avoiding his glance.

"That soon?" he asked.

"Yes." There was silence.

"If," the prince began. "If I changed, would you still go to sleep?"

"Yes," she said. "But you would sleep with me and we would dream together." She turned and started to hop away from him.

"Where are you going?" he cried after her.

"Back to the marsh. I also have some thinking to do."

He stood up. "But when will I see you again?"

"When it's time," she said, and hopped away. He did not try to follow her, but sat by the pond, sneezing occasionally, deep in thought.

The prince came into the house at dusk and joined his family for dinner. Both his parents noticed his flushed and troubled face, though each of his brothers was so elated from the day's company that they kept the conversation afloat despite the heavy ballast of his sighs.

That night he sat in his room, wheezing and surveying his books and other belongings. He examined two recent gifts from his brothers: a handsome woolen cloak with a porcelain fastening, and a scrapbook of award-winning recipes. He puzzled over one recipe in particular, a loaf that called for ground flies.

He also studied a miniature portrait of his family hanging over his bed. In it he stood, flanked by a brother on either side; his mother and father enclosed them like parentheses.

Midnight came and still he sat, leaning on his elbow next to a candle on the windowsill. His shadow leapt about on the ground below. There was a knock at his door. "Come in," he croaked without looking around.

The king walked quietly in and sat down on the bed near his son. "I saw your shadow from my window and I knew you were awake."

"Yes, I couldn't hiberna . . . uh, sleep."

"Do you want to talk?" asked his father.

"Oh, sire," said the prince, turning his feverish eyes to the older man, "I'm just so confused. Today I learned that I love someone who will always belong to a different world than mine."

His father tilted his head to one side. "I'm not sure we don't all have to live with that realization." He paused and asked, "So, she can't become your princess, eh?"

"No," said his son. "She only has the power to turn me into a frog! And I'm not so sure I can accept that condition."

"Did you expect her to accept the condition of changing into whatever you happened to be?"

"Yes, I did," said the prince. "And now that I know the enchantment can only happen the other way, I find . . . I'm afraid. Do you understand?"

"More than you know," said his father.

And that's when he told his son the story of his courtship of the queen. The prince listened with his mouth agape.

"Close your mouth," said his father. "You'll catch flies."

The prince swallowed hard.

Then the king said, "I'm not sure who had more changing to do: me, who left behind frog to become man, or your mother, who grew from a spoiled and self-centered princess to a capable, loving, generous queen."

The king continued, "Who we are at birth only lasts until we strive to be what we want to be. And after that, we can take on a new shape entirely. Of course it's a leap," the older man smiled, "but that's what our strong back legs are made for."

His son was silent. The king stood up and stepped to the window to look out over the marsh. Together their shadows hopped and danced in a pool of flickering light on the ground below.

The prince leaned close to his father, and the king wrapped an arm around his son. "Father," he whispered, "were you ever sorry to leave the other world behind?"

"Ah, but I didn't," said his father. "I still live in the same marsh where I was born. Where you were born. And I have my memories. And my dreams."

The prince searched his father's golden eyes, and saw that they were smiling. "Did changing hurt?" he asked, and the eyes told him "yes."

The king said: "It's the wondering, the anticipation that hurts. The change feels like letting go of something you've held tightly much too long."

They were silent together for a while longer, and then the king helped his son from the seat by the window and over to the bed. The prince lay down, and his father covered him with a blanket, and then took the seat by the window, to watch him sleep. Outside, the clouds scurried furiously past the moon and thunder rumbled in the distance. A late autumn rainstorm was rolling toward the castle.

The youngest prince slept through a dull gray dawn. It had been raining since sometime deep in the night, for the marshes were swelling with water. The trees lost many of their brightly colored leaves. At the edge of the fishpond, his frog-sweetheart sat blinking between rain-drops.

By now, the prince's face was hot with fatigue and fever, and his mother sat by his side and fed him broth whenever he stirred. Her husband had relayed their late-night conversation, and she found that she was holding on tightly to her son, knowing the cold weather was coming in. He slept for nearly a week.

It was early evening when his fever broke, and his mother was dozing in her chair by the prince's bed. He raised himself up on one elbow and reached over and touched his mother's arm. She awoke, startled, and then smiled at him.

''Mother, how long have I slept?''

''For six days.''

''Thank goodness. I dreamed that I slept through the winter. I was afraid I'd missed her.''

''No, my darling. You have plenty of time.'' She stood up. ''Can I get you anything?''

''No, I'm fine. Only, I want to get up and . . .''

She nodded and stepped to his bedside to hug him tightly and then let go. ''I'll leave you to your privacy.'' She walked to the doorway, and he called to her.

''Mother . . . I won't be going very far.''

She smiled at him and said, ''No, the marsh is just outside my window.'' She went out and closed the door.

He stood up and pulled on his boots under his night-shirt. Then he wrapped himself in the cloak his brother had made for him. On the way to the door, he glanced at the scrapbook to memorize the family recipe. He paused once more to gaze at the portrait of his family, then went out into the hall and down the stairs.

He pulled open the great door that led to the garden fishpond. As he strode across the grounds, his boots made a squishing sound with every step. The rain seeped down his neck. The pond stretched out in front of him, decorated with the leaves that had fallen beneath the torrent. He was relieved to see her perched on an island of lily pads in the middle of the pond.

He took two steps into the water, and his boots filled up and anchored there. Laughing, he hopped from foot to foot to free himself of them. He could feel his nightshirt soaking up the water, so he unbuttoned all the buttons and pulled it off beneath his cape. Folding it carefully, he laid it at the water's edge.

The prince walked forward into the pond. When he was wet up to his waist, he sat down in the water and his cloak floated around him, a huge lily pad, buoyed by air. He stood up again and it clung to him, heavily. Fingering the porcelain clasp to make sure it was caught securely, he stretched out in the water to swim toward the island where she waited.

He could see her between strokes. Seated on a lily-pad throne, she looked regal and very beautiful. The clasp pulled at his throat; his feet kept tangling in the cloak; and his strokes were impeded by the heaviness of it. She watched him, her golden eyes blazing, as he struggled toward her. He gasped in a breath and lifted his arm to stroke one last time, and then she saw the cloak enfold him like a shroud. She closed her eyes, called on the magic and dove.

The rain stopped before midnight, and the next day dawned sunny. The prince's boots were visible just below the surface of the water; an inquisitive carp was nosing in and out between them. The nightshirt lay folded where he had left it. The woolen cloak, littered with leaves, was caught on some rocks at one end of the pond. There was no other sign of the prince.

The king and queen stood in a window and listened to the quiet of the autumn marsh.

"I miss the sound of the peepers," said the queen.

"It's only till springtime," said the king. "They'll be back."

"I know," she said, and leaned into him.

Chamber music floated up to them in the window from the parlor below. A breeze picked up the music and carried it out to the marsh.

The frog prince and his princess sat on the bank in the forest of marsh grass.

"Are you ready?" she asked him.

He blinked his pop eyes and croaked, "Yes."

Together they burrowed into the mud. Settling into the cool and the damp, they nestled together. Their three lids closed one by one by one; the rhythm of their breathing and their heartbeats quieted and slowed.

And they began to dream.

—For Ed Stivender, Nancy Schimmel
and Koko the gorilla

Shell Story

George Mackay Brown

The seagulls came to the island pier.

The old wives came out with bowls, with crusts and bits of fat in them.

They threw the scraps to the gulls.

While the food still hung in the blue air, the gulls gobbled every fragment up.

"That's Tommy Ritch, that gull, that's my Tommy," said one old woman, pointing to a gull that was stretching his wings on the pier. "Tommy got his death off Yesnaby thirty-one years ago come June."

"Here you come again, Willie Anderson," said another old wife. "Look at him gobbling up that hen giblet. He was always hungry when he came in from the sea. My neighbor Willie, he was lost on the trawler *Nevis,* a long while ago."

"I think that gull is my brother Drew," said one old woman. "But I was only two when his ship went down off Iceland. So I don't remember him. I can't tell if it is Drew or not."

So the old wives spoke to the gulls after every dinner-time, calling them by the names of drowned fishermen and sailors that were kin or acquaintances.

One old wife, Charlotte, looked every afternoon into the gull-shrieking, gull-beating air over the village and every afternoon she shook her head. She could never see her man Jock Wylie in the white screaming gull-drift. Jock Wylie had gone down in unknown seas, the winter after they were married . . . Still Charlotte threw bits of bannock and bits of bacon to the gulls . . . And Charlotte was getting on for a hundred years old.

Still the village wives kept up their singsong.

"Here's a piece of bread for you, Bertie Ness . . ."

"You like chicken wings, don't you, Ally Flett? Take it . . ."

"I swear, Jerry Thomson, you're a greedier gull than you were a ferryman . . ."

"I bet you'd sooner have beer than this end of bacon, Dickie Folster . . ."

Old Charlotte threw her scraps to the gulls and viewed every one from her shaded eyes, and shook her head and went home.

One day there was such a storm that even the gulls kept to their crag ledges in the Black Craig.

Oh, it was a howling gale out of the east!

The fishermen and their wives and children stayed inside, behind their rattling doors.

They saw through their salt-crusted windows a woman struggling down to the pier. They thought every moment she would be blown into the white-crested waves. And, "It's Charlotte!" they cried in croft after croft.

Then the village folk saw that a solitary bird had fallen and furled on the very edge of the stone pier.

Old Charlotte took a piece of fine cake that she had kept from the last island wedding, full of fruit and nuts, fine flour and rum, and she put it into the seabird's beak. It seemed to be a bigger bird than the usual gull.

The bird ate the bridecake, and it flew three times round Charlotte's head, and then it swung away out to the open sea.

And the wind blew salt spray over the roofs.

The old woman knocked at every door along the village street.

When the man of the house tugged the door open—so fierce the gale blew—Charlotte said in a young sweet voice, "Jock my man, he's come back to see me at last from the wastes of ocean."

Orkney Lament

Jane Yolen

When Magnus swam easy in his blood
And the selkies sang his passing,
No one on the islands was surprised.
Living is the miracle, not death.
Between ice and axe
Lies but a little space.

   There were dolphins at the bow,
   And tunny down below.
   Earl Magnus is the sea.

When Magnus flew silent in his blood
And the curlews cried his passing,
No one on the islands was surprised.
Peace is the awkwardness, not war.
Between hawk and hand
Lies but a shield of skin.

There were eagles at the prow,
And osprey at the oars.
Earl Magnus is the dove.

When Magnus fell saintly in his blood
And the oxen wept his passing,
No one on the islands was surprised.
Growing is the prodigy, not rot.
Between stalk and root
Lies but a shaft of green.

There were blossoms on the bough
And petals on the ground.
Earl Magnus is the seed.

Raven, Jade and Light

Richard Kearns

She was Jade.

Nowadays, it is a word the People use when they mean *woman,* and also a kind of lustrous, precious stone of many colors and shades. Those are only echoes of Jade. Back then, back in the myth time, back when the world was a half-made thing, filled with pearl-dark mist and shadow, Jade was a Power of Earth, although none of us knew it, herself included.

I am Raven. I was a Power of Darkness, which was a good thing to be back then, considering that darkness is all there was, or at least it was everywhere, it touched every thing and filled every place.

And I am clever.

I have always been clever. I shall always be clever.

Not sly. Not cunning. Tricky. Always right. Always a jump ahead. Always a player of the game. Always a winner.

Always.

But Jade. Jade.

I tended the world back then, clipping here, pruning there, planting, a gardener of sorts before there were any gardens.

Jade first came to my river in the darkness. I caught the sweet tang of her scent, and I heard the cautious tread of her feet in the moss, in the dust, in the mud, pausing by my banks. She dipped something she had with her in my waters, and I heard it splash and gurgle and bubble and fill. I heard the wavelets slosh against its sides. Then I heard her strain to lift the thing, and the waters dripped and fell from it, making sounds like rain and yet unlike rain. She stumbled back through the forest—I could hear her breathing heavily, clumsily breaking twigs, her odors more pronounced, running away, taking part of my river with her.

I wondered if she was beautiful.

Beauty was not something we knew about back then, because everything was so dark, and we had no way of telling what we looked like. No one knew if there was any difference between a sea slug and a turtle, or between the way Hummingbird flew and the way Loon and his brothers tumbled through the air, between the dew that encrusts Spider's web and the wet mold that blankets unburied excrement. Only a few of us suspected there might be such a thing as beauty—Hawk; Otter; Wasgo, Father of Hunters; myself. The others laughed at us, but they could not stop us wondering.

She came back. An unchallenged thief always returns for more. I know this because I have often been a thief myself.

Her approach was more brash, filled with the arrogance of success, and I grew aware of her presence long before she reached my banks.

I waited among the rushes until she had dipped her strange object in my river, and then I asked, "Who are you?"—because I didn't know at that point she was called Jade, and even knowing her name, like knowing her scent, or knowing the fall of her feet, wasn't all it could be. It wouldn't really tell me who she was. Or if she was beautiful.

She bolted.

She had the presence of mind to hang on to her strange object and drag it with her back through the forest, but then there was a brittle, crunching sound, and the rushing of waters, making an awful muddy mess as she went, and an even more awful racket.

The entire episode was really very odd.

Trying to follow her through the darkness was useless, so I let her go.

I went to find my friend Wasgo, Father of Hunters.

He was outside his cave, dozing. I could hear his shallow, even breathing, and I could smell him. Wasgo had a peppery, dusty smell.

He slept as a wolf, which made me glad. It would have been more difficult to find him had he been as a killer whale, swimming, rolling through the waters, splashing anyone who came near, spewing seawater through the air with the breath from his blowhole.

I managed to land fairly gracefully on an outstretched long-needled pine branch I had recalled and memorized outside his cave.

"Wasgo," I said.

He didn't answer for a time, but the pattern of his breathing changed. "Raven," he finally said. "My friend." He arose, stretched (I could hear the popping of his joints), yawned (his teeth clicked as he snapped his jaws shut), and shook himself. The dusty part of his scent became stronger.

"Wasgo," I said, "a creature I know nothing of has come to my river and stolen my water."

"Not all of it?" he asked.

"No," I said. "Just a little."

Wasgo sat himself down and considered this.

"She has come twice now," I said.

"Twice?" he asked.

"Yes," I answered.

"And you think she will return?" he asked.

"I believe so."

"Good," said Wasgo. "When she does, let us catch her and kill her and eat her."

I shifted my grip on the pine branch. "Wasgo," I said, "I believe she might be beautiful."

"Hm," said Wasgo. "That changes things. You're sure about this?"

"Of course I'm not sure," I said to Wasgo. "How could I tell? How would I know? How would anyone know?"

"Ah," said Wasgo.

"That is why I have come to you," I told him. "You hunt. You are aware of the ways, the scents, the manners of more creatures than any of us. I hoped you might know who this was."

"Well, I certainly have never heard of any creature that would steal your water," Wasgo said. "How did she do it?"

"I'm not sure," I said. "She had a thing she immersed in my river, and somehow, when she brought it forth again, was able to carry the water away with it."

"Hm," said Wasgo.

"She made an incredible mess the second time," I told him. "There is now mud everywhere, and the normal smells are confused and disordered. There are also many sharp, thin pieces of something like shale scattered about, but her scent is washed away."

"An interesting problem," said Wasgo. "However, just because *I* don't know about this creature doesn't mean *someone* doesn't know about this creature. We must go and ask the others."

"We?" I said.

"Yes," said Wasgo.

"You are very kind, Wasgo," I said.

"You are my friend, Raven," Wasgo said.

"And you mine," I answered.

"Come perch on my shoulder," said Wasgo. "It will be easier for us to stay together if you do."

Hummingbird knew nothing.

Loon and his brothers only laughed at us, and said there was no reason anyone would want to steal water from my river.

Hawk had heard nothing about such a creature, but was intrigued.

It was Beaver who knew about her. Beaver had actually met her, and spoken with her.

"She is called Jade," Beaver told us.

"Jade," I said.

"Jade," said Wasgo. "Tell us what you know about Jade."

Beaver scratched herself and cleaned the spot with her tongue. "She came here a long time ago," said Beaver, "with a thing that smelled like an eagle's nest, but was not an eagle's nest. It was made with twigs and eagle down all twisted together, and it could hold many more eggs than any eagle woman would ever make at one time. I know all this because she let me examine her nest-thing.''

"Interesting," said Wasgo.

"Why would she show it to *you?*" I asked, my feathers a little ruffled.

"Perhaps because we are both women, and she trusted me," said Beaver, triumphant, relishing the fact that she had somehow done something about which I was jealous. "And perhaps because I mocked her. She tried to fill her nest with water from my pond and I laughed at her, because it all spilled out. Then I showed her how to fill the spaces between the twigs with mud, and let it dry, and then the water didn't run out when she filled it."

"So that's what she used," Wasgo said. "A nest."

I thought for a moment. "But it didn't sound like a nest might sound. At least not like any nest I've heard of. Certainly not an eagle's nest, which is a very crude affair, from what I understand. It never holds together well even when it's anchored, but to move it, to carry it—"

Beaver cleared her throat. "You're right," she said. "That was what was so curious. She came back here another day with something new, a kind of nest with no twigs in it. She told me it was made of clay, and let me touch it. It was hard, like a path that is used too often, like rock. Not soft and pliant like clay at all, even though it smelled like clay a little. Jade told me her nest-thing was hollow on the inside, and that it was possible to transport normally unmanageable items within the hollow, such as water, or berries, or seeds, or olachen oil."

The two of us were silent.

"She promised to help me make one," said Beaver. "But she never came back. That was very rude of her, don't you think?"

"Yes, it was," said Wasgo.

"Perhaps because you are both women," I said, "she did not trust you."

"You think she might be beautiful—don't you, Raven?" asked Beaver, annoyed.

"Yes," I said. "I do."

She laughed at me, a high-pitched chittering sound, dragging it out for a very long time. "And when you catch her will you eat her?" Beaver asked Wasgo.

"Perhaps not," said Wasgo, who then yawned and snapped his teeth shut, which made Beaver very nervous.

"Well, if you do," said Beaver, "bring me the hollow nest-thing. It has a very powerful magic which is worthless to you men. I wish to study it, in order to make my own."

"If I do, I will certainly bring you her nest," said Wasgo. "You have been very helpful."

"I am glad," said Beaver, who then hastily dove into her pond.

We walked through the forest together, Wasgo bearing me on his shoulder.

"So she is clever," I said, after a time.

"Yes," said Wasgo. "That explains your attraction to her."

"Not all of it," I said. "You have not heard her move. You have not tasted her scent."

"No," agreed Wasgo.

"And she might be beautiful," I said.

"Perhaps," said Wasgo.

"But an eagle's nest," I said.

"I have no wish to speak with Eagle about this matter," said Wasgo. "He is a hunter, but not a clean one. Not fair. He has no respect for the chase, for the game. And he hunts when it pleases him, to amuse himself, not to fill his belly, not to enlarge his spirit."

"For my part, I have no wish to speak with him either," I said. "He would try to eat me."

Wasgo chuckled. "Has he not tried before?"

"Yes," I said. "Many times. And he has always been either too slow or too stupid to catch me. Or both." I imitated Wasgo's chuckle, which amused him greatly.

"Eagle has little cause to love you," he said.

"We have had our misunderstandings, Eagle and I," I agreed. "Nothing we couldn't patch up, if we wanted to. Still, it would not be wise to tempt him at this point."

"What do you wish to do, then?" asked Wasgo.

"I have a plan," I told him.

"Why is it I am not surprised?" asked Wasgo. "But your plan—or, at least, my part in it—will have to wait. The hunger begins to grip me, and I feel the need to visit the Sea Lion people. It has been too long since I was there last."

"Good hunting, then, my friend, Wasgo," I said.

"As always," answered Wasgo. "But I thank you for your kind wishes, my friend, Raven. They are a blessing to me."

I waited in the boughs of a great hemlock tree by the banks of my river. Its spicy smell hid my scent, more than pine, more than spruce, more than the flowering crabapple. And the height let me listen carefully to the sounds of the forest. Also, odors came to me clearly on the breath of the wind.

She returned.

I knew she would.

I heard her walking softly through the woods, waiting, waiting, walking, carrying her magic nest-thing. I recognized her scent.

I listened to her pause beneath my very hemlock tree. Then she waded quietly into my river. I heard her begin to fill her nest-thing.

"Jade," I said.

She stopped. She didn't move.

"Jade," I said again.

"You must be Raven," she said, and her voice, like her scent, was sweet and tangy. "My grandfather warned me about you."

"What did he say?" I asked.

"He told me you were evil," she said.

"That's hardly fair," I said. "You don't even know me."

"I agree," said Jade, and I heard her begin to fill her nest-thing once again.

"You are very clever," I told her. "What is that thing you have made to steal my water?"

She laughed, and I have never heard a sound before or since that could ever compare to it. "It is called a pot," she said. "And this one is better than the last one I broke, when you frightened me."

"Ah," I said. "A pot. And why is it you are using your pot to steal my water? Are you trying to make a river of your own?"

She laughed once more, and I knew I wished to make her laugh again and again, just to listen to the music of it. "No," she said. "I wish to drink it. Grandfather wishes to drink it."

"You could drink it here," I told her. "There is no need for stealing."

I heard her lift the pot, now full and heavy with water, and I heard the drip and spill from it again, making those sounds like rain and yet not like rain. "Grandfather will not come to the river," she said, wading back to the shore. "So I am left to make do as best I can for both of us. Besides, it is not dignified to drink at a riverbank."

"I am very sorry to hear that," I told her.

There was a sudden great commotion from deep within my river, a roaring and a hissing and a swelling of many waters. Jade rushed into the forest.

Wasgo heaved himself ashore, mostly killer whale, peppery to the point of pungence, his transition to wolf not even half-complete. "That was her?" he asked excitedly. "That was Jade?"

I fluttered to the forest floor. "Yes!" I said.

"She smells wonderful!" he said, the change more complete now.

"Hurry! Hurry!" I said. "We must not lose her!"

Wasgo shook the wet from his shaggy coat, spraying water everywhere, soaking me, spattering mud and hemlock needles over everything. "I have the spirit of a fierce young bull from the Sea Lion people within me now," he said. "It fills me with strength and eagerness! Come—on my back! We shall catch her!"

"I am not so sure," I told him.

To hunt with Wasgo was an honor, it was a marvel. He knew the forest, he knew the places of the trees and the shrubs and the grasses and the ferns, the fallen logs, the boulders heavy with moss, the heaps of dead and rotting leaves, and avoided each of them. He knew all the paths that lay before us in the darkness, and his knowledge made him swift.

Pace. Stop. Pace. Turn. Lope a bit. Stop. Anticipate. Take a side path. Stop. Cast about to pick up the trail once more. Pace again. Lope again. Turn again.

He ran with his nose to the ground, panting, and I clung to his back as best I could, my wings spread and pressed along his flanks so I would not be swept away by low branches or snagged by knotted vines.

We heard Jade ahead of us, crashing through the underbrush, breathing hard, still carrying her filled and unbroken pot. Her scent was sharp with fear.

We were close.

We could hear her moans and grunts. She was weeping. And still she ran.

She made it to the clearing first, and her stride increased: a last, desperate sprint.

Wasgo sneezed.

He coughed.

"Smoke!" he said, and I could smell it now.

"Smoke!" I said.

Wasgo stopped at the edge of the clearing. "Smoke!" he repeated, and sneezed once more. "It is a foul thing! An abomination! It stings my nose! I fear it, Raven! I cannot remain here! It is perilous! It will bewitch me!"

"Go back, my friend," I told him, between his sneezes. I hopped from his back. "You can do no more. It is for me to take the chase from here. You must go back!"

"My eyes!" he said. "They burn!" He sneezed again.

"Go to my river," I told him. "Soak yourself in it. It will heal you."

"You must tell me what you find," he said.

"I promise, my friend."

He slunk away. I could hear his sneezing in the distance.

There was a lodge, as I expected. I felt my way along the planking, looking for a door, but could find nothing. No matter how many times I circled the lodge, no matter how carefully I felt, all I could find was unyielding, doorless walls.

There was a smokehole cut into its roof, but not even I could overcome the foul stench that poured out of it.

I remained in the clearing for days. Several times I could hear Jade, or Grandfather, leave the lodge and return, but it was always from the side opposite me, and when I ran to find the door, the walls seemed as solid as they had ever been.

I could hear them inside. The sweet, refreshing voice of Jade, and the dried-up, cackling, singsong voice of her grandfather. His voice reminded me of someone, but I couldn't remember who. And I never heard Jade laugh.

One day, when Jade had gone down to my river to gather up more of my water in her pot, I sat with my head pressed against the smooth planking of the unbroken lodge wall, listening. I could hear Grandfather inside, singing to himself, chuckling.

"I have a box," he sang, "and inside it is another box, and there are many boxes inside that, and in the very smallest box is all the light in the world, and it is mine, and I'll never give any of it to anyone, not even my granddaughter, because—who knows?—she may be ugly as a sea slug, and neither she nor I would like to know that!"

I blinked in the darkness. I could not believe it. "I did

not know the sea slug was ugly," I said. "But Jade *must* be beautiful. I shall steal the light and find out."

I left the clearing before she returned.

Wasgo was nowhere to be found, which was just as well. It meant he had put to sea, and was healing. I expected much time would pass before I could speak with him again, if what I had in mind was successful.

I fasted.

I gathered my powers, and prepared my magics, and I thought.

It was terribly unfair for Jade's grandfather to keep all the light in the world to himself. The rest of us needed it. The darkness that was everywhere was tiresome, and made for a horrible life, always to be blindly bumping around, never to see where we were going, never to look upon the world we were making.

And I had to know if Jade was beautiful. It was a fearsome gamble, a terrible risk to take, but I had to know—I had to know if *anything* could be beautiful.

I continued to fast. I polished my plans. I waited in my hemlock tree.

She came to my river again. Quietly.

She waded in, and began to fill her pot.

"Jade," I said.

There was silence.

"Raven," she answered. "Is the Father of Hunters near?"

"No," I told her. "But you should not worry. I would not let him eat you."

"Wasgo does not hunt unless he is hungry," she replied.

"There are other hungers aside from the one that lives

in the belly," I said. "I believe Wasgo was hungry for knowledge when last you met."

Jade considered this. "There may be merit in what you say," she said. She resumed filling her pot.

"Jade," I said. "I believe you are beautiful. And I believe I love you."

She hesitated, and clutched her half-full pot to her. "You cannot know," she said.

"I *do* not know," I told her. "But that does not mean I *can*not know."

"I don't understand," said Jade.

"Your grandfather has a box," I told her, "inside of which is another box, and inside of that another box, and many more boxes inside of that, and in the very smallest box he keeps all the light in the world. If we had that, we could find out."

"Grandfather will not share his light with anyone," she said.

"I know," I said. "I want you to help me steal it."

"Raven, I cannot do that," Jade answered. "I am afraid. Grandfather would be terribly angry if he found out."

"We still must do it," I said.

"Raven, you want *me* to love *you* because *you* love *me*," she said. "But I do not know if I love you. I do not know if you are beautiful. I could not bear to find out you were ugly. I must refuse. You cannot force me to love you."

"We shall see," I said, and I put forth my power.

I laid a mighty thirst upon Jade, and as she stooped to fill her pot with river water, I transformed myself into a hemlock needle and cast myself inside it.

She drank the entire potful, and me with it. I heard

her exhale, and felt her wipe her mouth with the back of her hand as I slithered down, deep inside her.

"Raven?" she said.

There was no answer.

She waited, then refilled her pot and headed home.

Jade was warm and soft inside. I grew sleepy, and my transformation began.

Of course, Grandfather could not see the changes that were taking place in Jade's body. She could tell something was happening, but she was unsure, and didn't speak about it.

My time arrived, and I came forth, Jade's firstborn son, Grandfather's first great-grandson.

Jade hugged me, and held me, and fed me, and cleaned me, and laughed until I felt sure my heart would break from sheer happiness. And Grandfather strutted about, all puffed up with pride, because there was no one else in the world who had a great-grandson.

They were both amazed at the variety of sounds I learned to make, many of which were shattering, blood-curdling, earsplitting, heartrending. And when I cried, the rafters would shake. They called me the Little Noisy One.

This was all as I had planned it. For I am Raven. I am clever. Always.

I grew older and stronger quickly, requiring less and less constant attention from Jade, which made her glad. The day finally came when Jade took up her pot and prepared to go to the river.

"What are you doing?" asked Grandfather.

"I am going to get water," said Jade.

"You cannot do that," Grandfather answered. "You cannot leave me here with *him*—I don't know what to do. Here—give me your pot. I will go down to the river."

"You would never go to the river before," said Jade.

"I know," he said. "But I will chance it now. You stay here and take care of my great-grandson."

"No," said Jade. "I have stayed inside this lodge all these many months, never leaving, while you have been in and out, in and out. I cannot tolerate it any longer. I must smell the smells of the forest, and feel the wind on my face, the drag of the river current on my calves, the mud between my toes. *You* stay and take care of your great-grandson."

"I will do no such thing," said Grandfather.

"You *will*," said Jade, stamping her foot. "If you wish to live in *my* lodge, you must help out, or leave this instant and go build your own lodge, cook your own meals, weave your own mats, make your own pots, and gather your own water."

"You do not show the proper respect," said Grandfather.

"It is *you* who is lacking respect," answered Jade. "You march around here all day, you boast to your friends that you are the only one in the world with a great-grandson, you bring them over here to listen to him, smell him, touch him, play with him, and of course they all must be fed and catered to. And do you ever lift even a finger to help?"

Grandfather sighed. "I am sorry, my granddaughter. It is just that when the Little Noisy One yells, my head aches. And his crying makes my legs wobble, my ears ring, my hands tremble, and my belly turn within me."

"Then you are not so different from anyone else," said Jade.

"Very well," said Grandfather. "Go to the river. But do not be gone long."

I smiled to myself as Jade walked out the door.

I waited only a few minutes after she left.

"My great-grandfather," I said.

"My great-grandson," he answered. "You can speak!"

"Yes," I said. "It is a thing I have learned by listening to you and my mother. I think you are better at it, so it was to you I wished to speak first."

"That is wonderful," said Grandfather. "I am honored."

"But tell me," I said, "what is this thing in the corner?"

"What thing in the corner?" he asked. "What are you talking about?"

"This square thing," I said.

"Don't touch that!" said Grandfather.

"I am not touching it," I said. "But tell me what it is."

"I will tell you," he said, "but you must promise to leave it alone."

"Why?" I asked.

"Because it is a box," he said, "and inside it is another box, and inside that is another box, and there are many boxes inside that, and in the very smallest box is all the light in the world, which is mine, and I will not let anyone else use it. It is too dangerous. We might find out we are all ugly, like sea slugs. You wouldn't like to find out your mother is ugly, like a sea slug, would you?"

"Of course not," I told him. "But I wish to play with one of the boxes."

"No," he said. "You must leave the boxes alone."

"Only one," I pleaded. "You have so many."

"No!" he said. "Absolutely not."

I let out a piercing, bloodcurdling scream that went on and on, until dust began to fall from the rafters.

"Stop it! Stop it!" he yelled. "I will let you play with the box!"

I stopped.

"But only one," he said. "And you must put it back when you are through."

I smiled to myself.

After a time, I spoke to him again. "My great-grandfather," I said.

"My great-grandson," he answered.

"The box you have given me to play with is much too small," I told him.

"Then you may not play with it any more," he said.

"I wish to play with two boxes instead," I said.

"You may not play with two boxes," he said.

"Why not?" I asked him.

"Because they are *my* boxes," he answered. "Besides, it is too dangerous."

I took a deep breath and screamed again, louder this time, an earsplitting scream, until dust fell from the rafters, and the woven cedar bark mats fell off the walls.

"Stop it! Stop it!" he yelled.

I stopped.

Grandfather sighed. "Very well," he said. "You may play with two boxes. But no more."

I let the time pass.

"My great-grandfather," I said.

"My great-grandson," he answered.

"I wish to build a mountain range of boxes, and play hunter among them," I said.

"You may not build a mountain range of boxes," he answered. "Play cave hunter among the boxes that you have."

"I have already played cave hunter," I told him. "It does not please me any more."

"Well, I will not give you more boxes to build a mountain range," he said. "You must find something else to play."

"I don't wish to play anything else," I said. "Why won't you give me more boxes?"

"It is too risky," he said. "All the light in the world is inside them, and it is mine, and I cannot let it escape."

"You only need one box in which to keep the light," I said. "Surely you will let me play with the others."

"No!" he said.

I screamed a heartrending scream, until the dust fell from the rafters, and the woven cedar bark mats he had put back in their proper places fell down off the wall again.

"Stop it! Stop it!" he yelled.

I stopped.

He sighed more deeply this time. "I will give you one more box to play with," he said.

I screamed again, a shattering scream, until Jade's two remaining pots burst, the one spilling salmonberries, the other spilling wheat grass seeds across the floor.

"Stop it! Stop it!" he yelled. "You may play with all the boxes except the last one, but you must cease this screaming!"

*   *   *

A strange glow filled the lodge—not enough to see by, except to discern the ruddy walls, and the large, dark shapes of the mountain range of boxes. I climbed among them for a while.

"My great-grandfather," I said.

"My great-grandson," he answered.

"I wish to play with the light," I said.

He was silent. I knew he was angry. "You may not play with the light," he told me.

"Why not?" I asked.

"Because the light is mine," he answered, "and I will not let you have it, and I do not care if you scream until the dust falls from the rafters, and the woven cedar bark mats fall down from their places once more; and you have already broken your mother's pots, so you cannot break them again. Anyway, my head is so close to splitting, you could not do anything to make it worse, so scream all you want, I do not care."

I raged and cried this time, and the tears rained down my cheeks, and the dust fell from the rafters, and the woven cedar bark mats fell down from the walls again, and the broken pot shards rattled, and the salmonberries Grandfather had swept into one pile all burst, and the wheat grass seeds he had swept into another pile jiggled and danced, and the fire went out, and the mountain range of boxes splintered, and the very planks that formed the walls of the lodge began to separate, one from the other, and the floor shook beneath us, and Grandfather's legs wobbled, his hands trembled, and his belly turned inside him.

"Enough!" he said.

I stopped.

"You are an evil child," he said, "and your mother will punish you severely when she returns."

I started to take another breath, but before I could fill up, Grandfather said hastily, "I *will* let you play with the light, just for a little bit. However, you must promise not to look at anything while you are playing with it, and you must promise to hide it away again before your mother returns, because if she were to come back when it was still out, and we saw her, we might discover she is as ugly as a sea slug, and both of us would be sad, and regret it deeply."

I smiled. "Of course, Great-Grandfather," I said.

Grandfather opened the final box, and pulled out a huge, shining, wonderfully radiant white ball, and tossed it through the air toward me. I only had time to catch a brief glimpse of his wrinkles, his hooked nose, his beady eyes, before I leapt into the air myself, changing from human to raven form.

I grabbed the light in my beak, and flew up, through the smokehole in the roof, and out. The ball of light was almost too big to fit through the smokehole; it scraped the sides, and sparks rose into the sky and stuck there, burning.

It was too marvelous, too powerful a thing to speak of properly. I flew over the world and saw it for the first time, the smoky green of the forests, the brighter greens of the meadows, speckled with reds and blues and yellows the way the stars now speckled the heaven above me.

The lakes and rivers and streams I flew over all reflected the light back to me, becoming things of white crystal shot through with pastel fires. To my left, in the distance, the ocean glittered at me darkly.

The mountains—oh, the mountains were purple and peaked with crisp white snow, with faint green misty forests folded in their skirts. A rainbow raced and sparkled through the air before me, the clouds turned pink and red and orange, and the sky itself blushed blue.

"Raven!" I heard below me.

It was Jade's voice! I looked for her.

"Raven!" she called. "Flee quickly. Grandfather Eagle almost has you! He'll eat you, and eat the light if he catches you! Please!"

I looked over my left shoulder and saw Eagle, my enemy, my great-grandfather—the angry glare in his eyes; the determined, powerful beating of his mighty golden-brown wings; his white and hooded head; his hooked, open yellow beak; his red tongue; his outstretched, taloned feet.

A piece of the light, cracked from our passage through the smokehole, broke off and fell into my river. It dimmed, bobbed to the surface again, then drifted skyward, appearing as a frosted, silvery disc.

I shot ahead, desperate, trying to think, still overwhelmed by the fresh sights below and around me. I could hear Eagle gaining.

Harder now, my wings churned the air, and I fought to reach the mountains in the east.

Still Eagle gained on me.

I was a dark streak across the sky, and the rainbow thundered before me, the earth echoing its desperate roar. The mountains were so close!

No time left to change my mind. No time to be surer. This would have to do.

I let the light go and tossed it east, then veered sharply west myself. Eagle would have to choose between us. I hoped he was too stupid to know which of us would be the more important prey.

I heard his final scream of rage as I swung low, seeking forest, seeking trees, seeking cover. He could not decide between revenge and greed, and lost us both. Furious, he circled in the sky above me.

The light turned hot, then incandescent, and sailed ever higher.

Jade was waiting for me by my river. I looked upon her for the first time. We looked upon one another.

"Raven," she said.

"Jade," I answered.

Neither of us could speak for several moments.

"Jade," I said again, "there is a thing I must tell you." I hesitated. "You are beautiful—more beautiful than the knobby fingers of my hemlock tree raised black against the bright red sky at sunrise, more beautiful than the flowers that shine among the meadow grasses, more beautiful than the rainbow that boomed across the world as Eagle chased me, more beautiful than the stars, more beautiful than the sun. I love you."

She smiled at me, and I trembled. I was afraid. I was sure she would find me ugly.

"And you, Raven," she said. "You are beautiful also. You are black, like night, but the light glimmers from you where there would be shadows in others. I love you also."

"Jade," I said.

"But you tricked me, Raven," she said. "I have become your mother. The thing you hoped for between us—the thing I hoped for, too—is no longer possible. It would be wrong."

"There is still the love," I told her. "And the knowing—I know now you are beautiful, when I didn't know before. I know now there is such a thing as beauty, when once I could only hope. And knowing all that is much better than any pleasure.''

She knelt and picked up a dirty brown round thing with handles. ''This is my pot,'' she said. ''This *is* ugly. I must learn to make pots that are beautiful.''

''I am sure you will succeed,'' I said. ''You are very clever.''

Jade laughed for me. *''Your* cleverness has destroyed my lodge,'' she said. ''I must go build a new one—many new ones, I think. And I will make them all beautiful.''

''One at a time, I hope,'' I told her.

''Maybe,'' she said. Then she sighed. ''I'm afraid Grandfather Eagle will never love you.''

''Eagle is a fool,'' I told her. ''He is selfish and mean, and has made the world a miserable place for a very long while.''

''That is true,'' she said. ''But it is also true there is good in him, and time will bring it out.''

''Perhaps,'' I said. ''But I do not think the goodness will ever be between him and me.''

''Perhaps,'' she answered.

There was silence again.

''Well, I can see you wish to leave,'' I said.

''Yes,'' she said.

''Good building, then, my mother, Jade,'' I said. ''Good painting. Good planting. Good weaving. Go in beauty.''

''I am sure of it,'' she answered. ''But I thank you for your kind wishes, my friend, my son, Raven. They are a blessing to me.''

I was very weary and sad.

I remained within the hemlock tree, and rested, and thought, and considered the bright colors of the world.

Before long, I smelled the smell of dust and pepper. "Wasgo," I said, and looked upon him for the first time. He was a mixture of day and night, moonlight smeared over darkness, and things not unlike starlight streaked his fur.

"Raven," he answered. "My friend."

"You are beautiful, Wasgo," I told him. "And you are healed from the smoke."

"Yes, of course, thank you for asking. And you, Raven, are beautiful also," he said. "You have been very busy. I want to hear the full tale of it—you owe me, if you recall."

"Yes," I answered. "Gladly."

"Come," he said. "Sit on my shoulder. We will visit the others and see if they are beautiful also."

"We?" I asked.

"Yes," said Wasgo.

"You are very kind, Wasgo," I said.

"You are my friend, Raven," Wasgo said.

"And you mine," I answered.

"We shall visit Beaver first," he said, as we trotted off together. "And even if she is beautiful, I shall tell her she is ugly. It was shameful the way she mocked you about beauty."

I imitated Wasgo's laughter, and he was pleased.

"Raven, Jade and Light" is a retelling of part of the creation myth cycle of many northwest coast Native American tribes, including the Haida, the Tlingit, the Tsimishian and Kwakiutl peoples.

while i was in the woods

Susan Solomont

while i was in the woods
leaning against a red tree

i met a red man   full of walking

his arms were like redwood
his bows were birches

his gaze over rivers was like the
sun piercing a cloud

his voice
rumbled like
trees splitting   under thunder

white spirit birds flew
up & down his back

165

he knew what volcanoes
have in their heart

my life is written on   gravestones
law tablets   iron statues

his laws were   delicate   birdbones
ripples on lakes   bending of rushes
shifting of sand   crackling of fire

when the sun's finger   points down the clouds
the ancestors chant   like a swaying forest

Desert Angel

Sandra Rector and P M F Johnson

A faint scrabbling noise interrupted Loon's prayer.

Careful not to disturb Dorissa, he eased out of bed and stepped outside. The shadows of dawn obscured the desert floor.

That sound haunted him these days, a rustle like paws moving along a ridge. He looked around, uneasy, but saw nothing unusual. Was his mind playing tricks? The wind was fitful; had it caused the disturbance?

The corn needed watering. That should be done before the day grew hot. He hurried to finish his daily petition to the angel. "It shouldn't have happened, I know that. Please tell my wife and daughter how sorry I am."

His shack rested on the abutment under a concrete bridge. The angel's image was painted onto the opposite wall; its peeling white wings and blue gown were faintly ashimmer in the creamy light.

Surely it was blasphemous to pray to the angel, but her mysterious presence beneath this isolated, rural bridge was the only *milagro* he knew, and he thought God, in His remoteness, would not fault a man who made a few requests closer to home.

In the shack, Dorissa grunted and drew the bedcovers closer about her big comfortable self. Loon stopped in mid-prayer to gaze at her with a mixture of tenderness and guilt. He stepped away from the door so he wouldn't disturb her sleep.

"It's lonely here," he explained to the angel as he walked down the path. "Dorissa helps me forget when I think maybe the memories'll . . ."

A stone chittered down a slope. More scrabbling came from the ravine and something pale vanished into the brush. He felt a cold pang of dread. A ghost?

The breeze stirred and Loon shivered in the brisk morning air. Aside from Dorissa, he hadn't seen another person nearabouts in at least three years.

His grandmother once said this time between darkness and light was when spirits visited. Loon bent, pinched up some loose caliche and rubbed the soil on his forehead to gain the earth's protection from insubstantial creatures.

As he did so, he caught the faint scent of rosemary.

A shiver ran through him. Guadalupe's favorite herb. The herb of remembrance.

Guadalupe stood at the door of the kitchen, the pork hissing and crackling behind her as it cooked, the scent of rosemary wafting through the air.

"I forbid you to go," she said, angrier than he had ever seen her. She brushed away a strand of her black hair with the back of her hand. "You'll get yourself killed, just like my father. I'm not ready to become a widow at such a young age."

"I have no choice," he said, angry at her for not under-

standing a man had his duty. "If I refuse, they'll call me a coward who hides behind his wife's skirt."

A gust of wind brought Loon back to himself. Was the mysterious creature the ghost of his wife? That would explain the scent of rosemary, the intensity of his memories. Would she forgive him? He must know. Hopeful, he searched the earth nearby for tracks.

Nothing. His frustration mounted. The tracks had to be here, but he found no trace even of an animal. The only prints in the clay soil were Dorissa's, smudged and indistinct. He felt an unreasoning anger that her tracks were in the way.

Determined, he searched farther up the dry wash, but saw no footprints, no animal spoor, no evidence of any kind of intruder. He came to the end of the arroyo and the top of the ridge. Still nothing.

Down the other side of the ridge lay a narrow plateau, and atop it, a mound of earth and timbers half covered with blown sand. A few blackened beams still stuck into the air after all these years. Farther on, the land dropped away to a muddy river. Beyond the river rose a wall of mountains, dark, sullen, cruel.

Loon quickly turned his back on the sight.

Disgusted with himself, he gave up the search for tracks—the creature was unreal. He had lived in this empty land too long, and his mind had been affected. Like the angel, he had faded, become insubstantial.

"Where are you?" Dorissa called.

Loon turned at the sound of her voice. "I'm right here," he said, and waved.

He labored back up the side of the ravine to his shack. The sight of her standing in the doorway filled him with a shock of pride at their lovemaking of the night before.

The wind carried a fine cloud of dust along the flatland. The breeze blew steadily, as it always did at sun-rise.

Dorissa waited. Her wiry black hair was white at the temples, lending her an aura of wisdom and dignity. She wore a black shawl and a long, purple dress. He felt honored, and a little awestruck, whenever she came to him.

As the sun rose, he slipped his arms around her and kissed her neck. She pushed him away. "I don't know what to make of you," she said. "You're always off in your own world."

"I'm sorry." He picked up the sack of cornmeal to start breakfast.

"And stop always saying you're sorry. I don't believe you."

"I'm sor . . ." His face grew hot.

He fed wood into the fire, and poured water into the pot. He felt her eyes on him. He dropped the ladle, picked it up again.

"You gave me no answer last night," she said softly.

He squeezed his eyes shut. "I do care for you."

She put her hands on her hips. "Proof exists some-where?"

Stung, he went to the door and gazed across the des-ert. The faded soil ran in endless lines across the flats, modeled and sculpted by the winds, broken everywhere by low brush—chamisa, junipers, the holed, porous skeletons of staghorn cactus.

"What is it you always search for?" she asked, a hurt in her voice.

"I thought I saw something earlier," he said. "Too big for a coyote."

"Maybe you saw a dog."

"Or a wolf," he said, with a shrug.

"Wolves are extinct." She started to make up the bed. "At least around here. Maybe way back up in the mountains some haven't been killed."

He nodded, turning to the fire.

She finished with the bed and stood up, a determined look on her broad face. "Well, Lorenzo, have you decided whether you will move from this place and come live with me?"

He cleared his throat, but found nothing to say.

"You didn't answer last night, either," she said. She laughed a bitter laugh. "Oh God, I haven't built up much strength these last few years." Her face was etched with pain. "Do I have enough strength to leave you?"

"Why not just stay?" he asked.

She glared at him with disbelief. "Because I cannot live this way and neither should you. Five years, you've lived under this bridge."

Her words hurt, but he recognized what she meant. He forced himself to sound calm, businesslike. "I don't blame you for not wanting to live here," he said. "We're too different and . . ."

"You old fool," she interrupted. "We're exactly alike. We've had the same hopes, we've had the same losses."

They were both silent.

"Do you hate him?" Loon asked at last.

She nodded yes, paused, then shook her head no. "I forgive him," she answered slowly. "All our children at once. All my little ones, gone. Who can blame him for leaving? But it shows how much easier it is to keep a distance from yourself and those who cause you pain."

"I'll never hurt you," Loon said.

"The people who say that hurt you most deeply," she

answered. "Still, I weary of loneliness. I need relief from that."

"Look," he said, in a voice not quite his own. "I'm doing better now. The corn is good this spring. It'll be a good harvest. I even built a whole other side of the bed, just for you."

To his surprise, she began to laugh.

"What?" he asked.

"You, silly," she said, and placed her arms around him. She pulled him close.

Desperate, he looked deep into her eyes. "Will you stay?"

She pressed her finger to his lips. "For a little while," she whispered, her voice a promise. "If you're good."

On a fierce impulse, he lifted her and laid her on the bed.

They lay together afterward, her hand across his chest. He thought about what she said. He had been here five years, unable to leave. If Guadalupe or Elise came back, he wanted them to be able to find him.

Guilt blanketed him. He shifted until he faced the wall of the shack, his back toward Dorissa.

"Please don't go, Papa." Elise stood between them, clutching her doll, her face pale and serious. She looked just like her mother.

Guadalupe gazed at him steadily. "We need you here."

"I go for you and our little one," he argued. "If I don't protect you, who will?"

"They only raid for food down by the villages, never out here. They'll not bother us if you leave them alone."

"They're bandits," he said. "They won't just go away. If we let these evil men break one law, they'll break others."

*"I don't care," she said. She slammed down his dinner and
walked away.*

*That night, he ached to hold her, to tell her that he loved her
and would be back in a few days. She rolled away from him
and faced the wall.*

They lay awake all night, back-to-back. Neither spoke.

The next morning he put on his uniform defiantly.

"You were thinking of her again, weren't you?" Dorissa said sharply.

"No," he lied.

"You always become stiff and untouchable, as though
you don't like me."

"I like you just fine." A terrible sorrow, an inability
to think had overtaken him.

She got out of bed.

Uneasy, he rolled over.

"You're hopeless," she said, snatching up her
clothes. "You won't try to change."

Would he lose her too? He came to his feet and spoke
before he thought. "I love you," he said, his voice
breaking on the unexpected words.

She held her dress in front of her, blocking him.
"How like you to say that for the first time this way.
Taking all the goodness out of it." She quickly shivered
into her dress, strapping her belt around her waist with
passionate movements. "I'm at a loss. I don't know
what to do with you. You think you're the only one with
troubles? Everyone has troubles every day, my friend.
Ah, I can't think here. I'm going home to care for my
sheep."

"I'll walk you," he said, hurriedly slipping into his
pants.

She was already at the door. "Don't trouble yourself."

"It's no trouble."

She confronted him. "I don't want you."

He stood, paralyzed by her rejection.

"I won't return," she said. "This place, your loneliness, it's all a shrine to her. If you care for me, you'll come. You can tend the sheep, and be a decent farmer once more. We'll live in my trailer. You're gentle, you work hard, you listen to me. I like that." She paused. "Too many reminders of death linger here." She glanced out the door. "Look at that ghost on the wall."

"It's an angel," he objected. "From God."

"It's a ghost. I hate it. I will not make love in a coffin."

Her chin was set. "If you want a live woman instead of a dead one, be quick. I'm going home. I can't stay here and watch while you destroy yourself."

She left.

He shouted after her. "Leave me, then. What do I care?"

He watched until she was out of sight, then slumped on a chair, his face in his hands.

He awoke suddenly. What was that noise?

He looked out the door of his shack.

The moon was high in the sky, towering over the black forms and groping arms of the dead cacti like a glaring priestess. Against a backdrop of junipers, a pair of amber eyes glowed.

He grabbed his knife and charged outside.

The eyes were gone.

The scent of rosemary lingered in the desert air.

Heat waves rippled across the dirt yard as he marched past the house with the other soldiers. His daughter stood at the window, clutching her doll. Her face was streaked with tears. Guadalupe was nowhere in sight.

He and the other soldiers were going to defeat the bandits of the mountains. Their show of strength was sure to drive off the ruffians. But the soldiers found only empty huts. The bandits had slipped away, forewarned.

Later that night, the creature reappeared at his doorway, as big as a wolf, gray in the moonlight. The tang of rosemary burned his nostrils.

He forced back his excitement so as not to frighten her, but he could not contain himself. ''Are you a ghost?'' he asked in a voice that sounded strange and common to his own ears. ''Are you Guadalupe returned to me?''

The animal disappeared.

He hurried outside to set a trap. By the light of the moon, he dragged out a heavy metal cage he'd found years ago, and kept to trap wild turkeys. He triggered the door to spring shut. Carefully he camouflaged the trap with brush and leaves.

Only then did he admit what folly his plan was. No creature would be so incautious as to invade an area recently disturbed, and reeking of man.

The crazy part of his mind argued that if the beast were his wife, the angel would deliver her to him.

The rational part of his mind made him bait the trap with a rabbit he'd snared yesterday. Even if the beast were just a wolf, he told himself, catching it would safeguard Dorissa's sheep.

He went back to his shack, and lay in his bed. Hours passed, but he couldn't sleep. The thought of Dorissa disturbed him. How nice it would be to lie down beside her, to sleep in a real bed. To have a future again.

He missed her and rose suddenly, wanting to go to her, but halting. Was it his pride that stopped him?

Despondent, the soldiers shambled home from the moun-
tains. They rounded a last bend and Loon saw, below, the
greasy smoke on the horizon. He broke ranks, and began to
run. No. Please God, no. The stench hit his nostrils. He saw the
hollow in the air where his home should have been.

He didn't want to remember any more. He ran from
his shack, his arms wrapped around his head.

The night was old, the sky pale in the east.

He stood on the dark ground, and gradually grew
aware of movement to his left.

Something was in the cage.

Excited, he hastened over. A huge grey wolf paced
back and forth, fiercely turning about on itself in the
cramped space. The scent of rosemary filled the air.

Loon came closer. The wolf paused, stared up at him
with pale, baleful eyes. Steady, determined, like Guadalupe.

''Guadalupe, oh my beautiful Guadalupe.'' He sighed
in his relief and reached into the cage to caress her.

Fangs slashed.

Loon screamed, and leaped away. The wolf growled.
Its neck hair stood on end.

Loon stared in disbelief at the blood flowing down his
arm. Had she tried to kill him? His own wife? Scarlet
liquid flecked the earth at his feet. Stumbling to his
shack, Loon pressed a bandage against his wound, and
weakly sank down on a chair.

That was only an animal out there, he said to himself.
A dangerous animal.

Angry, he picked up his knife, and bound it to a stout
length of wood. It was only a wolf, a predator. His wife
would never have hurt him. They loved each other. He
would dispatch the beast, or it would threaten Dorissa's
sheep. He would kill it from a safe distance.

He approached the cage and tried not to gaze into the wolf's eyes, but when the beast did not growl, he couldn't help himself. Guadalupe's eyes had been hazel in the daylight, green by lamplight. These eyes were amber.

Running, running, ashes crunching under every step, he came home. There lay the blackened beams, there the trampled garden.

In the center of the broken herbs sprawled his daughter's doll, its little head hacked off, ripped and bloodied, its body mutilated.

The wolf stared at him, steady as a lover. Suddenly it didn't matter if this beast's eyes were amber, or green, or hazel—Loon knew. This was Guadalupe. The strong smell of rosemary was proof. There was no mistake. He had come to her and she struck at him. She did not want to be with him any more. Was she still angry?

Surprised, he hunkered down on his haunches. Why had it taken him so long to learn? After years spent mourning and praying, all he had accomplished was to hold Guadalupe here with his grief.

At last he stood, and walked slowly up the ravine to the ridge. In the growing light, he looked down at the burnt timbers. On a bare spot where the garden used to be, a lone hollyhock had grown up, raising its shaft of pink flowers to the heavens.

Guadalupe was gone. She wanted to be gone. It wasn't that she was angry. She slashed at him because she wanted him to let her go. If there was any life after death, that life must have its own purpose, and all anyone could know was that its purpose was separate from this world.

Abruptly, Loon turned back. He headed for the cage, walking faster and faster. When he arrived, mindless of the wolf's fangs, he yanked the clasp free that held the cage closed and flung open the door.

The wolf leaped through the opening and disappeared into the underbrush. Again he caught the faint tang of rosemary.

He smiled.

Then he returned to the shack to gather his clothes, his water gourd, a small packet of seed corn. At the doorway, he paused to examine the angel one last time. He was surprised to see she had faded almost beyond recognition.

Whistling, Loon stepped onto the path to Dorissa's sheep camp.

Behind him, the wind blew soft trails of dust into the abandoned cage. His were the only tracks.

The Hell Gamblers

Jessica Amanda Salmonson

"Don't pose as a brave man, Hwa Li! There is none of us would spend a night in the Hell King's temple. You are no braver than the rest of us."

"You think that way?" complained Hwa Li to the company of young men gathered in the bamboo garden. They were at the beginning of their scholarly careers and would one day become wise men, if they lived so long. Hwa Li said, "We are learned men! We ought not believe such things as send the ignorant fleeing through the night. Who that was not afraid of ghosts was ever hurt by one? They have only what power we allow them. Did not Confucius say so?"

The other boys nodded with general agreement, not wishing to admit to any fear of ghosts. But the original speaker—a slight young man with a guileless face but guileful disposition, whose name was Kwan Fo—was not easily convinced.

"Your argument has two flaws," said Kwan Fo.

179

"First, it is easy to say what you have said while avoiding places where ghosts are apt to appear; so your fearlessness is but a sham. Second, even allowing that ghosts can cause no injury to those who are unafraid, we are not in this case speaking of ghosts, but of the King of Hell, who nightly fetches offerings left for him by day. To sleep in his temple is to be mistaken for an offering. You would be carried away into Hell never again to be seen. Therefore it is not cowardly for us to say we would never sleep in such a place. Rather, it is wisdom to avoid folly. But for you to tell us you could sleep there without shrugging, that is an idle boast."

"Ha! You think so? But I say the King of Hell doesn't go there in the night. The monks slip into the place under cover of darkness and claim the offerings for themselves! That's what I have to say. They make weird noises to keep the inquisitive away. If I were to find a comfortable spot where the monks couldn't detect me, I could sleep the whole night unmolested. If harm came to me, it would be because the monks found me out. If I took a weapon with me, they could not do a thing even if they found me. These things being true, it would be perfectly safe to sleep in the Hell King's temple."

The others were only half convinced. Certainly they would not like to sleep in the temple to test Hwa Li's supposition.

"Then you will do as you have said you can," advised Kwan Fo, "or else we will know that your hypothesis rests upon vain boastfulness. I will lend you my sword, that is an heirloom, and you may keep it as winnings of a bet—supposing you do not flee the temple before dawn. If you are not brave enough, then you must give me your silk-embroidered shoes. The rest of your possessions will be divided among the others here. Lo

Wei has admired your hairpins; they'll be his. Ma Heh can have your silk shirt. Lo Bin can have the porcelain-coin belt you wear on fine occasions. Your pants will be burned in a kettle as offering to the insulted Hell King. Then you will promise to walk naked through the streets.''

The others laughed in agreement.

Hwa Li tried to suppress unseemly feelings of fury and annoyance, but his face became red from his emotions.

Kwan Fo added, ''As we are magnanimous, you may run naked instead of having to walk.''

''It is too easy a bet,'' said Hwa Li evenly, sounding self-assured and authoritative. ''What else will I win besides Kwan Fo's sword? Lo Wei, you like my hairpins so much; but what if you cannot win them? What can you lose? You will shave your head if you lose! Ma Heh covets the silk shirt? What if you cannot have it? Will you tattoo your shoulders against your family's wishes? Good! As for my porcelain coins! They are only decorations. But will Lo Bin put his purse of gold against them? Ha ha! You are not brave enough to bet against me! All right, the bet is off.''

''No, no, you cannot get off so easily,'' said Kwan Fo. ''Lo Bin agrees; we all do. You must sleep in the Hell Temple tonight. This is the night of the Fire Holiday, after all, the time when would-be scholars are burnt into charcoal down there in the Hell country. If you cannot escape the Hell King before dawn, it'll happen to you at once!''

''Ha ha! I'll make plans to spend Lo Bin's purse! Part of it will pay the tattooist for Ma Heh's shoulder designs! I'll cut off Lo Wei's hair with Kwan Fo's precious sword! What fun it will be!''

"We'll see who wins," said Kwan Fo. But no one else was laughing.

His four companions escorted him that very evening, amidst the final visitors to the Hell Temple. The four soon after took their leave; Hwa Li was secretly left behind. He had slipped unnoticed into a recess behind the statue of a minor demon at one side of the main hall's entry.

Gaunt, head-shaven monks moved from door to door sealing the place for the night. When they, too, had parted, and Hwa Li was alone, he began to doubt the wisdom of his bet. The pure philosopher should not find it necessary to test his theorems empirically. Really, he oughtn't be here at all! That was Hwa Li's thinking.

His teeth chattered, but it may have been only for the sake of the temple's chilliness. There were protracted squeaking noises, like faraway tortures, tracing the length of the ceiling. The patter of a myriad tiny feet rushed upward within the walls. Such sounds were amplified in the vast hollowness of the temple.

To tell the truth, Hwa Li wanted to run right out of there at that very moment. He was afraid the monks had placed thick braces outside the doors and he was trapped.

On the other hand, he didn't want to lose all his favorite things and have to run naked through the village and feel humiliated for the rest of his life.

He tried to talk himself out of being frightened, remembering the lecture he had given his fellows early in the day.

After a while, Hwa Li peered from behind the statue, expecting at any moment for the monks to return and fetch the offerings left for the King of Hell.

At the far end of the long room, upon low ornate lacquered tables in front of the incense brazier, innumerable offerings were pleasingly arranged.

The fuming incense sent thin, ghostly shapes here and there. These smoky wraiths drifted and transformed themselves. They had smoke-ring mouths and eyes in their expanding faces. These frightful illusions slowly dissipated and were replaced by others.

Behind the glowing brazier stood a row of demons with swords upraised. They were made of wood and represented the Hell King's twelve captains. Coals from the brazier cast faint shadows behind the demons and made their faces appear to frown then smile.

Hwa Li imagined to himself what it would be like if the twelve captains sprang to life, dashed the length of the room, snatched him from the nook in which he was hiding, and hacked him to bits with their weapons. Having such a fancy, Hwa Li began to quake, and took hold of Kwan Fo's family heirloom, wishing he had more sword skill than was the case.

The walls and ceiling were in darkness. Hwa Li became as quiet as a mouse when he heard a noise. It had to be one of the monks coming to get the Fire Holiday offerings and transport them up the hillside to the monastery.

A secret door opened somewhere; Hwa Li couldn't see it. Then, shambling forth into the dim glow of the brazier, an enormous man appeared. He was hardly more than a shadow. His back was hunched. Unexpectedly he turned his head and Hwa Li saw the eyes were glowing the same color as the coals in the brazier! Hwa Li stifled a whimper and told himself the eyes merely reflected the faint light.

Then the horrible shadow-thing asked, "Is that Hwa Li over there?"

Strange to say, hearing his own name called out, Hwa Li was caused to feel a great sense of relief. It was not one of the monks after all, for they knew nothing about him. It had to be some freakish man hired by his friends to come and startle him and make him lose the bet.

"It's Hwa Li, all right," said Hwa Li, bold as could be.

"Well, I'm gathering up some things to take to Hell with me. Do you want to help me carry them? Or will I have to take you there by force?"

Hwa Li came out from behind the statue and strode forth with nonchalance. It was not easy to be calm, because the hunchback man was very big and ugly, and his teeth were abnormally long with incisors like a wild hog's. His hair was a thick stubble covering his face and head. His hands were thick and the knuckles fat.

"I'm ready to go right now," said Hwa Li, "except that I have a bet to win with some friends. I cannot leave the temple until dawn. At that time, I'll win some money, this sword I'm carrying, and concessions from my fellow students."

"You're a gambler, then? So am I," said the exceedingly ugly man. "Your game conflicts with mine, for I must claim everything that is mine before sunrise, whereas you must stay here until after. I admire you and would like to test your gambling ability. Look there in that pile, an old set of gambling tiles has been given to me by a gangster who hopes to be forgiven a lot of sins. Shall we use them to play a game?"

"I wouldn't mind, but what shall I bet?" said Hwa Li. "All those things on the table are yours. But I have only this sword and the clothes I am wearing."

"Those are good things to start with," said the creature. "Get the tiles."

Hwa Li went to the pile of offerings and took up the tile set. He dumped the tiles on the floor and sat down opposite the monster. They played swiftly, the brazier's light showing them their own game.

"I've lost the sword and my clothing," said Hwa Li, chagrined. He took off his clothes and gave them to the monster. The monster held the sword, admiring it.

"It's an old sword," said the strange fellow who posed as the Hell King. "I'm glad to have it."

"It's not really mine unless I stay past dawn," said Hwa Li.

"I don't mind," said the monster. "I'm a big gambler, after all. It will be too bad if I cannot keep the sword, but the game was still worthwhile. However, I think you have something else you can bet—the hair of the young student friend of yours, Lo Wei. That, too, is not yours if I take you into Hell before dawn. I'll nevertheless consider it as collateral."

They played another round, and Hwa Li's bluff failed. He lost Lo Wei's hair.

"You play well but not well enough, it seems," said the monster. "Have you anything else?"

"Not with me. I have some nice porcelain coins at the dormitory where I'm living. But they'll belong to Lo Bin if I don't stay past dawn. As you are a big gambler, will you accept as collateral something that may not be mine when it comes time to pay the debt?"

"Ah, but if you do stay past dawn, you get Lo Bin's gold, am I right?"

"That's exactly right," said Hwa Li, thinking the ugly man very foolish to be letting on how he knew all the students who put him up to this stunt.

"Well then," said the monster. "That sweetens the pot for me! I'll bet the rest of those offerings against your porcelain and your gold coins. If I win, it will be a lot for me. If you win, and stay past dawn, you keep everything, even the Fire Holiday offerings."

"The monks might keep me from taking the offerings," said Hwa Li, scratching his naked body and rubbing his chilly shoulders.

"Oh, I'll see to that," said the monster. "In any case, what you're really hoping to win by betting with me is permission to stay past dawn, in which case I forfeit you as the best offering in the temple. Too bad for me if that happens!"

"But I get the other offerings in addition to permission to keep myself?"

"I said so."

"Then it is a good bet," said Hwa Li, selecting tiles from the heap.

This time he had a good selection and thought he had a good chance to win. But he failed. The monster said, "That's three rounds lost to me. I now own everything you have. It would not be fair to demand the tattoos off Ma Heh's shoulders, unless you can think of some rationale for me to take them. I suppose I could wait until he dies; but his family might be disturbed if I appeared at the funeral and ripped out his arms. Then again, if you cannot stay past dawn, he won't have to tattoo himself after all, and there'll be nothing for me to claim. It looks as though you've run out of things. I have you now! We'll go to Hell. Let's go!"

The monster began to shift his bulk and stand, but Hwa Li suggested a final game. "Why not one last round to see if I go free? If I lose one more time, I'll help you carry everything into Hell. If I win, then I get my clothes back and permission to stay past dawn.''

"You're already mine to take to Hell. You cannot bet yourself.''

"I see,'' said Hwa Li. Then, having pondered briefly, he said, ''What I'm betting is my labor, to help you with all those nice offerings. It's getting close to dawn. You might not have time to get everything. If I don't help, you'll have to leave a couple of things behind. Maybe you'll have to leave everything, since you'll have your hands full of me, if I am kicking and screaming.''

"Let me get this right,'' said the monster. ''If I win a fourth round with you, then you will help me get my things and come with me quietly. But if I don't play the game at all, you'll cause a big nuisance and keep me from getting anything but you?''

"That's right.''

"And if you win the fourth hand, I give you your clothing and let you off entirely.''

"I also get the sword back, and the gold coins I'll be winning, and Lo Wei's hair.''

"That's too much!'' complained the monster.

"Very well,'' said Hwa Li. ''Try to take me to Hell right this minute. I don't mind. I'm only disappointed that you aren't such a big gambler after all.''

The monster's eyes glowed bright and he sat back down by the tiles.

It was a long round and Hwa Li thought he would lose this one, too. But it didn't matter, he reasoned, because dawn was coming pretty soon, at which time the whole charade would be over. As it happened, he did win that round, and the big monster put the sword on Hwa Li's side of the tiles, gave him back his clothes, then began to stand up.

At that moment, it was dawn. The monster disappeared, Hwa Li didn't see quite how, and what was more, all the offerings piled by the brazier were gone. This puzzled Hwa Li, but he gave it little attention as he dressed himself and left the temple brandishing the sword that was now his to keep.

His friends were waiting for him. Hwa Li said, "It is my plan to be magnanimous and let you off, Ma Heh, for it would be a shame to upset your family so much as to make you tattoo your perfect shoulders. As for you, Lo Bin, though by rights I own everything in your purse, I know your family saved hard to give you that allowance, so you may keep it. Lo Wei, please don't bother to cut off all your hair. It looks so nice, and, since I must see you every day, I don't want to see you bald. But Kwan Fo started all this, so I'll keep his sword that he was so eager to bet. It serves him right for sending that ugly ogre of a man in there to gamble with me all night. The rest of you had a hand in that, too, I'm sure, but Kwan Fo is always the ringleader. From now on, don't listen to him so much!"

Now the students were caught between relief and joy to be let off from their debt, and confusion regarding the information about the ugly man. They protested this part of his speech. But Hwa Li scolded them. "Don't argue about it, and don't deny it! Admit you've been found out."

But they would admit nothing and Hwa Li was disgusted.

However, that night, there was a loud clap of thunder in the mountains. All the students in the dormitory were awakened by the presence of a big, dark, horrible-looking creature who was easily recognized by his boar tusks as the King of Hell. He strode past the beds of the quivering students. He walked to the pallet on which Hwa Li was sleeping.

"Hwa Li!" exclaimed the King of Hell. "I had such a good time last night, I had to come and thank you. I have brought you this present!" He placed a box of finely carved gambling tiles at the foot of the pallet. "If you ever want to gamble with me again, let me know! You have my admiration!"

Then there was a second clap of thunder and the King of Hell vanished. Hwa Li's friends were impressed and began to explain to the other students how Hwa Li had spent a night gambling with the Hell King. Soon everyone gathered around Hwa Li's bed and ogled the extraordinary game tiles. Lo Wei, Lo Bin, Ma Heh, and even Kwan Fo boasted in their friend's behalf and sang his praises. But Hwa Li didn't hear a word of it. He was spread out unconscious on his bed, his mouth foolishly agape.

Japanese Fan with Waterfall

Carol Edelstein

I picked Lake
  Chaugagagog-manchaugagog-chaubunagungamaug
out of the hat, but I threw it back.
I wanted something blacker
to cut into the black hills. How useless
is the imagination!

Thousands of black and gold butterflies
  land on one tree—
the very same tree I picked and threw back,
in a different season. How useless
is the imagination!

This Japanese fan? For some reason I kept it.
When you unfold it—go ahead, try—you see a girl
  in a flowery kimono, walking alone
over the red bridge.

I believe this bridge with its high, arched railing
must exist. And when the girl pauses
  to catch her breath,
or to start a short conversation with the waterfall,
it does talk back, usually with remarks like

"We are no longer young," or, "That is no
  surprise,"
but once, sharply, with "Move along!"
which proves that even folded up
  (yes, the clasp is a bit tricky)

her power makes the air move.
  How useless is the imagination!
Just put it back where you found it,
on the middle shelf by that dark lump
  which is actually lava.

A Most Obedient Cat

Tappan King

It began with a small *yargling* noise from the back of the
house. A moment later, I heard Beth calling:

"Tappan, could you come here a minute?" There was
a brief pause, and then she continued, "Right now?"

"What is it, honey?" I called back

"Sybil has brought us—a present." There was a note
of humor in her voice, tinged with just a hint of panic.

I'd been busy doing cultural research (okay, I was
watching MTV), and I didn't feel much like getting up.
But something about the way she said "present" told
me it was time for me to be husbandly.

So I put on my best Imperturbable Male smile and
sauntered back to my office, to find our little black cat,
Sybil, looking up at me proudly, a forest of waving legs
bristling from her mouth.

"Yargle-yargle!" said Sybil. And, without a moment's
hesitation, she placed her prey gently at Beth's feet.

It was about the size of a baseball, which made it half

the size of Sybil, who was at that time barely six months old. It had a half dozen jagged black legs, a tiny head with nasty jaws, and a back that might at any moment sprout wings. My gonads instantly sought refuge in my abdomen.

"What is it?" I asked.

"I don't know," Beth answered between clenched teeth. Beth is not afraid of anything on two legs or four. Six is pushing it. "Make it go away."

It twitched. I jumped, and made a noise that would have been a scream—if men screamed.

"I'll take care of it," I heard myself saying, as reckless machismo won out over common sense. I walked quickly (all right, I *ran*) to the kitchen and found a plastic margarine tub. I dropped it quickly over the creature and slid the lid underneath, but not before a leg grazed my hand.

"Yeesh!" I shrieked, nearly dropping the thing. When my heart finally stopped hammering, I marched the offending arthropod out the back door, tossing it unceremoniously into the lilacs.

"Sybil," Beth was saying quietly as I returned, "thank you very much for the present." She was a tower of strength now that the creature was gone. I, on the other hand, was turning to jelly . . . "But you aren't to bring such things into the house. Do you understand?"

Sybil looked up, perplexed and a little hurt.

"I'll make it simple for you, Sybil," said Beth. "No bugs!"

Sybil paused thoughtfully, nodded slowly, and then solemnly answered *"Eep!"* as if she'd understood perfectly what Beth had said. Sybil has always been a most obedient cat.

A moment later, she cocked her head, as if struck by a thought, and suddenly dashed outside.

We stared at each other for a moment and then simultaneously collapsed in helpless laughter. We might not have laughed so hard if we'd known what was in store.

For it was summer in Staten Island, and the yard around our ramshackle Edwardian on Westervelt Avenue had suddenly turned into a jungle. The maple spinners that had sailed so gracefully and innocently down in the fall had taken root in the spring rains and burgeoned like triffids in the backyard. Unnameable weeds had unfurled overnight, and the wan patch of lawn overlooking the street had become an impenetrable thicket, providing a lush habitat for all manner of creeping and crawling things.

For a young kitten just learning to hunt, it was a particular sort of heaven.

The humid heat of that June morning turned into the balmy cool of the evening, as breezes blew off the harbor up Bay Street, bringing with them the scent of brackish water and garbage barges, the cries of seagulls and Run-DMC.

I was making up a batch of my patented Terrific Cheese Sauce in the microwave for a broccoli casserole when I heard a small shriek from the back of the house. I found Beth standing in the doorway of my office, clutching the door frame.

"Sybil," she asked warily, "what have you got?"

"Yargle!" answered Sybil. *"Yargle-yargle-YARGLE!"*

Between her paws was a bilious green garden spider the size of a small grapefruit. It had bulging, malevolent eyes and a swollen abdomen that looked as if it concealed billions of tiny spider eggs. Sybil watched proudly as it advanced inexorably on Beth's sandaled toes.

Beth moved a few feet backward without traversing the intervening distance. Beth does not like spiders.

"Tappan," Beth said calmly. "Would you please kill that thing? *Now?*"

"Kill it? Me?" I asked, in a display of unbridled raw courage. Beth gave me a withering stare from her perch atop the dining room table, and I quickly said, "Right. I'll take care of it right now."

"Thank you," said Beth politely. "Let me know when it's gone."

By this time the spider had scuttled under a chair, where Sybil was batting at it playfully. There ensued a miniature Keystone Kops chase between me and the spider, as I crawled about for several minutes under my desk, armed only with a Cool Whip container and a pizza box lid, while Sybil watched my efforts with obvious pleasure and approval.

Finally, I cornered the thing behind a bookcase, convinced it to crawl onto the cardboard, and dropped the container over it before it could change its mind. Then I scooped it up and charged down the back porch steps to the patio. On the way out the door, the clothesline brushed my arm, and I panicked, flinging box, container, and spider over the fence into the neighbors' yard.

Sweat-soaked and grimy, I returned to the kitchen to find Beth scraping cheese off the inside of the microwave.

"How about some Chinese takeout?" she said brightly, sitting down at the kitchen table.

"Great idea," I answered. "How does chicken with cashews and snow peas sound?"

"*Eep!*" said Sybil. She had followed us into the kitchen and was regarding us reproachfully.

"Yes, I know we took away your spider, Sybil," said Beth. "But I distinctly told you no bugs in the house, didn't I?"

"Um, technically, it wasn't a bug, honey," I interjected. "After all, spiders are arachnids, not insects . . ."

"*Eep?*" asked Sybil.

"Whose side are you on, anyway?" Beth said, flashing me a tight grin. "Now listen to me, Sybil," she continued in a grave tone of voice, "you are not to bring bugs—or spiders—into the house again. Do you understand?"

Sybil gave a contrite "*mew*" and jumped up into Beth's lap.

An hour or so later, we heard a strange *gleeping* sound. Shortly thereafter, Sybil entered with a large toad in her jaws. She let it drop, and it hopped toward me, one leg dangling loose, with Sybil in close pursuit. Beth and I looked at each other, shook our heads.

"Well, it certainly isn't a bug," I said. I scooped the toad up with a bit of newspaper, and it followed the other critters out into the night.

"Sybil," I said slowly when I returned, "listen carefully. No toads—and no frogs," I said, just to be sure.

The next day, she brought in a lizard.

It had great bulging eyes and little balls on its toes, and a long stripy tail which it proceeded to shed in a futile effort to escape Sybil. After I had disposed of it, I picked Sybil up and held her in front of my nose.

"Sybil, it's not that we don't appreciate the presents," I told her. "And we don't have any problem with you killing and eating things. That's your job, after all. We know you are just trying to be a proper carnivore, as nature intended. We'd just prefer it if you didn't bring them into the house. So no more lizards, okay?"

"Eep!" replied Sybil.

On Sunday, we heard the *yargling* again. This time I got there first.

Sybil stood with her right paw on the neck of an evil-looking black snake, over a foot in length.

"What has the Mighty Huntress brought us this time?" called Beth from the living room.

"A snake," I answered. "A very large snake."

"A snake?" she answered. "Let me see!" Beth is not afraid of snakes. In fact, she finds them kind of interesting. I don't share her fascination. "Do you want me to take care of it?"

"No, that's okay," I answered breezily. After all, my male pride was on the line. I got a large pair of spaghetti tongs from the kitchen and grabbed the snake behind its head. Holding it at arm's length, I tossed it out into the bushes and slammed the door behind it.

"Eep?" said Sybil. She poked about under the sections of the Sunday *New York Times* in a vain search for her serpent. *"Eep?"* she repeated plaintively.

"I'm sorry, Sybil," I said, "but you're not to bring snakes into the house. Okay?"

She nodded gravely.

The next day she brought us a worm.

She carried it into the living room and placed it at my feet, looking up inquiringly. It was large and brown, with a segmented body and red splotches all over it, and it writhed about in a most disgusting fashion.

"She's testing us," said Beth.

"What?"

"She's testing us," she repeated. "She wants to see how snakelike something can be without being an actual snake."

I laughed. "Don't be silly," I said. "It's all just coincidence."

"I'm not so sure. Sybil," said Beth sternly, "you are not getting the message. No bugs. No spiders. No toads. No snakes—or snakelike objects—in the house. Got it?"

Sybil lowered her head onto her paws, obviously ashamed of herself.

Since it was time for Sybil's six-month checkup, we thought we'd ask Dr. Hand, our stunning red-haired New Wave East Village veterinarian, if Sybil's behavior was anything worth worrying about.

"It's perfectly normal," Dr. Hand told us. "Female cats are genetically programmed to teach their young how to hunt. Sybil thinks of you as her kittens," she said brightly. "When she brings you live prey, she's just trying to show you what you should be catching." She flashed a dazzling smile. "She probably thinks you're both a bit slow . . ."

Things were quiet for several days. Then, one sultry evening, Sybil was out late, missing her dinner. We called her several times, but she was nowhere to be seen.

Finally, around ten-thirty, we heard a heartrending squeal, and a moment later Sybil bounded in with a large field mouse in her jaws, and let it go at my feet.

It scurried under the couch. Beth and I spent the next half hour chasing it about the house with a dustpan and broom as Sybil watched the proceedings intently. At last we caught the cowering, timorous beastie behind the refrigerator and let it out the kitchen door.

Sybil was indignant, but Beth was inflexible.

"No mice, Sybil," she told her sternly. "If you want to catch mice, there are perfectly good ones in the basement. There's no need to bring new ones inside."

"*Eep,*" Sybil muttered sullenly.

The next morning she turned up with a strange mole-like creature with a star-shaped nose. The following day it was a huge Norway rat, mercifully dead. The day after that it was a groundhog, fully as big as she was.

"Perhaps we didn't make ourselves clear," I said to Sybil as we prepared for bed that night. "When we told you 'no mice,' we meant no mice, no rats, no voles, no groundhogs—in fact, no rodents of any kind. Do you understand me, Sybil?"

But Sybil had fallen asleep.

Beth and I looked at each other, shaking our heads. "Well," she said philosophically, "at least we'll never starve . . ."

Whether our words had had an effect on Sybil, or the hunting had gotten sparse, there were no further incidents that summer.

But the next spring it began again. First with a big black beetle, and then with a gray squirrel that was almost (but not entirely) dead. Eventually, we had to sit Sybil down and give her the lecture all over again.

"Sybil, you remember what we told you last year. No bugs, no spiders, no snakes, no reptiles or amphibians, no mice or rats or voles or weasels. In short, you are not to bring vermin of any kind into this house, alive or dead."

Sybil just stared at us with a puzzled expression, until I had a sudden inspiration, and grabbed up a paperback copy of the *American Heritage Dictionary* which was lying nearby:

"Vermin," I read aloud. "Noun. Any of various small animals or insects, such as cockroaches or rats, that are destructive, annoying, or injurious to health."

"*Eep!*" Sybil replied brightly, as if that made it all much clearer. She was, as I've said, a very obedient cat.

Not *perfectly* obedient, of course. She did test us from time to time over the next few years.

There was the greylag gosling that must have somehow gotten separated from its flock. And a Vietnamese potbellied piglet that we figured must have come from the couple who owned the fruit stand down the street. A full-grown ring-necked pheasant. And one day she even brought in a live catfish, still gasping for breath. Our only guess was that she'd stolen it from the corner fish market, but it seemed far too lively for that.

And then there was the night when Sybil refused to come in at all, and I'd left a window propped open, hoping she'd come back by herself. I woke to a horrible clatter, and padded downstairs in my robe to find Sybil tussling with something near the back door. I saw it in the flashlight's beam for only a few moments, just long enough to make out what looked like a broad beaver tail, wide webbed feet, and a bright ducklike bill. Then it scuttled over the windowsill and was gone.

Despite her faults, however, I'll say this for Sybil. In all those years, she never once directly disobeyed us by bringing in forbidden prey. Nor did she ever repeat herself.

Until we moved to Arizona . . .

You see, a couple of years ago, we left Staten Island and moved into a large house in Tucson on an acre of land near the foothills of the Catalina Mountains. Our part of town has so far escaped the developers' bulldozers, and we've got wild Sonoran desert on all four sides of the place: great saguaro cactus and prickly pear, mesquite and acacia trees, verdant paloverdes, and sturdy creosote bushes. It was a perfect habitat for a wide variety of desert creatures—and a prime hunting ground for Sybil, who had by now grown into a slim, sleek, seven-year-old pygmy panther.

It might have been that she felt that our injunctions were purely regional, or only applied to certain narrow subspecies. Or maybe there was something in the wild, untamed nature of the place that was a challenge to her. Whatever the reason, Sybil once again began to bring in prey.

It started innocently enough, with a small cricket, dropped quietly just inside the patio door, that scuttled off into Beth's office with Sybil in hot pursuit, scattering manuscripts left and right as she stalked it about the room.

Before we had the sense to remind her that we'd said "No bugs!" she'd brought in a bewildering succession of bizarre insects, which our Audubon guide told us were an agave billbug, an Arizona blister beetle, an Aztec pygmy grasshopper, and a hideous creature called a tarantula hawk, which was neither a tarantula nor a hawk, but a horrid sort of wasplike insect with crimson wings and a mean disposition.

"Sybil," Beth sighed, "I don't care if they have wings or not. Six legs make it a bug."

Sybil responded by catching a series of not-quite-bugs, including a millipede, a scorpion, a tarantula, and a ghastly five-inch-long ten-legged critter with enormous pincers known locally as the Jumping Vinega-rone.

When we finally had the sense to forbid *all* long-leggedy beasties, we got a number of snakes, toads, and lizards of the most exotic sort, culminating in the discovery of a disgruntled-looking crimson Gila monster who'd curled up in one of my slippers in the back of the bedroom closet, in an attempt to hide from Sybil, the Scourge of the Desert. We had the local fire department dispose of it, though the young man who carried the thing away said it was probably more scared of us than we were of it . . .

It was inevitable, I suppose, that Sybil would once again work her way up the evolutionary ladder. When we outlawed amphibians and reptiles, she brought in birds. When we forbade birds, she rounded up rodents: chipmunks and ground squirrels, pocket mice and pack rats. We tried to deal with it all in a spirit of realism and good humor.

Until the day Sybil brought in a baby bunny . . .

We have several species of rabbits around our house, from black-tailed jackrabbits the size of small mules to desert cottontails, a hapless, suicidal species that is best described by the term "dumb bunny." One hot, dry afternoon, Sybil marched in with a baby cottontail in her jaws. It was screaming in terror, making more noise than I'd ever imagined a rabbit could make. Beth had tolerated the lizard tails in the dining room, little rat feet under the bed, the bird wings hidden behind the refrigerator. But she drew the line at baby bunnies.

"Sybil!" she commanded. "Drop it!"

To our surprise, Sybil complied immediately. Which left us with a panic-stricken baby bunny careening about the house, squealing at the top of its tiny lungs. I cornered it with a spatula and wooden salad bowl and spirited it out into the backyard.

Ten minutes later, Sybil brought it back.

I caught it again, and carried it out across the road, hiding the rabbit in a stand of ocotillo.

Half an hour later, I heard a disturbingly familiar squeal. Sybil, the Scourge of the Desert, had followed my scent and brought the bunny back again. When I took it away from her for the third time, she responded with a disgusted growl, obviously questioning my sense of gratitude, and sulked for the rest of the afternoon.

So Beth and I sat her down and had a long people-to-cat talk with her. We began by acknowledging the differences in our worldview. It was understandable, we told her, that she should consider this house her den. And we appreciated her efforts to teach us how to catch nice yummy bunnies. But we also hoped she would understand that we didn't much care for little gobbets of flesh strewn about the carpet. Needless to say, she had trouble accepting this.

Finally, Beth laid down the law:

"From now on, Sybil, you are forbidden to bring any of your favorite treats into the house. Do you understand? No rats, no mice, no lizards or toads, no Gila monsters or chuckwallas, no iguanas or snakes, no beetles, no bugs, no spiders or scorpions—and above all, *no bunnies!*"

The expression on Sybil's face was as close to human frustration as I have ever seen on an animal. She grumbled and muttered to herself for days afterward, as if she were looking for some way to keep her little midnight snacks. But this time we'd left her no loopholes.

Or so we thought . . .

*   *   *

The monsoon season hit in mid-July, after record heat and months without a trace of rain. When the rains come in Tucson, they come with biblical force, transforming gullies into lakes, dry washes into foaming rivers. The pounding thunder loosens every knotted muscle in your body, and the wet ground gives off a heady, spicy scent of life reawakened after a long sleep.

Sybil spent most of the season camped at the back door, watching the rain sluicing off the brick patio, looking up at us with an expression that implied we had personally called down the rain. When the rains finally ended one afternoon in August, the winds sweeping the clouds eastward across the Rincon Mountains just before sunset, leaving a perfect double rainbow behind, Sybil bounded out into the still-damp desert with a triumphant cry.

In the summer, we rise early, with the sun, and retire early as well. Usually Sybil would come in for dinner around sunset. Once in a great while, she'd stay out till nine or nine-thirty. This night, she was still missing at eleven. It was understandable, of course. She'd been cooped up indoors for almost a month, and there was a bright, nearly full moon, making for ideal hunting conditions.

But there'd also been coyotes around the house of late. One brazen creature had even come up and pressed his nose against the front window, as if to ask: "Any cats inside?" We feared the worst.

I finally shooed Beth off to bed around midnight. I left the patio door ajar, turned off most of the lights, and sat up in front of the tube with a book, waiting for Sybil's return. I must have dozed off, because it was well after three by the clock on the VCR when I next opened my eyes.

I'd been awakened by an odd *whuffling* sound. It sounded a bit like a horse snorting, and a bit like the furnace turning itself on. I sat stock-still, listening carefully, and suddenly caught a whiff of an acrid, sulfurous scent coming from the direction of the kitchen, followed by a loud metallic clatter.

I got up quickly, tying my robe about me, and headed for the kitchen, even though every instinct for self-preservation screamed at me to stay where I was. As I approached, I saw an intermittent orange glow, and then heard a blood-chilling sound:

"Myrgle!" cried Sybil. *"Myrgle-myrgle-MYRGLE!"* Her normal *yargle* of triumph seemed oddly muffled. A moment later, I saw why.

She was holding something in her mouth, by the scruff of its neck, the way a mother cat holds a kitten. In the pale moonlight, I could barely make out what it was . . .

Until it burst into flame.

A small curl of ruddy fire issued from its snout, bathing it for a brief moment in amber light. What I saw was a small reptilian creature, deep bottle-green in color, with tiny front claws and stout, taloned hind legs which it kicked frantically in the air. It had a long, scaly tail ending in a leaflike blade. A small pair of leathery, bloodred wings fluttered uselessly at its shoulders.

The flame startled Sybil, and in that brief moment the creature struggled loose, rising up awkwardly toward the ceiling fan. Sybil leapt after it, but was unable to catch it. It clung frantically to the blades of the fan, its deep-set eyes reflecting the crimson timer light on the Mr. Coffee, and snorted a small cloud of noxious gas in my direction.

Without thinking, I turned on the kitchen light to get

a better look at the thing, starting the fan blades whirling at the same time. It took off suddenly, startled, buzzing my head on its way out of the kitchen, flapping off toward the living room. Sybil turned to me and howled, though I'm not sure if she was angry that I'd caused it to escape, or pleased that she could chase it again.

Whoever it was who originally built our house had a lot of imagination and a strange sense of humor. The living room is two and a half stories tall, with a gigantic twelve-paned picture window that looks north toward the mountains. Suspended from the ceiling on a heavy black chain is a massive wrought-iron lighting fixture—a cylindrical cage of iron bars nearly six feet in height with a large black-light bulb running up the center—that resembles some sort of medieval torture device. In her more charitable moments, Beth refers to it as the "Iron Maiden."

The hapless creature had crashed into the Iron Maiden on its desperate flight into the room, wrapping itself around the chain, and setting it swinging back and forth madly like the pendulum over the pit. Sybil began prancing around under it in a vain attempt to frighten it down. This only served to make the creature more agitated, and it belched forth another burst of flame that charred the paint on the chain.

There was a bit of a stalemate for a while, with me throwing things at the dragon (for it was clearly a dragon) in an attempt to dislodge it, and the dragon coiling itself ever more tightly about the Iron Maiden's chain. When I poked a broom at it, it singed the straw with its breath, and retreated toward the window, tangling itself in the drapes, and then burning itself free, sending me running for the mop bucket to douse the smoldering curtains.

Finally, I jammed a metal dustpan on the end of the pole we use to skim dead bugs out of the pool, and gave it a solid *whack*. It fell stunned to the floor, and I covered it quickly with a large steel bowl just as it started to recover, sliding it slowly along the carpet toward the door while Sybil batted at it playfully.

"Having fun?" said a voice behind me.

Apparently the commotion had waked Beth. She was surveying the chaos from the dining room, with a bemused expression reminiscent of an attendant at a Halloween party for the feebleminded.

"Um, Sybil caught something," I said, clamping my hand down on the bowl, which had started to rise up from the floor.

"*Eep!*" said Sybil proudly.

"What exactly did she catch?" Beth asked slowly and patiently.

"Um, it's kind of hard to explain . . . *Yeow!*"

The metal bowl had suddenly started to get hot. The palm of my hand began to blister. I wrapped my hand up in a nearby rug and pressed down on the bowl again. A bright red spot was forming on the side, and little wisps of flame were darting out from under it. I had to do something—fast.

"Honey," I said calmly, "could you get the hose?"

"The hose? Are you sure you're okay?"

"I'm fine," I said. "The hose, please?" Shaking her head, Beth went outside, turned on the faucet, and stretched the garden hose inside the living room.

"Okay, now spray it at the bowl, quick!"

"You want me to spray the bowl . . ."

"Humor me," I snapped. A moment later, I was hit in the face with a spray of water.

"Oops! Sorry!" said Beth, laughing apologetically,

aiming the stream downward. As the water hit the metal, clouds of steam rose up, there was a snarling sound, and the bowl began to shake under my hands. Sybil, who had jumped out of the way just as the water hit, was edging back to get a better look.

I lifted the edge of the bowl, and a single claw reached out. Quickly sizing up the situation, Beth stepped closer, directing the spray under the edge. A few moments later, the creature had stopped moving.

Beth knelt down beside the bowl and lifted it slowly. "Let me see," she said. The dragon lay sprawled on its back in the middle of the soggy, blackened carpet, making pitiful burbling noises, limbs straggling, tail limp, eyes glazed.

"Oh, the poor little thing," she said. "I hope it's all right." At that moment, I felt her compassion was somewhat misplaced.

Sybil took a couple of steps closer.

"Get back," said Beth sharply, without turning around. "Leave it alone, Sybil."

"*Eep*," said Sybil contritely.

"What do you think we should do?" she asked, her voice filled with concern. "I've never resuscitated a baby dragon before. I'm not sure it would survive the trip to the pet clinic."

I never got a chance to answer. Across the patio there was a sharp cracking sound, followed by a loud thud. Then the ground began to tremble . . .

Sybil ran to the open door, stopped short, and puffed up three times her normal size, arching her back, hissing, and emitting a long, low growl.

Two gleaming circles, as big as streetlamps, were drawing closer. A huge, hulking shape was shouldering its way across the patio, flattening the fence, snapping the lawn chairs like twigs. A great, scaly head loomed into view, emitting first a guttural roar and then a swirling ball of fire that scorched the walls and shriveled the plants.

At the sound, the baby dragon coughed, snorted, spat steam, rolled over, and wobbled to its feet, making a desperate dash for the door, nearly bowling Sybil over. Wailing, it scrambled up its mother's massive back, latching onto the great fin at the back of her neck. With a belch of acrid smoke, the momma dragon turned slowly, picking its way back across the yard, trampling the remains of the wooden fence as it lumbered off toward Redington Pass.

The morning after the incident, we held a Family Meeting.

"Okay, Sybil," I told her. "You win. If you really have to catch mice, or lizards, or birds, we're willing to put up with them once in a while—even baby bunnies. But please—no more dragons, okay?"

"*Eep!*" Sybil promised, sealing her side of the bargain.

To our surprise, our insurance paid for the damage, which was relatively minor, all things considered. When we told the adjuster it had been caused by "ball lightning," he didn't question the statement at all. Perhaps Sybil isn't the only cat out there with unusual hunting habits.

By and large, Sybil honored her agreement with us. Once in a while—usually on birthdays or holidays—she'd bring us a nice juicy pack rat or a yummy lizard, which we'd accept graciously so as not to hurt her feelings. But she never again brought in a dragon.

She was, after all, an extremely obedient cat.

*   *   *

A year ago, Sybil suddenly started to decline, becoming listless, refusing to eat, not going out. A blood test revealed that she was suffering from diabetes, a condition that usually affects older, more sedentary cats. To our great relief she responded immediately to insulin, though it took us over six months to get her medication properly balanced.

We were reluctant to let her out hunting, fearing that she might not get back in time for her shots, or go into shock and perhaps become prey herself. But when we kept her cooped up in the house, she got worse; when we let her out to hunt, she got better. So we decided to take our chances, though we were sick with worry every time Sybil stayed out late at night.

But one night she didn't come back.

We scoured the area, driving around the neighborhood, looking for any trace of her. Hours turned into days, and days into weeks, and we finally accepted that Sybil had probably tangled with something that thought *she* was a tasty treat. Though it didn't make it any easier, there was some consolation that the Scourge of the Desert had died as she'd lived, a Mighty Huntress to the last.

After a decent interval, we got kittens: two tiny balls of fur, a brother and sister, John Storm Drinkwater (aka "Storm"), an affectionate little fellow in a gray and white tuxedo, and Violet Bramble (aka "Bramble"), a rambunctious calico who looked like she'd been hastily rendered in a swirl of pastels. We were a bit more strict with them, hoping to avoid some of the problems we'd had with Sybil. We weren't entirely successful . . .

*   *   *

I was up in my office the other day, working on a story, when I heard a faint *yargling* sound from the dining room. A moment later, I heard Beth's voice.

"Bramble," she said sternly, "what have you got? Give it here."

There was a bit of commotion, then a long silence. Finally, I heard Beth speaking in low, measured tones:

"Now listen carefully, Bramble. You are not to bring elves into the house. Do you understand? No elves, no faeries, no brownies, no wee folk of any sort at all! Do you understand me, Bramble?"

"Eep!" she replied indignantly, as if offended that we would doubt her.

And, to be fair, she *has* kept her word—at least about the elves . . . She is, after all, a *most* obedient cat.

The Dovrefell Cat

Diane Duane

In the midmorning of the world, when the dragons still flew, there lived a hunter who hunted the steep fjord-forests of the west of Norway. That was a wild, lonely country, where one could stand under pines a thousand years old and look out over the hundred thousand isles scattered toward the Norwegian Sea; and the valleys and shadowy woods of that country were full of beasts, strange and otherwise.

The hunter was not afraid of most of the creatures living there. He knew them well, Arctic fox and snowshoe hare and ptarmigan and sable, ermine and snow lion; and he knew something of how to deal with goblins and trolls, and how to avoid the dark things that laired in the places in the wood where fir needles crowded so close that no snow ever fell.

The hunter was a silent sort, and used to being alone. But he intended not to be that way forever. His idea was to find some strange beast in the wood, and tame it.

Then he would take it down south to the King of Denmark, and sell it to him for a great price, and so make his fortune; buy a house, and settle down, and have friends who would come to call.

The hunter kept his grey eyes open, and travelled far and wide. Once late in the year his wanderlust took him far out of the woods, closer to the seashore, where the snow fell fierce and bergs climbed the beach on the backs of bitter waves. And it was on such a beach, white with sand and snow, that the hunter found the white bear cub, all alone and crying for its lost mother.

It was very small. That was as well for the hunter, for a polar bear much older than a cub sees only one use for man—food—and cannot be tamed. But this one was hardly weaned as yet. The hunter caught it without hurting it, and fed it his own dried meat soaked in water, and (when he could get it from the farmers he guested with) he gave it milk from farmstead cows, for the bear was *very* young, and the milk made it glad. The hunter was pleased. He thought that when spring and summer and fall had come and gone again, the bear would be big enough to sell. Then he would take it south to the King's great seaport market-city—the Cheaping-haven, as it was called—and offer the bear to the King. He would make his fortune, and be famous, and settle somewhere far from the white wastes.

So spring and summer and fall went by, and the hunter and the white bear cub travelled the length and breadth of the northern countries together. In spring they fished in bitter-cold streams just breaking free of the ice; the bear was better than the hunter at this, and caught them many a fat trout. In the long days of summer they stayed in the cool of the shadowy forests, moving at their ease, while the hunter caught martens for their fur, and red deer for venison. In fall they lingered to enjoy the last of the fair weather, raiding the occasional bee-tree for honey: and they met trappers moving north, who looked at the bear with wonder.

And at last winter came round again, and they began to make their way south together, the hunter and the white bear. It was no longer the tiny cub it had been. It was a great shaggy-coated beast, blue-eyed and wise-eyed, that followed the hunter like a dog. The hunter began to be sore of heart. He was a poor man, with nothing to live on but what he caught and could sell or eat. The bear was always hungry, so it was a trouble to keep fed, and its sale would bring him a great deal of money. But when he looked at the bear across the camp-fire of an evening, and it ate what meat he could find, and licked his hand afterwards; when he turned in the night and found its broad warm back bumped up against his; when it nosed him awake in a silent morning, breathing bear-breath on him, and pawed him merrily to get up and greet the day—at those times the hunter did not want to sell the bear, not for all the gold in the Cheaping-haven, not for the King's own crown.

But still they went south together—the hunter partly out of habit, the bear because its friend was going that way. The year grew very old, and the days very short. In those high northern parts of the world, when Midwinter grows near, the sun only rides above the horizon for four or five hours out of the twenty-four. Dark things come out of the woods then, reveling in the shadows and troubling the houses of men. Those nights, when the hunter fell asleep, many a time he woke in the starlight to see the great white bear drowsing by the fire like a great shaggy toy, one half-closed blue eye resting on him; and he was very glad the bear was with him still.

They were still travelling when it got to be Yuletide—that time of year which is Christmas now, but was just starting to be Christmas then. People would travel from their lonely farmsteads to some neighbor's large house, and eat and drink and dance and make bonfires to celebrate the days slowly getting longer. But first there would be Midwinter Eve, a terrible night when monsters would run loose, and ghosts would fly and the evil sort of witches do all the harm they could. It was a bad time to be out in the open, away from a friendly hearthfire. People made it a point not to travel then, and to be all gathered together by the time night fell. They considered that there was safety in numbers.

The hunter and the bear were still up on the high fells far north of the Cheaping-haven when Midwinter Eve came. Now, the hunter was brave, but not foolhardy. When he realized what night it was, he decided to turn in at the nearest farmhouse and ask their hospitality for a night. Farmsteads were few and far between up on that fell, the Dovrefell, but the gleam of firelight shines a long way in those empty places. The hunter and the bear made for the light of windows, and came to a great farmstead, and the hunter knocked on the big house's door.

There had been much hectic laughing and singing going on inside, and now it stopped dead. This puzzled the hunter. After a little he saw someone peer at him from a window; and after a little while more the door was unbarred, and men and women (and some children staying up late) looked out at him and the bear in astonishment.

"That's not a troll!" one of the youngest children said. She sounded slightly disappointed.

"Come in!" said the people inside, and they pulled

the hunter inside, and made respectful room for the bear as it shambled in and snuffled at the house smells. Well it might have, for there was a feast laid out, as they still lay out in the northern countries at Yule—fish of every kind, fresh and pickled and smoked and dried, and lobsters, and chickens, and sausages and hams, and black bread and brown, and rice puddings, and cheeses, and butter and cream, and enough ale and beer to swim in. The farmfolk gave the hunter a chair, and hot ale to drink, and more food than he usually saw in a week. The bear helped itself to a whole smoked salmon from the sideboard, and settled down with it at the hunter's feet, very pleased with itself. Then the farmers all drank the hunter's health, and began eating and drinking again, and doing it very quickly.

"Forgive me," said the hunter, a little later (for it had been a long time since he had had ale), "but why should I have been a troll?"

The farmers and the farmers' wives and their children all looked embarrassed, even those who were still eating. "It is because," they said, "this whole area is infested with trolls, and every Yule Night they come in a great crowd to wherever feasting is held, and they ride the roofs, and scream and yell, and eat everything and drink everything, and kill whatever man or beast they can catch. So we are feasting, but very quickly, and as soon as we finish we are all going to take our horses and cows, and run and hide in the woods and the caves. Of course we would offer you hospitality for the night if we could, but if you stay here, the trolls will kill you too."

Now, the hunter was extremely sorry to hear this. What with the ale inside him and the warmth outside him, he was getting very reluctant to do anything at all, much less run away into the woods and hide in a freez-

ing-cold cave all night. While he was thinking this, the
bear got up and went to the sideboard and ate a five-
pound firkin of butter, and swallowed a roast chicken
whole, and then put its head in a huge bowl of pickled
cod and started work on that—sneezing at the dill and
garlic, but not slowing down.

The hunter watched this, and thought for a few moments, while everyone else kept eating. "Listen here,"
he said at last, "I have an idea. I'm a wandering man,
and I have no house of my own to bid you to, to thank
you for this feast. As my guest-gift to you, let me rid you
of these trolls."

Then there was great noise of people crying "Yes,"
and "No," and everything else imaginable; and the
hunter drank his ale until they quieted down. After that
came more arguing, and many entreaties, but the
hunter's mind was made up and he would not budge.
And eventually the arguing stopped, for it was getting
on towards midnight, and the wind was rising. So the
farmers said their last goodbyes to the hams and the cold
lobster, and dressed for the cold and went out, leaving
the hunter by the fire with a fresh hornful of ale and an
amused look. Several children who wanted to wait and
see the trolls eat him had to be removed by force.

The bear settled down beside the hunter with a
smoked ham and began gnawing on it meditatively.
There they sat together, waiting for midnight. There
were no clocks in that part of the world in those days;
you told midnight by the way the stars stood, or by the
way your heart tightened when midnight came. As it
grew close, the hunter took the ham away from the
bear—carefully—and shoved it under the room's tall
tiled stove. The bear, unconcerned, squeezed and curled
itself under too, till only a little of its white furry back

showed, and then went back to gnawing the ham bone again.

Then the hunter's heart tightened, and the wind began to scream, and the hunter went to the side of the room where there was a lockbed. This was a sort of bunk bed built into the wall, with a thick wooden shutter that came down and locked from the inside, and little peep-holes to see through. Very quickly the hunter took all the best food and drink, in bowls and pitchers and platters, and put them in the lockbed. Then he climbed in and made the shutter fast—not forgetting to take the ale horn with him.

There the hunter drank comfortably for some few minutes, while the wind howled and wailed outside; and then something hit the roof, *bump,* and the hunter realized that the howling was not all wind, but voices. That was when the door burst open, and in came the trolls.

There were about a hundred of them, and they were so ugly that hardly even their mothers could have loved them. Some of them had tails. Some of them had extra arms, or legs, or heads. A few of them had given up heads entirely. They came in all sizes, and they were all either the color of dirty snow or of mud, except for the ones that were completely covered with bristles. Their teeth were yellow and their nails were long, and if any of them had ever had a bath, it was an accident. What the dark stuff was under their nails, the hunter tried not to consider. He made a hurried prayer to the young hero-God who died to save men from the dark things; and if he then made another one, out of habit, to brave old Thor the Trollbasher, perhaps it was understand-able.

The trolls swarmed all about the big room, screaming

and howling, tearing down the hangings and knocking over the furniture, until they saw the food. Then they screeched with delight, and leapt onto the tables and the sideboard and began eating everything left in sight, and also rolling in the food and throwing it on the floor. They sat in the rice puddings, they hit each other with dried herrings, they danced with garlands of sausages around their necks.

One of them, a troll with no nose and a mouth that went halfway around his head, snatched up a fireplace poker and stuck a sausage on it, to toast it at the fire. As he squatted there he chanced to look sideways, and what should he see under the nearby stove but some white fur showing, like the fur of a cat.

"Look, look, everybody," he screamed, "a cat! A cat!" And all the other trolls screamed in wicked delight too, for trolls like nothing better than to seize some helpless creature and tear it limb from limb; but they always torment it first if they can. "Kitty, kitty," screeched the troll, "does it want a nice sausage?" And he poked the white fur, hard, with the fireplace poker.

The fur jerked, and vanished further under the stove. The troll howled with laughter, and got down on his hands and knees to peer under. Back in the darkness beneath the stove there were two glints of green fire, very big and round, that could have been taken for the eyes of a cat frightened to death.

"Puss, puss, come have your sausage!" screamed the troll, and jabbed under the stove with the poker again. That was when the bear came out.

Trolls are even louder when they're frightened than they are when they're pleased—but being loud did not help them. They climbed what curtains had not been torn down, they tried to squeeze out through little windows, they jammed together in the door, so many at once that no one could move. They hid under overturned furniture and even under the stove. None of it did them any good. Only a few of them got away. The bear found all the rest.

A surprisingly short time later it was quiet again. The hunter came out of the lockbed with his ears ringing. He poured himself another cup of ale, and went to scratch the bear behind the ears. It looked up at him, a very cheerful and satisfied look, and went back to washing its paws. The bear was not hungry any more.

The hunter cleaned up the mess as best he could, and put out all the food and drink he had saved, and shut the door and built up the fire again, and sat down beside it. That was how the farmers found him when they came back, with the sun, on Yule morning: snoozing comfortably in the chair, with the bear stretched out in the middle of the floor on its back, with its feet in the air, and its stomach *very* full, and one eye open.

Then there was real rejoicing, and the farmers unlocked their storehouse and loaded the tables again, and there was singing till the rafters rang, and dancing till they shook; and the hunter's health and the bear's were drunk so many times that they are still probably alive somewhere. Indeed the feasting went straight on through the day and the dark, till towards midnight everyone was too full to eat another bite—except the bear, who had finally gotten up around elevenish and was nibbling on another half-salmon. Contentment reigned.

—until something went *bump* against the door, and everyone's heart tightened.

The hunter stood up with the ale horn in his hand. "Yes?" he said, very loud. "Who is it?"

"It's the trolls," said a voice from outside—a nasty voice that was frightened, and trying to hide it.

"And what do you want?" said the hunter.

"We want to know—do you still have your cat in there, that you had last night?"

The farmers all stared at each other. The bear looked up with interest, and licked its chops. "Yes," said the hunter. Then he had a thought, and said quickly, "And what's more, she had kittens this morning, and they look like they're going to be bigger than she is, and all the neighbors hereabouts are taking one apiece. Want one?"

There was screaming from outside. "No," yelled the troll, "and we're never coming back, so don't bother saving us one just in case!"

And the screaming dwindled away to nothing, and the night was quiet again.

The trolls never did come back; and the hunter knew this for certain, for the farmer whose Yuletide he saved made the hunter a present of a snug bit of land on the eastern side of the Dovrefell, by a little lake. There the hunter built a small neat house, and though he still wandered and hunted the forests as he loved to do, he always came home again. The bear went everywhere with him, and in later times his children and grandchildren drowsed against it by the fire in the winters, and swam with it in its cold blue lake in the summers. And it must still be there, for even now some people in the north of the world put a little food out "for the Bear" at Yuletide, and the food is always gone in the morning. And who would dare to take it?

Certainly not the trolls . . .

The Newcomer

*t. Winter-Damon and
Thomas Wiloch*

See that man in the window
watching us?
Don't stare!
I know that man.
I know that man well.

When you look in his
left eye you see a black
raven crouched in
a shattered tree.
I know that man well.
He is the newcomer.

Don't stare!
I know that man.
His right eye shows you
the minute face of a screaming
child.

Don't stare!
I know that man well.

His hair is a bristling
sea of lances, his mouth
the dungeon's leering door.
His forehead's curvature
is a line of shorn, naked jews
shuffling to the final chamber.
I know that man.
I know that man well.

Don't stare!
His teeth are glistening steel
autopsy tables.
As he reaches forward to shake your hand,
you see the curve
of his hand
is a bloody scimitar.
I know that man.
I know that man well.
He is the newcomer.

Don't stare!
His skin is the skin of the slain lamb.
His heart is carved of adamantine stone.
I know that man.
I know that man well.

Don't stare!
His loins are the capon's,
the gelding's. His blood
is soured wine, his issue is
the locust plague, stripping bare the wildwood.

I know that man.
I know that man well.
He is the newcomer.

Don't stare!
He has scorned Our Lady,
chained Our Lady, branded Mystery
upon her brow, Our Lady
of the Tides and Moon.
She is no mystery.
And neither is he.

I know that man.
I know that man well.
He is the newcomer,
the man in the window,
watching us.
As the constellations wheel across the sky,
he watches us.
The newcomer.
Our Father in the heavens.

Don't stare!
Don't stare at us!

The Executioner
Rose Kremers

"This is the Lifetree? How can its branches spread so far? How does it get water? Does it bear fruit? Why are its leaves *ocher* instead of green?"

I unpack our lunch. On the cool side of the tree, a family of gypsies sleeps in the sand while its black-spider caravan bus recharges in the sun: *IRng—IRng—IRng—*. They are fortunate to own a vehicle, but, then, gypsies are more affluent than the rest of us. I travel via cart because Mission is impoverished; however, as we are cloistered, I am the only one who travels anywhere, and the ancient mule and I are used to each other. We have to take the sunny side of the tree, but, nevertheless, the sun is shade-dappled and not unpleasant.

Liora is full of our neighbors. "Who are *they?"* She whispers in her usual dramatic staccato as she studies gleaming black boots, scarlet blouses, glittering jewels, raven hair, tattooed faces. Until now, she has known only the Mission Sisters.

Even in sleep, they exude the exotic. They pillow their heads on their money. They are a father, a mother, two sons, a daughter, tangled together in the sand. Gypsies value their young. She takes it all in, Liora does, absorbing this surprise.

"Hush your questions. Eat your cheese."

Liora stuffs her mouth. Her eyes dart to the gypsies, who are stirring awake. "How long until we arrive? Shall *I* be allowed to read scripture? Will late devotions last so *long* into the night? May I wear an amber robe?"

I lie. "I cannot say. I know only to deliver you to Greeble. Beyond that I know nothing."

Liora cannot keep her eyes to herself; she peers around the tree.

"Would you like being gawked at while you sleep?" I mutter.

"Oh, but Sister Mala watches us *all* the time, even as we disrobe."

Startled, I sit up straighter. "How do you know?"

"We see her peering through the *peep*hole."

"You're supposed to be sleeping."

She protests. "No one sleeps. Nighttime is the *only* pleasant time novistas have together."

I am struck silent at this truth.

"Don't you think this tree is *odd?*"

"Odd? What do you mean, odd?" I pour water into Liora's cup and into my own.

"Well, just *one* tree growing in a vast desert?" After her first burst of hunger is satisfied, Liora remembers to eat with decorum, delicately pinching off one bite of bread at a time with long, creamy fingers. She is too excited to sit still, but, because of my mission, I curb my criticism.

I watch her pretty hands. Perhaps trained as a lutist,

her curiosity channeled into song, she would have better suited us, and my assignment made unnecessary. But we are top-heavy with artistes and have no means for yet another.

I explain as best I can. "The roots of a Lifetree grow straight down, sometimes for miles, in their search for moisture. This one must have found an underground pool to have grown so large. At one time, there were hundreds of them scattered over the desert, all of them hand-planted by the Voorhees. After their defeat at Broughm, the plantings stopped. This is the only one left here. It is considered sacred by all who travel this road. Tradition says that if this tree dies, earth will be consumed again in firestorm. Before we leave, we will utter a pencha and sprinkle a cup of water onto its trunk in homage."

Liora has eaten, is now lying on her back staring up into the branches. "Please tell me more."

I grow cross. "I weary of your incessant queries. You well know the principal duty of a novista is to absorb the Code of Silence."

She turns stricken eyes on me, leans up on an elbow. "Forgive me! I thought as we were away from the Mission . . . that is, I didn't know the Code extended this far . . ."

"Once you have been ensconced, the Code follows wherever you go. But no matter." I gather together our lunch things, pack everything back into the leather bag, dust my hands. Behind us, the gypsies have awakened. They strike a coilfire to roast sausages. The odor of broiling meat grips my gut. I have not tasted meat for so long that I feel I will perish if I cannot have one bite.

"Look at *that!*" Liora saves my life by interrupting my

thoughts. "Oh, yes, look!" She has straightened to a sit, is pointing upward.

My glance follows hers. I see nothing, and then I see it.

"Ohhhh. Isn't it *beautiful?* What is it?"

I find myself staring into the benign blue eyes of an ocher-colored creature. It has near-human hands, a bushy tail, and whiskers. It smiles at us. I am startled. All undomesticated creature life had perished during the century of global wasting. What is this thing? Exultation floods me and I stand nearer to examine it. It does not run away.

Liora, as usual, is ecstatic. "Do you see it? It thrives on the *leaves* of the Lifetree! See it munch?"

A sickness enters my soul. The giant tree has countless limbs that are covered in thousands of hand-size leaves. But anyone who knows anything about Lifetrees also knows that once a leaf is plucked then a new leaf can never grow back, and that if too many leaves are destroyed, the tree will wither and die. Even now, I can see the dead places the creature has caused.

"There is its mate. Do you suppose they have *babies?*"

I jerk my head toward Liora. How could she know of such a thing? She has been cloistered since the age of three, brought to the Mission by a vagabond who found her abandoned at the side of a road. Only her fairness saved her from the usual fate.

"Really, Liora . . ."

"Ho there!"

We turn startled eyes toward the gypsy father. He is short and thick and solid, bandy-legged, heavy-featured, merry-eyed. He smiles at us, and his teeth are white and even in his swarthy face.

"I see," he nods toward my cart, "that you are from the Mission. Might you barter an extra loaf?"

We have loaves. My cart is laden with loaves. The Cloister is noted for its fine bread; while in Greeble, I will sell it. Nevertheless, I am tempted to refuse. Commoners never win in negotiations with gypsies: that is a known fact. I glance at Liora. She is staring past the father to the elder son just now in full manhood. He in turn is staring at her, or, rather, is staring at her sweeping, pale hair. Liora's expression is so telling that I lower my gaze. She has never before seen a young man.

Liora's expression decides me. I turn toward the gypsy. "Gladly," I say. "What have you that I might want?"

The wife is squatting at the fire, her varicolored skirt drawn between her knees. She is barefoot and her feet are dirty; she wears gold ankle bands and gold rings in her nose. She smiles up at me and her black eyes sparkle. Unlike the rest of us, gypsies have much to smile about.

They also play false. Everyone knows that. I am too clever to fall for her charm and do not return her smile.

"You could share our meal." The father-gypsy's eyes crinkle as he gestures toward their fire.

Neither do I return his smile. Sharing his meat is nothing to him, for he stole it from an unwary vendor. Now he would get free bread as well.

As I open my mouth to tell him we have already lunched, I notice that Liora has entranced even younger-son. The daughter, near Liora's age, perhaps a bit older, perhaps sixteen, although Liora is much taller, as tall, in fact, as elder-son, comes to stand near the father. The son's black eyes flash a raw and naked and timeless message as he watches Liora's heavy, bright hair shift in the breeze.

"Liora, get a loaf." My words astound me.

My response startles Liora back to reality. A slight flush colors her high cheekbones; thick, pale lashes fall over sapphire eyes. She glides to the cart and returns, her motions fluid and graceful.

I savor the forbidden food: meat bursting out of its casing, hot juices filling my mouth. Looking at me, Liora laughs aloud. Her laughter is pure and sweet and real. She never could contain joy.

"What is this food? Why don't *we* eat it at the Mission? Might I have more? Where *does* it come from?"

The gypsies look at Liora. They know, now, what Liora is, what I am, foundlings dedicating our lives to silence, sisterhood, sacrifice, and selflessness in gratitude for bread, a roof, a gown, a life, providing we first meet the appropriate criteria, which Liora has not. That is the real reason we are on our way to Greeble. Once vows are spoken, a Sister enters Sanctuary and never again sees another person outside the stone walls of the Mission, and Liora is of that age. I am the one exception; I am the Worldly Liaison and must know how to get along in the secular world, but I have sworn in blood that I will never utter a single word of the outside world inside Mission walls. For that, my tongue would be cut out and I would be cast out.

As he looks at Liora, pity flashes in father-gypsy's eyes. Elder-son stops chewing to frown. Sister looks on in horror.

Liora stares back at them, not understanding. The Mission is the only home she has ever known.

"Ah," the father remarks, rubbing his belly. "The

best bread on earth. No one can bake bread like the Sisters.'' When he eyes my cart, I grow uneasy.

"And now, we shall music! Bring me my songer!''

I open my mouth to protest, then, remembering my assignment, close it again. Glancing upward, I see the pretty creature poised on a branch, looking down at us, joining our gaiety.

Music begins. Liora whirls around and around as she is twirled from one hand to another to another. She is breathless and laughing and her bright hair streams out and around, tangling in elder-son's hands. She has not danced before; nevertheless, she knows the steps, the rhythm.

Finally I protest. "We must go. We have already tarried too long. Liora, bring the mule.'' I smile at the family. "Thank you,'' I tell them, but they won't know what I mean.

They watch us until we pass over the hill, are still watching as we ascend the next one, and I wonder what I will be missing from the cart when we arrive at Greeble.

The city is sin-infested, smoke-filled, squalid. Narrow, twisting streets teem with humans and camels and dogs and dung. Urchins beg, stick-arms outraised; no one pays them any heed. To display their wares, whores lift their legs on street corners. Thieves pilfer; I lay my whip on one who thinks to filch from me. Open, sunken, sewer canals pour their reeking loads down the middle of the streets; in the past, I have glimpsed babies floating in them. I have often wondered where it all goes when it gets to the end of where it is going. For once, Liora is silent, but her stricken eyes speak volumes. I drive the mule deeper inside the city and rent a stall.

Within the hour, the load of Mission bread is sold. I conceal the money inside my blouse. With it, I must buy a cartload of fine flour.

We sleep in the cart; at dawn, we rise, we wash, we eat our bread and cheese, and then I drive to the fair.

The world of reality does not sit well on Liora's shoulders. She is affronted, repulsed, frightened. When we arrive, the fair is already crowded. Beautiful, pale Liora looks around, looks around. For the most part, she has stilled her questions and I am glad, as I have no answers. We push through the crowd and find the proper line, but for some reason, I am indecisive. This time, my duty burdens me, disheartens me. Perhaps I am getting too old for this task. I have tended to this matter many times and it never affected me before, but this time, with Liora, it does.

Liora notices them at once, sees the long, wailing, surging line of them.

"Who are *those* children? What are they *doing* up there? What is the *matter* with them?"

"Those are," I explain, "throwaways."

"But," she dramatizes behind her hand, "they haven't any *clothes*. And they weep. Is that bundle a *baby?* Where are their mothers? Are they hungry? Do we mean to give them bread? Why, that thing is a chopping block. And what is that object hanging there? A kind of *cleaver?*"

I rub my brow: I have a horrid headache. It must have been the meat. A procurer pushes past, stops, turns back to us. His eyes rake Liora. He looks at me with raised brows.

I mean to nod. Instead, I am caught up in a fit of coughing until he moves on. I reconsider. I have the cart, the mule, a full purse. I know bread; it is the only thing I have to offer. I look at Liora, beautiful Liora.

For the first time in memory, I waver at this unpleasant task. Unfamiliar grief wells upward. I have no family. My daughters are the foundlings brought in a never-ending stream to the Mission. We accept perhaps one out of fifty; that is all we can afford. The rest of them end up here.

Reality, resolve set in. I am old. I know my duty.

The auctioneer mounts the dais. I grasp Liora's arm, take a forward step.

I see them then, see the scarlet blouses. The gypsies are here to pickpocket. Without hesitation I fish out the Mission purse, turn to Liora, and press it into her hands.

"Do you see the gypsy father? You must go to him. Give him this purse. Tell him . . . tell him . . . that Sister sent you. You must stay with him now and not get lost. Be obedient to him as you have been trained."

"Why . . . ?"

"Go!" I shove her away and press myself backward into the swell of humanity.

She has lost me. I see her sapphire eyes, wide and frightened, search for me, search for him. Because I am gone, he is all she knows.

The Lifetree welcomes with cool, loving arms. The odor of sizzling meat still hovers in the air. Feet flash with dance. Black eyes bore into blue. Lovely, pale hair whips around a tall, slim body, entangles in a dark boy's hands. They are there to this day, impressed in the unrelenting sand, forever shadow. I see them often.

I crawl upward through the branches. The creature is tame, not ever having been human-hurt. I cradle it in my hands. It preens and stretches and smiles.

With my bread knife, I puncture its throat, allow its lifeblood to drain onto the tree. I toss it down to the sand, search for the mate. Then I find a nest containing eight young.

I dig a hole at the base of the Lifetree, throw in the dead, cover them with sand, wipe my bloody, dusty hands on my thighs, leaving dirty streaks behind. I am glad I did what I did. My mule is eager to be gone, to be home.

Bloodtide

Mary A. Turzillo

The daughter was not quite right in the head, but she was pretty. So the mother was not surprised when the girl walked down the long slope of the beach one evening, toward the moon, toward the roaring sea's heart.

The mermen got her. That's what the mother thought. And certainly the mermen could make the daughter happy.

She was right on both counts.

Maybe I have given the wrong impression. The mother was not coldhearted; she did plunge into the waves to find the daughter, to pull her back to the mortal land.

Still, how can a woman fight the ocean? The surf crashed around her in deceptive colors, playful with deadly power, but the girl was gone. Battered by driftwood, her legs slashed by broken conch shells, the mother struggled back to land for help. By the time the townspeople came, it was too late. The daughter had gone to sea without ship or sail, wearing only a smock printed with little purple birds.

Her wedding dress, the mother called it, after that.

The daughter had always been simple, a fool, and worse than a fool. The schoolmistress despaired of educating her. The girl would look out the window and a dreamy expression would come into her black eyes. Then, when no one seemed to see her, she would get up and drift out the door. Often she would take off her shoes, to move more quietly. Even in winter, she would go barefoot to the wharf to watch the boats.

The mother would hug her and stroke her straight black hair. "My moonstruck baby, what will I do with you?" she would sigh. But the daughter had done for herself; she had gone to sea on foot, in her thin print smock.

Now she had come back.

One morning, she simply walked out of the waves. She was changed, you know, even prettier than before. Her dark hair was wet, sleeked against her head, tendrils like calligraphy against her cheek. Her eyes looked more intelligent, but the mother knew that was all an illusion. Even the mermen could not penetrate that thick skull.

"Mama," said the daughter, and tried to embrace her.

The mother recoiled. The daughter's flesh would be cool, lifeless now, she thought.

"Mama, kiss me, the way you used to. I can't hurt my own mama, can I?"

But the mother was reluctant. She was still a pretty woman, and she thought the touch of the dead girl would blast her beauty.

"Oh, my poor lost baby, the sea got you. Let the sea keep you."

Benign wonder dawned in the daughter's eyes. "You

think I'm dead? You think I drowned out there? My husbands would never let me drown."

The mother took time to look at her. The daughter had been fair-cheeked, and of high color, easily embarrassed and easily blushing. She was the same now, except thinner in the face, and fuller in the breasts and hips. She was still wearing the printed smock, but it was worn to shreds, loops of frayed fabric hanging like ribbons on her body. And the mother saw that she wore pearls and coral—necklaces, rings, earrings, fobs, anklets, bangles, even rings for her toes—the gems all carved with delicacy. The effect was as if they were organic to the girl herself, a second skin or chitin.

"You would be twenty, if you had lived," whispered the mother.

The girl laughed, her loud simpleton's laugh. "You still think I'm dead, but I'm not. I went back where I belonged. Now, Mama, didn't you fish me out of the sea when I was a little baby? Why shouldn't I go back there to marry?"

"No. I never got you out of the sea."

"You did. Out of a little basket washed up on the shore. I heard my father tell it, when he thought I wasn't listening."

"No," whispered the mother.

The girl sighed and put down the mother-of-pearl box she was carrying. She went to the mother and forced an embrace.

"You're as warm as if you were alive," said the mother.

"I *am* alive. Alive and married, and I have many children. I came back to give you a present." And the daughter picked up the box, holding it out in both hands.

The mother took the box and stood a long time look-ing at the girl. But she didn't open it. "Come in the house. I'll make tea and scones like we used to have before you went to sea."

They went inside, and the mother baked scones and heated tea. As they ate, the mother told her daughter the gossip of the town.

But after a while, she fell silent. The two listened to the surf murmur and gulls keen. The daughter, never one to talk much, gazed dreamily out the window of the cottage, at the horizon.

"I have to go back, Mama." And she rose and slipped out into the sea-misted evening, leaving damp foot-prints on the floor as if she had just walked out of the surf.

The mother continued to sit a long time, holding her tea mug as if it were a rope end thrown to a woman fallen overboard. Then she put the dishes in the sink and opened the box. It contained a necklace of green coral and black seed pearls, with earrings to match, and a tiny pelican carved out of white coral. The mother put the necklace and earrings on. In a mirror, she saw they became her very well.

But she put them away and never wore them again. She feared she was going crazy, feared she had not really seen her daughter.

The daughter came back, not often, but about as often as a child will who has grown up and moved to another country. Each time she brought a piece of jewelry or some trinket. Sometimes these contained precious stones; sometimes, only pale blue sea glass or clustered sea beans.

The mother never wore them, never put them out to show. She was afraid of their witchery.

In time, the mother opened an inn, where she served chowders, lobster and shrimp dishes, and fish prepared in many ways. She had a few rooms where people could sleep in worn, cool sheets. She placed a vase of sea grass and wildflowers in each room. When the guest went in to sleep, he would always find the window ajar, and the room chilly and a little damp. The flowers made the air fresh, hinting that morning would be sunnier.

One night a traveler came late, and the mother's hired boy rented her a room overlooking the sound. When the mother came home to work on her account book, the traveler slipped up behind her and laid a hand on her shoulder.

The mother looked around in fright, and recognized her at once, though the young woman was thinner now, and her eyes were red with weeping. Yes, it was the daughter.

"You've killed my child and served him up to guests in your inn," she told her mother.

The mother straightened the spectacles on her nose. "Your child? A merchild?"

The daughter nodded. "You did not know it for my child because it was more sea creature than human."

"Are you sure?" the mother asked finally.

"Do you know me? Does a mother know her own?"

The mother certainly recognized her own daughter, though the girl was dressed in tatters, was haggard with sorrow. She asked, very low, "What do you want me to do?"

"Nothing. There is nothing you can do. My husbands

came and mourned the child this morning. You didn't see them. My son, my son!''

''What should I do?'' asked the mother again. ''Are all sea creatures your children?''

The daughter stopped crying and looked at her in surprise. ''No. I have only two hundred children. This one was the eldest.''

The mother clutched her daughter's hand and begged a third time, ''Tell me what I should do.''

The daughter pulled her hand away and wiped her face on the back of it. Her hair had dried, stiff with salt, against her neck, in patterns like a child's scribbling. Her mouth twisted with bitterness. ''Drink the sea and die.''

The girl did not come back with gifts after that. And though the mother continued to run the inn by the sea, she was superstitious about food and made someone else prepare the seafood dishes. She buried the bones and claws of sea creatures eaten in her inn far inland, where no mermen could know about them.

Late in life, when her hands had become arthritic claws, too crippled to prepare food or beds for strangers, and when the inn itself had fallen into disrepair, the mother found the mother-of-pearl box with the necklace and earrings. She ransacked her cupboards, releasing the scent of sea grass, looking for the other gifts her daughter had brought her.

She took them to an old man in town, a pawnbroker, a dealer in curiosities.

''See these? Are they worth anything?'' She dangled a handful of them in front of him, then put them on the counter.

He picked through them. "These are nothing." He dropped them back in the carved box and delved in his pockets for a dirty handkerchief, with which he wiped his spectacles and then his nose. "Beachcombings. Sea glass, shells. Somebody has glued them together, strung them with package twine." His eyes grew beady. "Where did you get them?"

She did not answer, only wrapped the box and went home.

With crooked pain, she climbed up to her attic. She wanted to find a basket, to offer her daughter's gifts back to the sea.

It took her most of the afternoon to find it. She heaped the things in it, and, a tarpaulin over her arm, shuffled down to the water's edge.

The wind that afternoon was not as blustery as the day her daughter had gone to sea, but the sky was overcast. She waded out in the turbulent water, spray dampening her face, undertow dragging at her frail ankles, and placed the basket in the surf. Then she walked back up the beach to spread her tarpaulin on the gray sand.

She watched the basket bob in the waves, until the swelling water carried it away. A crude thing, out of reeds and willows, festooned with faded ribbons. Just big enough to hold a three-month-old child.

Tale of the Crone Goddess

Bruce Boston

When I came to the caravan I was
virgin, I was peachbud, the flowered
garland still fresh upon my brow,
the gold chains of travel on my ankles.
The wagonmaster glowered with umber eyes
set deep within his frown, and said that
I was chosen to guard the torch, by day,
by night, to feed the oil in its socket,
to take the cloak from my shoulders and
offer each burgeoning tongue of flame
a shelter from the wind, to stand close
by as the rippling air rose against my
cheeks and darkened my pale braids.

I took this honor within my breast.
I forgot the boots of my father. I
forgot my mother's eyes, her words
of entreaty. Atop the wagon, swaying

to the music of hooves and wheels,
I kept the torch and my hands and
thoughts did not waver in their task.

The small, dirty boys came to me,
running within the rutted tracks,
tossing rings for my attention.
Women with other lives and lovers
walked below as I saw their bellies
swell in turn, spilling the bloody living
fruit, throats taut with the birthpang,
dull hairs sprouting about their lips.
Forests passed. Rivers forded. The night
a spinning cape, the torch blown fat
or lean. The dark hairs curling from the
slits on the wagonmaster's gloves, the
roughness in his touch I learned to
tame and covet with my clever limbs.

Still my eyes did not waver, to stare
through sunache, the flail of rain,
the softly-hissing snow, to gather
the leaves and strip the bark and
draw forth the oil to feed the flame,
for I was chosen, a goddess no longer
human, my white feet, my body pure
and as sacred as the torch itself.

Until the years turned hard. And hard
as I tried I could not yearn them back.
Strands of gray stained my darkened braids.
My vision dimmed. Wrinkles found my neck,
my shoulders. I cried in the night and
my voice grew ragged as the milkweed leaf.

Now the wagons are still.
The master visits no longer.
The torch flickers within my breast.
And in the night there are rumors
of a girl come to the caravan.

Transmutations

Patricia A. McKillip

Old Dr. Bezel was amusing himself again; Cerise smelled it outside his door. The shade escaping under the thick, warped oak was blue. A darker shadow crossed it restively: he must have conjured up his apprentice, who had been among the invisible folk for five days. Cerise planted the gold-rimmed spectacles Dr. Bezel had made for her firmly on her nose, and opened the door.

As usual, Aubrey Vaughn, slumping into a chair, looked blankly at her, as if she had fallen through the ceiling. She noted, with a sharp and fascinated eye, the yellow-grey pallor of his skin. She slid her notebook and pens and the leather bag with her lunch in it onto a table, then opened the notebook to a blank page.

"I'm sorry I'm late," she said in her low, quiet voice. She added to the velvet curtains over the windows, for Dr. Bezel beamed at anything she said and rarely listened, and Aubrey simply never listened, "At least I'm not five days late."

But this time Aubrey blinked at her. He could never remember her name. She was a slender, colorless wraith of a woman who appeared and disappeared at odd times; for all he knew she was conjured out of candle smoke and had no life beyond the moments he encountered her. But gold teased him: the gold of her spectacles catching firelight and lamplight among laughter, sweat, curses, music . . He made an incautious movement; his elbow slid off the chair arm. He jerked to catch his balance and felt the mad, gnarled imp in his brain strike with the pick, mining empty furrows for thought.

"You were there," he breathed. "Last night."

Behind her spectacles, her grey eyes widened. "You can see me," she said, amazed. "I've often wondered."

"Of course I can see you."

"How long has this been going on? Dr. Bezel, he sees me. You will have to dispose of one of us."

"Yes, my dear Cerise," Dr. Bezel agreed benignly, peering at his intricate, bubbling skeleton of glass. "Now we will wait until the solution turns from blue to a most delicate green."

"You were there," Aubrey persisted, holding himself rigid to calm the imp. "At Wells Inn."

"You are beginning to see me outside of this room? This is astonishing. What is my name?"

"Ah—"

"You see, I had a theory that not only am I invisible to you, the sound of my voice never reaches you. As if one of us is under a spell. Apparently even my name disappears into some muffled thickness of air before you hear it."

"I can hear you well enough now," he said drily. He applied one hand to his brow and made an effort. "It's a sound. Like silk ripping. Cerise."

She was silent, amused and half annoyed, for on the whole, if their worlds were to merge, she preferred being invisible to Aubrey Vaughn. He was seeing her clearly now, she realized, as something more than a mass and an arbitrary movement in Dr. Bezel's cluttered study. She watched the expression begin to form in his bleared, wincing eyes, and turned abruptly. His voice pursued.

"But what were you doing there?"

"Now see," Dr. Bezel said delightedly, and Cerise forgot the curious voice in the chair as she watched a green like the first leaves flush through the bones of glass. "That is the exact shade. Look, for it goes quickly."

"The exact shade of what?" Aubrey murmured, and for once was himself unheard and invisible. "Of what?" he asked again, with his stubborn persistence, and, unaccountably, Dr. Bezel answered him.

"Of the leaves there. Translucent, gold-green, they fan into the light."

"What leaves where?"

"No place. A dream." He turned, smiling, sighing a little, as the green faded into clear. "I was only playing. Now we will work."

What leaves? Aubrey thought much later, after he had chased spilled mercury across the floor and nearly scalded himself with molten silver. Dr. Bezel, lecturing absently, let fall the names of references intermittently, like thunderbolts. Cerise noted them in her meticulous script. What dream? she wondered, and made a private note: Green-gold leaves fanning into light.

"Also there is a well," Dr. Bezel said unexpectedly, at the end of the morning. Aubrey blinked at him, looking pained. Dr. Bezel, distracted from his vision by Aubrey's expression, added kindly, "Aubrey, if you tarnish the gold of enlightenment with the fires and sodden flames of endless nights, how will you recognize it?"

Aubrey answered tiredly, "Even dross may be transmuted. So you said."

"So you do listen to me." He turned, chuckling. "Perhaps you are your father's son."

Cerise saw the blood sweep into Aubrey's face. Prudently, she looked down at her notebook and wrote: Well. She had never met Nicholaus Vaughn, who had enlightened himself out of existence; he had not, it seemed, misspent his youth at Wells Inn. Aubrey said nothing; the sudden stab of the pickax blinded him. In the wash of red before his eyes, he saw his bright-haired father, tall, serene, hopelessly good. Passionless, Aubrey thought, and his sight cleared; he found himself gazing into a deep vessel, some liquid matter gleaming faintly at the bottom.

"Analysis," Dr. Bezel instructed.

"Now?" Aubrey said hoarsely, bone-dry. "It's noon."

"Then let us lay to rest the noonday devils," Dr. Bezel said cheerfully. The woman, Cerise, was chewing on the end of her pen, deliberately expressionless. Aubrey asked her crossly,

"Have you no devils to bedevil you?"

"None," she answered in her low, humorous voice, "I would call a devil. I am intimate with those I know."

"So am I," he sighed, letting a drop from the vessel fall upon a tiny round of glass. Unexpectedly, it was red.

"Then they are not devils but reflections."

He grunted, suddenly absorbed in the crimson unknown. Blood? Dye? He reached for fire. "What were you doing at Wells Inn?" he asked. He felt her sudden, sharp glance and answered it without looking up, "In one way, I am like my father. I am tenacious."

"You are not concentrating," Dr. Bezel chided gently. They were all silent then, watching fire touch the unknown substance. It flared black. Aubrey raised his red-gold brows, rubbed his eyes. At his elbow, Cerise made the first note of his analysis: Turns obscure under fire. Aubrey reached for a glass beaker, poured a bead of crimson into a solution of salts. It fell as gracefully as a falling world.

Retains integrity in solution, Cerise wrote, and added: Unlike the experimenter.

The puzzle remained perplexing. Aubrey, sweating and finally curious by the end of the hour, requested texts. Dr. Bezel sent him out for sustenance, Cerise to the library. There she gathered scrolls and great dusty tomes, and, having deposited them in the study, retired beneath a tree to eat plums and farmer's cheese and pumpernickel bread, and to write poetry. She was struggling between two indifferent rhymes when a beery presence intruded itself.

"What were you doing at Wells Inn last night?"

She looked up. Aubrey's tawny, bloodshot eyes regarded her with the clinical interest he gave an unknown substance. She said simply, "Working. My father owns the place."

He stared at her; she had transformed under his nose. "You work there?"

"Five nights a week, until midnight."

"I never saw—"

"Precisely."

He backed against the tree, slid down the trunk slowly to sit among its roots. "And you work for Dr. Bezel." She closed her notebook, did not reply. "Why?"

She shrugged lightly. "I have no one to pay for my apprenticeship. This is as close as I can get to studying with him."

He was silent, eyeing the distance, his expression vague, uncertain. The woman beside him, unseen, seemed to disappear. He looked at her again, saw her candle-wax hair, her smoky eyes. It was her calm, he decided, that rendered her invisible to the casual eye. Movement attracted attention: her inner movements did not outwardly express themselves. Except, he amended a trifle sourly, for her humor.

"Why?" he asked again, and remembered her in the hot, dense crush at the inn, hair braided, face obscure behind her spectacles, hoisting a tray of mugs. She wore an apron over a plain black dress; now she wore black with lace at her wrists and throat, and her shoulders were covered. He tried to remember her bare shoulders, could not. "What do you need to transmute? Surely not your soul. It must be as tidy as your handwriting."

She looked mildly annoyed at the charge. "Why do you?" she asked. "You seem quite comfortable in your own untidiness."

He shrugged. "I am following drunkenly in my father's footsteps. He transmuted himself out of this world, giving me such a pure and shining example of goodness that it sends me to Wells Inn most nights to contemplate it."

Her annoyance faded; she sat quite still, wondering at his candor. "Are you afraid of goodness?"

He nodded vigorously, keeping his haggard, shadow-smudged face tilted upward for her inspection. "Oh, yes. I prefer storms, fire, elements in the raw, before they are analyzed and named and ranked."

"And yet you—"

"Cannot keep away from my father's one great passion: to render all things into their final, changeless, unimpassioned state." The corner of his mouth slid up: a kind of smile, she realized, the first she had seen. He met her eyes. "Now," he said, "tell me why you study such things. Do you want what my father wanted? Perfection?"

"Of a kind," she admitted after a moment, her hands sliding, open, across the closed notebook. She was silent another moment, choosing words; he waited, motionless himself, exuding fumes and his father's legendary powers of concentration. "I thought—by immersing myself in the process—that perhaps I could transmute language."

A brow went up. "Into gold?"

Her mouth twitched. "In the basest sense. I try to write poetry. My words seem dull as dishwater, which I am quite familiar with. Some people live by their poetry. They sell it for money. The little I earn from Dr. Bezel turns itself into books. I work mostly for the chance to learn. I thought perhaps writing poetry might be a way to make a living that's not carrying trays and dodging hands and stepping in spilled ale and piss and transmuted suppers."

His eyes flicked away from her; he remembered a few of his own drunken offerings. "Poets," he murmured, "need not be perfect."

"No," she agreed, "but they are always chasing the perfect word."

"Let me see your poetry."

"No," she said again swiftly, rising. She brushed crumbs from her skirt, adjusted her cuffs, the notebook clamped firmly under one elbow. "Anyway, the bell has rung, Dr. Bezel is waiting, and your unknown substance is still unknown." He groaned softly, a boneless wraith in the tree roots, the shadows of leaves gently stroking his father's red-gold hair. She wondered suddenly at the battle in him, tugged as he was between noon and night, between ale and alchemy. "Do you never sleep?" she asked.

"I am now," he said, struggling to his feet, and groaned again as the hot, pure gold dazzled over him, awakening the headache behind his eyes.

Dr. Bezel, bent over an antique alembic and murmuring to himself, remained unaware of their return for some time. "How clear the light," he said once, gazing into the murky, bubbling alembic. "It reveals even the most subtle hues in water, in common stones, in the very clay of earth." Cerise, flipping a poem away from Aubrey's curious eye, made another note of Dr. Bezel's rambles through his dream world: Clarity. Something within the alembic popped; a tarry black smeared the glass. Aubrey winced at the noise and the bleak color. Dr. Bezel, surprised out of his musings, sensed the emanations behind him and turned. "Did you see it?" he asked with joy. "Now, then, to your own mystery, Aubrey. Cerise has brought your texts."

Aubrey, sweating pallidly, like a hothouse lily, bent over the scrolls. While he studied, Cerise ventured a question.

"Is there language, in this lovely place, or are all things mute?"

"They are transmuted," Aubrey murmured.

"Puns," Cerise said gravely, "do not transmute: there are no ambiguities in the perfect world."

"Nor," Dr. Bezel said briskly, "is there language."

"Oh," she said, disconcerted.

"It is unnecessary. All is known, all exists in the

same unchanging moment." He poured a drop of the
tarry black onto a glass wafer. Aubrey gazed bewil-
deredly at his back.

"Then why," he wondered, "would anyone choose to
go there?"

"You do not choose. You do not go. You are. Study,
study to find your father's shining path, and someday
you will understand everything." He let fall a tear of
liquid onto the black substance. It flared. The smell of
roses pervaded the room; they were all dazed a moment,
even Dr. Bezel. "It is the scent of childhood," he said
wistfully, lost in some private moment. Aubrey, saturated by Wells Inn, forgot the word for what he smelled.
Driftwood, his brain decided, it was the smell of driftwood. Or perhaps of caraway. Cerise, trying to imagine
a world without a word, thought instantly: roses, and
watched them bloom inside her head.

Aubrey, after some reading, requested sulphur. Ap-
plying it to his unknown and heating it, he dispersed
even the memory of roses. Cerise, noting his test, wrote:
Due to extreme contamination of surroundings, does
not react to sulphur. Neither does his unknown. She
drew the curtains apart, opened a window. Light gilded
the experimenter's profile; he winced.

"Must you?"

"It's only air and light."

"I'm not used to either." He shook a drop of mercury
into a glass tube, and then a drop of mystery. Nothing
happened. He held it over fire, carelessly, his face too
near, his hand bare. He shook it impatiently; beads of
red and silver spun around the bottom, touched each
other without reacting. He sighed, ran his free hand
through his hair. "This substance has no name."

"Rest a moment," Dr. Bezel suggested, and Aubrey

collapsed into a wing-backed chair patterned with tiny dragons. They looked, Cerise thought with amusement, like a swarm of minute demons around his head. He cast a bleared eye at her.

"Water," he ordered, and in that moment, she wanted to close her notebook and thump his head with poetry.

"We are not," she said coldly, "at Wells Inn."

"Look, look," Dr. Bezel exclaimed, but at what they could not fathom. He was shaking salts into a beaker of water; they took some form, apparently, before they dissolved. "There is light at the bottom of the well. Something shines . . . How exquisite."

"I beg your pardon," Aubrey said. Cerise did not answer. "How can I remember," he pleaded, "which world we are in if you flit constantly between them?"

"You could frequent another inn."

"I've grown accustomed to your father's inn."

"You could learn some manners."

Silent, he considered that curious notion. His eyes slid to her face, as she stood listening to Dr. Bezel's verbal fits and starts, and writing a word now and then. Limpid as a nun, he thought grumpily of her graceful, calm profile, and then saw that face flushed and sweating, still patient under a barrage of noise, heat, the incessant drunken bellowings of orders, with only the faint tension in her mouth as she hoisted a tray high above heedless roisterers, betraying her weariness. He rubbed his own weary face.

"I could," he admitted, and saw her eyes widen. He got to his feet, picked up a carafe of water from a little ebony table. He went to the window, stuck his head out, and poured the water over his hair. Panting a little at the sudden cold, he pulled his dripping head back in and heard Dr. Bezel say with blank wonder,

"But of course, it is the shining of enlightenment."

"Where?" Aubrey demanded, parting plastered hair out of his eyes as if enlightenment might be floating in front of his nose. "Is it my unknown?"

"It is at the bottom of the well," Dr. Bezel answered, beaming at his visions, then blinked at his wet apprentice. "From which you seem to have emerged."

"Perhaps," Aubrey sighed. "I feel I might live after all."

"Good. Then to work again. All we lack now is a path . . ."

Path, Cerise wrote under her private notes for Dr. Bezel's unknown. Or did he speak of a path to Aubrey's unknown? she wondered. Their imponderables were becoming confused. Aubrey buried a drop of his under an avalanche of silvery salts, then added an acid. The acid bubbled the salts into a smoking frenzy, but left the scarlet substance isolated, untouched.

"Sorcery," Aubrey muttered, hauling in his temper. "It's the fire-salamander's tongue, the eye of the risen phoenix." He immersed himself in a frail, moldy book, written in script as scrupulous as Cerise's. Dr. Bezel, silent for the moment, pursued his own visions. Cerise, unneeded, turned surreptitiously to her poem, chewed on the end of her pen. It lacks, she thought, frowning. It lacks . . . It is inert, scribbles on paper, nothing living. I might as well feed it to the salamander. But, patiently, she crossed out a phrase, clicked words together and let them fall like dice, chose one and not the other, then chose the other, and then crossed them both out, and wrote down a third.

"Yes," she heard Dr. Bezel whisper, and looked up.

"There." He gazed into a beaker flushed with a pearl-grey tincture, as if he saw in it the map to some un-named country. Aubrey, his head ringing with elements, turned toward him.

"What?"

"The unknown . . ."

"In there?" He eyed the misty liquid hopefully. "Is that the catalyst? I'd introduce my unknown into a solution of hops at this point." He reached for it heedlessly, dropped a tear of crimson into the mystery in Dr. Bezel's hand.

It seemed, Cerise thought a second later, as if someone had lifted the roof off the room and poured molten gold into their eyes. She rediscovered herself sitting in a chair, her notebook sprawling at her feet. Aubrey was sitting on the floor. The roof had been replaced.

Of Dr. Bezel there was no trace.

She stared at Aubrey, who was blinking at her. Some moment bound them in a silence too profound for language. Then, a moment or an hour later, she found her voice.

"You have transmuted Dr. Bezel."

He got to his feet, feeling strange, heavy, as if his bones had been replaced with gold. "I can't have."

She picked up her notebook, smoothed the pages, then held it close, like a shield, her arms around it, her eyes still stunned. "He is gone," she said irrefutably.

"I couldn't transmute a flea." He stared bemusedly at his unknown. "What on earth is this?" He looked around him a little wildly, searching tabletop, tubes, alembic. "His beaker went with him."

"No, you see, it was transformed, like him, like your father—it is nothing now. No thing. Everything." Her voice sounded peculiar; she stood up, trembling. Her face looked odd, too, Aubrey thought, shaken out of its calm, its patient humor, on the verge of an unfamiliar expression, as if she had caught the barest glimpse of something inexpressible. She began to drift. He asked sharply,

"Where are you going?"

"Home."

"Why?"

"I seem to be out of a job."

He began to put his unknown down, did not. He was silent, struggling. Her mind began to fill with leaves, with silence; she shook her head a little, arms tightening around her notebook. "Stay," he said abruptly. "Stay. I can't leave. Not without knowing. What he found. How he found it. And there are unknowns everywhere. Stay and help me." She gazed at him, still expressionless. He added, "Please."

"No." She shook her head again; leaves whirled away on a sudden wind. "I can't. I'm going back to buckets and beer, mops and dishwater and voices—"

"But why?"

She backed a step closer to the door. "I don't want a silent shining path of gold. I need the imperfect world broken up into words."

He said again, barely listening to her, hearing little more than the mute call of the unknown, "Please. Please stay, Cerise."

She smiled. The smile transformed her face; he saw fire in it, shadow, gold and silver, sun and moon, all possibilities of language. "You are too much like your father," she said. "What if you accidentally succeed?" She tore her notes out and left them with him, and then left him, holding a mystery in his hand and gazing after her while she took the path back into the mutable world.

Last Day in May
Grammar Lesson

Barbara Van Noord

I am reading now
with a pencil in my hand
because sometimes
writing and reading are one.
The lesson plan called
only for parsed verbs
and adverbs rising
on slantwise stalks.
But it turns out
the paragraph is
full of water lilies
each round, and one
leading into another.
Under one, a frog
which wants to be a verb,
passive or active,
darts out its tongue.
A fly enters the tutorial

by the same window
through which we,
dear reader, will
soon depart, writing
our way out.
The fly takes the lead,
bouncing above
the subtitles.
A long tongue
unfurls from
under the thickish cream
of the blossom.
Quick as a blink
it disappears again
while the lily pond
looks still
so smooth
on the surface;
there really are
no anchors here.
We do drift
tranquil on a tranquil
summer's raft,
little adverbial
objects, little
adverbial phrases
bundled together
by prepositions.
Is it too much
to ask, that we
leave by the window?
That great
godlike noun
through which

the world
may be viewed,
need only
be prefaced
by the adjective
open
for us to understand
that viewing
is not likely
to be enough
and to cause desire
to haunt us
until we drift up
like an answer
and go.

The Spinner

Martha Soukup

Rianna lived alone on the other side of the hill outside town. Each month she went down into town to bargain for wool of sheep, hair of goat, for flax and cotton. Each day she spun them into yarn and thread. Each week she took what she had spun and sold it to one of several women who wove it into cloth they themselves sold. She had moved to this town two years ago, when her mother died, because her own had too many spinners. The hillside was pretty, and she was busy and content.

Rianna traded with a dressmaker for her clothes. She knew herself to be a poor cook, and her housekeeping was none too good. She spun only, but she could spin anything human hands could spin.

When she tired of spinning wool, goat hair, and flax, she would spin other things, just for her fun: fur from the coats of her sleepy dog and of the two fat fluffy cats who slept at his flanks; hair from the manes of horses; fibers she pulled from the drying pods of plants that grew along the edge of the swamp. Not all of these made supple yarn or strong thread, but most of what she spun from them she was able to sell or trade.

It was spun dog and cat fur that brought Rowan to her door.

"Spinner, can you spin me gold?" he asked. A bag, full and light, was slung over his back.

She did not know him, but she had seen him, sometimes, at a distance, walking through the hills at twilight. She recognized him by the fine fair hair that swirled around his shoulders in the strong afternoon breeze. He was a woodcutter who came to town less often than she.

"That is just an old story," she said.

He grinned. His eyes were hazel. "That's too bad, for gold is what I need." He swung his bag to her doorstep and opened it. "What can you do with this?"

It was full of the pods of a plant she had not seen before. She took one and pulled lint from it. It was very light and fine, and shone in the sun like the woodcutter's hair. "Where did you get these?"

"They grow deep in the woods, where I sometimes go to cut old, thick trees," he said. "My name is Rowan. They tell me you are Rianna the spinner, and you can spin anything."

"Everything I have tried," she said. She twisted and pulled the plantstuff; she spun it between her fingers to look at the thread it made.

"I have seen a shawl knitted from your dog-fur yarn. Someone bought that. Would someone buy this, if you spun it?"

"Perhaps," Rianna said. She liked the look of the lint. She took the bag and went to her wheel. The lint pulled easily from the pods. In a minute or two she had enough to wrap around the distaff. She spun. The thread shone on the spool.

"Pretty enough," she said, "but none too strong." She thought a moment, then tsk-tsked to her cats until one came. She took the purring animal in her lap and combed long brown fur from it. "This is a trick I have played with before," she said. The fur went around the distaff with what the woodcutter had brought, and she spun the two together. The yarn wound onto the spindle and she nodded.

"Better," she said.

"What can we sell it for?" he asked.

"Whatever people will pay for it. Why do you want gold so much, woodcutter?"

"There is a maid in town I would marry," he said. "She will have me, but her father will not let her go to a man who has only his axe and a cabin he built with his own hands, strong as that cabin may be. If I show him gold in my hand, and perhaps some for his purse, he will show me his blessing."

He was straight and strong and warm of eye. Rianna could see how a town girl might be willing to move to a dark cottage in the woods for that warmth. "I will need many more of these plants," she said. "Do you have animals?"

"Cats," he said. "Why?"

"If we use mine, I take a larger share of the gold," said Rianna.

The woodcutter grinned again. "You'll do it."

"And you will have to wash and soak the lint," she said, standing from her stool. "It is not a job I like. I can show you how."

The woodcutter laughed and swept her up in his arms. She blinked at him, startled. "We will be great partners," he said, releasing her. "It's a fair day brought me to your door." Rianna tilted her head to see the cloudy sky, and smiled at the woodcutter's back as he strode down her walk.

Rowan had five cats, all of a litter and all pale orange. In a few weeks' time he brought their fur to her, and many bags more of the woodland pods. The cat fur was long and seemed to wind through Rianna's fingers of itself. She spun thread that shone like gold. The woodcutter came to her door at odd hours late in the evening, gave her a bag or two, and left.

Rianna took some of the thread to the weaver. The cloth it yielded was lovely, and, as it did not need to be dyed, would never dull in color. A merchant's wife said she would take enough to make two gowns.

The season passed and she had as much lint as she could want, and not enough fur to go with it. Still the woodcutter came from time to time. He would sit by the fire and watch her spin, as she carefully admixed the one fiber with the other to keep color and texture true.

"You are a marvel," he said. "Truly you could spin anything."

"Anything I have tried," she said again, and they laughed together. It was now an old joke between them.

"You spin gold," he said. "It is gold to the eye, we will have gold for it, it *is* gold. You have spun out the most precious stuff, all to help me."

"I'll take my share," she said.

"We share everything."

"Half and half," she said.

"Half and half," he said, and kissed her.

Rianna's lips warmed to his, but she remembered, and said, "You have a maid in town."

"Not now."

Not anymore, or not yet? Rianna wondered, as the woodcutter reached up and unpinned her plaited red hair; he pulled her hair loose and she was unspun. She fell into his arms like a tree.

Each night the woodcutter came to her until spring, when his cats gave off fur. Now she spun the last of the golden thread; now they carted it together to the weaver, receiving for their labors two small bags of coins.

Rowan did not come back to watch her spin, not that night, nor the next. She thought she should go to see him, until a farmer told her, as he piled wool down from his cart, that a wedding was being planned in town. "A woodcutter and a merchant's daughter, imagine that."

"Imagine that," Rianna said. Her fingers felt numb, counting out coins. "Imagine that." The thought of tall Rowan dancing at his wedding with a giggling town girl filled her mind. She wished that she could not imagine it. "When is the wedding?"

"In six, no, in seven weeks' time, I hear," said the farmer chattily. He waited for a response Rianna could not make.

The next day she spun from the time she roused herself in the morning until late into the night, when her eyes stung and her head was heavy. It was working so that made her eyes sting. She spun without ceasing for a week and another, dust building unnoticed in her cottage, hair slack and unplaited to her waist, and then she had nothing left to spin.

And still Rowan had not come to say goodbye.

Rianna could not sleep, she could not eat. "It is not fair," she thought, "that he forgets me. He may leave me and abandon our partnership, our friendship and our pleasure, but he should not forget me." The thought persisted in her mind like a knot she could not undo. She brushed her dog until it yelped and cried and her cats until they hissed and clawed, seeking more wool to spin, but she could not keep herself busy.

The weaver came to her cottage. "When will you have more golden thread?" she asked. "All the women in town ask about it, with the merchant's wife showing off the golden dress she'll wear at her daughter's wedding."

"Is that who bought the dress?" Rianna asked.

"It is," said the weaver. "But we will not sell the cloth so cheaply again. The merchant has shown the cloth to a visiting noble from the court. I told him if he would have more to sell to them, it would cost at least twice what he paid before. He did not flinch. Will you spin more thread for me?"

"I cannot," said Rianna.

The weaver frowned. "Do not hold back on me now, girl," she said. "We have been together from the start. The merchant made his bargain with me."

"I cannot," Rianna said again. Rowan no longer brought the plants he found deep in the woods. Rowan no longer came at all.

"If you cannot bring me that thread," said the weaver, "see if I buy any thread from you again. Everyone spins. One spinner less means nothing."

By the next week Rianna still had nothing to spin. She went to town, hair bound carelessly and skirts hanging crooked. She discovered the weaver had spread stories she was mad, that she had made a dark bargain for her skills. No one would look at her eye-to-eye.

"I am not mad," she thought. "But if I cannot work,

I will be mad before the summer is out." She went from farm to farm in bare feet and trampled skirts to plead for flax and wool. From farm to farm she was turned away.

She found herself, near night, in the fringe of the woods, at the door to Rowan's cabin. Her rap was so faint it could barely be heard, but he opened the door and looked at her silently.

"They will not let me spin," she said. "They want the golden thread. They think I am mad. Without your pods I have nothing. Without you I do not sleep. You must help me find the pods."

"I am preparing for my wedding," said the woodcutter. "I have no time to hunt for pods."

"You know the woods and I do not. You must help me," she said. "With all that was between us."

"There was nothing between us." Rowan's voice was mild. "We have split the gold and our business is done."

"Something is yet between us," said Rianna.

"Go home," he said. "You can spin anything, spinner. Find something else to spin." He shut the door firmly.

The sun was nearly down and Rianna stumbled on her way to her cottage, cutting her feet and bruising her shins. In the dark she finally reached her home; in sobs she fell beside her wheel. She had nothing left to spin. She had nothing left. She had nothing but the ache in her heart and the memory of what was gone.

She turned her wheel.

She went to her little dresser and took a hairbrush from the lowest drawer. In it were caught Rowan's fair golden hairs amid her red ones. She brought it to the wheel and spun the hairs all together. They made the barest thread. But she could not stop spinning. Memories seemed to flow from her fingers. She spun how he had touched her, she spun how he had whispered to her, she spun how he had cried out. She spun her hopes and she spun her joys and she spun her tears. She could spin anything, and they were all she had to spin. She spun until the dawn.

There was nothing to see upon the wheel, not even the fair golden hairs or the red ones, but she took what she could not see between her fingers and twisted it upon itself. She twisted a cord of love and need, pain and want.

She tied one end of the cord to her wrist, wound the rest around her forearm, and went again to Rowan's cabin. He was not there. She pulled a handful of her red hair and tied it around the handle of his door, and went home to wait.

That afternoon Rowan came to her door. "I found this around my door handle," he said. He held the lock of red hair. "My future father-in-law came visiting and asked what it was." He threw the hair to the floor. "Stay away from my home. Our lives have gone their two ways and there is nothing between us, spinner. Forget me."

Rianna unspooled invisible cord from her forearm and grabbed the woodcutter's wrist. He made one startled noise before she tied the cord above his hand. Her unsteady heart took a new jump at the moment she knotted the knot.

"If there is nothing between us, then go," she said.

"I will," he whispered. He turned to leave. He took three steps. He stopped.

"Ah, Rianna!" he cried out. "Ah, what is it you have

done to me?'' He turned back to her, his eyes wide and
wild.

"Go," she said, with difficulty, each memory of the
two of them sharper and more painful than ever before.
"Go, now, if you can!"

"I cannot go," he said. His breath was ragged. "God
help me but I cannot." He caught her face in his hands
and kissed it. He fell shaking at her feet.

She took him into her cottage and in time made him
stop weeping. She promised he would not have to leave.

Three paces was the length of the cord. From that
moment Rowan did not depart three steps from her side.
At times, when he turned or rose or sat, she thought she
could see a glint of gold wind from his wrist to hers. At
times, out of the corner of her eye, she thought she saw
it growing deeper into the flesh of his arm.

Three days he wept at odd moments. Three nights he
called the name of another woman in his deepest sleep.
Three mornings he woke and stared at Rianna as though
wondering who she was. Each morning she kissed him
until the confusion slipped from his eyes, replaced with
need, and then with hope, and then with trust. Each day
he wept less. Each night he called out another woman's
name less frequently. And then, at last, he breathed
only, "Rianna."

Another week she kept the woodcutter at her side. For
long hours he would lay his head on her lap and she
would stroke his hair, feeling a peace she hadn't known
before. She did not spin and did not miss it. She had
enough gold to buy food for a year.

But she did not forget why she had spun him to her.
After three days and a week she said, "Rowan, do you
love me?"

"Ah, God, Rianna, I cannot live without you. You go

through and down to the bottom of me. Ah, Rianna, I do not understand how I did not see it before. I will always love you.''

She had spun the man to her. She could spin anything.

Now he had started talking, he would not stop. Every word he said, her heart echoed. ''We can live on love. Surely we can live on love. And if we have need of anything else, we can go to the woods together and gather that plant, and you can spin it for gold. But never leave my side, Rianna. You cannot leave me.''

He was the man who had broken her heart. He was the man on whom she planned revenge. He was the man she could love for the rest of her life. She picked up her heavy shears.

''You must never go,'' he said.

''I will go if I can,'' she said, and marveled at how steady her hand was as she cut the invisible cord between them. All color left Rowan's face, and he collapsed to the floor.

''You cannot leave,'' he said hoarsely. ''I cannot let you go. Rianna!''

She knew that he would never recover from her, and that now she could never recover from him.

''There is nothing between us,'' she said.

She turned and walked from her cottage; and she never returned in her lifetime or yours.

Weaver's Cottage

Terri Windling

A portrait of a place.
A house entered, and learned, and loved
with all the senses, the
cool light of reason, the
heat of the heart.
I touched the living flesh of its walls,
the crooked shipyard timber bones,
the granite carried from farmyard and moor and
piled by hands that four hundred years
have returned to Devon soil. I felt
the touch of the ghosts in the stone. I saw
the past as rising damp and
mist rolled down from Meldon Hill. I heard
hearts beat in walls of cob, the
past listening, hushed and still, while
fiddle and drum made music
to rise with the smoke
to the roof of straw.

Weave, he said.
Ribbons of color unfolded from my fingertips. Blue
when I filled a brush with paint, gold
when I opened a library book, earth brown
when I brewed my tea and carried it to the
    parlor. White
when I opened the morning mail. Ribbons of silver
covered my desk, words hammered out like jewelry
to lie upon the page. Forest green
and claret red as we lay abed in the moonless dark.
Weave, he said; that's why this is called
Weaver's Cottage, didn't you know?
This is your work. To weave it together.
To weave daily life into art.

Oldthings

Will Shetterly, P.J.F.

Jeffy got silver bullets, Jill got a matched pair of big golden crosses, and I got a lousy wooden stake. I sat cross-legged on the floor, looking at this three-foot-long pointed stick, and said, "What's this? A carve-your-own-cane kit?"

Poppa Fred had his sense of humor removed when he was four, I think. He said, "You know what it is, C.T."

Mother Dearest said, "There's a mallet, too."

"Oh, great," I said. When I shifted some wrapping paper, I found a hammer made of polished oak, like the stake.

"Frederick made it himself," Mother Dearest said. "For you."

Poppa Fred looked away like he didn't care.

Jeffy and Jill had collaborated on their presents for everybody: string necklaces with crude wooden crosses set between bulbs of garlic.

"See?" said Jeffy. "It's like, two-in-one."

"It was my idea," bragged Jill.

"That's great," I said. "You can pick your teeth with the wooden piece, and with that stinky garlic around your neck, you won't have to take a bath ever again."

Jeffy said, "No, C.T., the garlic's s'posed to keep off—" He stopped then 'cause Jill had begun to cry. Mother Dearest hugged her, of course, and made a face at me like I'd said something wrong. Poppa Fred just kept looking away at the window like he could see right through the wooden shutters.

And Grams kept on staring at the fireplace like no one was in the room at all.

I'm not always so grouchy, especially at Krizmiz. It's just that this was the first Krizmiz since Gram's brain went south. I loved her more than anyone, 'cause she'd known so much. Mother Dearest and Poppa Fred were trying to give us an old-fashioned Krizmiz, but they didn't understand it the way Grams did.

Grams knew the old stories about Krizmiz back before Thingschanged. Then Krizmiz wasn't a day of giving each other secondhand junk or stupid ugly homemade things. Before Thingschanged, Krizmiz was a season of its own. Stores put up decorations three months in advance, and the whole country worked together making wonderful stuff for everyone to buy. And on Krizmiz, everyone in the country got lots and lots of the wonderful stuff, and everyone was happy.

But after Thingschanged, none of the wonderful stuff worked, not the 'lectrical stuff or the mot'rized stuff. People went back to the country, 'cause in the cities, there were riots and fights and folks starving. And it was all made worse 'cause after Thingschanged, the Oldthings returned.

It was a drakla that got Gramper. It would've got us all

if Grams hadn't known what to do. There were lots of draklas for a while, men in dark suits and women in soft, shiny dresses, but the worst was when Gramper came back. Grams did what had to be done. She taught us all what to do, before she had her stroke.

Besides draklas, there were witchers, wolf-folk, dusty bandaged people, ghosters, and stiff, slow shufflers with glassy eyes. The safest thing was to stay in at night, so that's what we usually did. If an Oldthing did catch one of us out of doors, we took care of it—the same treatment worked on all of them.

Krizmizeve was a cold, windy night. Jeffy and Jill and I decided to sleep in the living room in front of the fireplace, near Grams. Jeffy and Jill were still mad at me, so they put their blankets on the far side of Grams's cot. It'd been a long day for the twins. They fell asleep almost immediately.

I lay there, watching the fire dying and listening to Grams breathing and wondering if things would ever get better for any of us. I was almost asleep when I heard a clompety sound on the roof like fat eagles had landed there. I remembered that the draklas and the witchers could fly. That woke me up completely. My Krizmiz stake was lying beside me, so I grabbed it and lay there, clutching it in both hands.

And then I felt stupid. We hadn't seen a drakla in two years, or a witcher in near as long. I told myself whatever I heard couldn't be an Oldthing. And even if it was, all the doors and windows were bolted. Nothing was going to get into our house. I looked at Jeffy and Jill and Grams, and I smiled, thinking I'd have to do something nice for the twins 'cause their stupid garlic crucifixes must've taken a lot of work. And I started to go back to sleep.

The fire was very low, hardly more than cinders, and my eyes were almost closed, but something made me look around again. I prob'ly heard a change in Grams's breathing, but I can't swear to that. I can swear to what happened next, though.

Two heavy black boots oozed out of the fireplace.

I don't know why I didn't scream. Maybe I still didn't believe it. Maybe the Oldthing in the chimney had some power to make people drowsy. I think that was it. I think if I'd been completely asleep, I wouldn't be here to tell this story.

After the black boots came bloodred trousers, and then a matching crimson coat edged with bone-white fur, and finally a bloated, grinning Oldthing stood in front of our fire. It was too fat to have squeezed down our chimney—Jeffy or Jill couldn't have squeezed down that chimney—yet there it was. Its eyes were black beads, and its bloated cheeks were bright red as if it'd fed on something's blood, and in its ash-white beard, its soft mouth twisted into a triumphant leer.

Grams spoke. "Sa? Tah?"

It spun, maybe even more startled than me, and faced her. Grams hadn't talked in months. She sat up in her cot and she smiled madly, and she twitched while she tried to say something to the Oldthing or to the rest of us.

The Oldthing brought a red-gloved finger to its thick lips and grinned. In its other hand, it clutched a sack that'd grown to be as large as the Oldthing itself, maybe larger. It stepped closer toward Grams, still making the gesture for silence. It pointed at Jeffy and Jill, sound asleep, as if Grams should understand.

But I understood then. It didn't matter whether it had something in that sack to deal with us or whether it wanted to stuff us all into the sack to carry us off. Grams had done all she could by speaking. It was up to me now.

"Satan!" I yelled, leaping out of bed in my nightdress with my Krizmiz stake ready.

The Lord of Night whirled toward me. Its eyes and its maw gaped in surprise. I plunged the stake toward its heart as it staggered back toward the chimney. The point grazed its chest, but I was too slow. I knew that it'd escape, and return with its servants, and everything would be my fault.

Then it stumbled. Something had struck it in the head. I glanced at the twins' bed, and Jill grinned back. One crucifix lay on the floor at the feet of the wounded Oldthing. The other was in Jill's cocked hand, ready to throw.

A shot rang out. The Oldthing stumbled, clutching its leg. I saw Jeffy fumbling to load another silver bullet into his .22, but it didn't matter. He'd given me the time I needed. I hurled myself forward as Grams cried out again.

When Mother Dearest and Poppa Fred came into the room, they saw that they'd given me a fine present. Jill said, "C.T. killed it," and I smiled, shy and proud all at once. Poppa Fred nodded at me. Before he could say anything, we heard a clattering on the roof.

We ran into the yard, all except Grams. A team of antlered deer were launching themselves into the sky, dragging a blood-dark sleigh behind them. Poppa Fred's blast of silver buckshot took out the leader. With it hanging in the traces, the rest were easy targets.

We smoked and ate the stringy little deer, all except the mutated one with a glowing nose. In the Oldthing's sack, we found toys and tools and clothes and all kinds of wonderful things, just perfect for each of us. Since we didn't know who it'd stolen them from, we had to keep them for ourselves.

That would've been the most perfect Krizmiz ever if Grams had lived. We found her in the living room. I find it comforting to know that the last thing she saw was me killing the evilest of the Oldthings.

Before her stroke, Grams had often said that if we survived the bad Oldthings coming back, good Oldthings might follow. I think she was right. Early this spring, when the last of the little deer had been eaten and we were afraid we'd all starve, a giant rabbit with a basket of eggs showed up on our lawn. That gave us meat for a month.

It's a fine new world. I only wish Grams was here to see.

About the Authors

Carol Jane Bangs is the author of two collections of
poetry, including *Bones of the Earth* (New Directions).
Director of Centrum, the prestigious summer writing
conference in Port Townsend, she lives in Washington
with her boat-building husband and two children.

Marvin Bell is a prize-winning poet, author of ten books
of poetry, and the Flannery O'Connor Professor of Letters
at the University of Iowa. Among his many awards are
the Lamont Prize of the Academy of American Poets,
Guggenheim and National Endowments as well as
Fulbright appointments to Yugoslavia and Australia.

Bruce Boston has published fiction and poetry in many
magazines and anthologies, including *Amazing, Asimov's,
Year's Best Fantasy and Horror,* and *Year's Best Horror*. His
poetry has won many awards, including three Rhyslings,
given each year by the Science Fiction Poetry
Association. His first novel, *Stained Glass Rain,* has just
appeared from Ocean View Books.

George Mackay Brown was born in 1921 in Orkney in
Scotland and has spent all his life there. He is the author
of many novels, volumes of short stories, books of

279

poetry, plays, two nonfiction books, and children's stories. He writes a weekly column for the *Orcadian* and his stories and poems and plays are frequently broadcast over the BBC.

Milbre Burch is a professional storyteller and recording artist who performs her material throughout the United States. Known nationally for her work as a monologuist and performer, she has delighted audiences from Maui to Martha's Vineyard. She lives in California with her journalist husband and young daughter.

Diane Duane's many novels include several Star Trek books, the *Door into Shadow* series, and the popular young adult books *So You Want to Be a Wizard* and its sequels. She has also written Saturday morning cartoon scripts and numerous short stories. She lives with her novelist husband Peter Morwood in Ireland.

Carol Edelstein leads a writers' workshop in Northampton, Massachusetts, where she lives. She has published poetry and stories in a number of journals and anthologies including, most recently, *Flash Fiction*.

Barbara Hambly describes herself as a novelist who writes sword-and-sorcery, only branching into short stories in the past year or so. She has also written Star Trek novels and novelizations of the TV show *Beauty and the Beast* as well as fantasy and historical fiction. She holds a

master's degree in medieval history and lives in Los
Angeles.

Richard Kearns has been working in publishing for more
than twenty years. He is currently a freelance writer,
editor, and graphic designer in the Los Angeles area,
where he has also been an aerobics instructor for the
past ten years. He has written award-winning short
fiction and is now at work on two novels. He lives with
his professor wife in Los Angeles.

Tappan King, author (with Viido Polikarpus) of the
acclaimed novel *Down Town,* was for a time editor of the
magazine *Twilight Zone.* He is the author of a number of
published short stories, as well as an SF novel, *Escape
Velocity,* to be published next year. He lives with his
editor wife in Tucson, Arizona, along with three cats.

Rose Kremers, a member of Wyoming Writers, lives in
Niobrara County, Wyoming. A graduate of Colorado
State University and a former English teacher, she and
her husband and two sons own a cattle ranch. Her story
''The Executioner'' won the prize for best short story at
Boskone, a Massachusetts science fiction/fantasy
convention.

Ursula K. Le Guin has won the Nebula, the Hugo, the
World Fantasy Award, and the National Book Award for
her novels, short stories, and poetry. Such books as *A*

Wizard of Earthsea, The Left Hand of Darkness, and collections of stories such as *The Compass Rose* have brought her international acclaim. She lives in Oregon.

Megan Lindholm lives on a small farm in rural Roy, Washington. A novelist (*Cloven Hooves, Wizard of the Pigeons,* and others), she also gardens and raises poultry. Her four children range in age from one to twenty-one.

Patricia A. McKillip is the award-winning author of *The Riddle Master of Hed, The Sorceress and the Cygnet,* and other novels. Born in Salem, Oregon, she currently lives in Roxbury, New York.

Sandra Rector and P M F Johnson are a husband and wife writing team who have sold short stories to a number of anthologies and over two hundred articles to such publications as *East/West* and *Washington Post.* They live in Boston, Massachusetts.

Jessica Amanda Salmonson is a well-known fantasy and horror novelist who has often written about a fictionalized medieval Japan as well as about women in the martial arts. A critic of the cultural scene, she also publishes with the small presses, often helping reestablish the reputations of women writers long hidden. She lives in Seattle, Washington.

Delia Sherman is a teacher and a novelist who lives in the Boston area. Her recent novel, *The Porcelain Dove,* has garnered much critical acclaim. Her short fiction has appeared in all the major genre magazines.

Will Shetterly, P.J.F. is a novelist *(Elsewhere, Cats Have No Lord)* as well as a writer of comics *(Captain Confederacy).* He co-edited, with his wife Emma Bull, five collections of short stories about the magical city Liavek. He is also the publisher of SteelDragon Press, which produces limited-edition books as well as CDs and tapes. He lives in Minneapolis.

Susan Solomont has published poetry in a number of literary magazines. She is a professor of English at Springfield College in Massachusetts.

Martha Soukup is a San Francisco short story writer whose work has been nominated for the Hugo, the Nebula, and the World Fantasy Award. A past secretary of the Science Fiction Writers of America, she does not claim to be working on a novel.

Mary A. Turzillo, a 1985 Clarion graduate, has sold a number of stories to magazines and anthologies. She is also—as Mary T. Brizzi—the author of critical   ` biographies of Anne McCaffrey and Philip José Farmer. She teaches at Kent State University and lives with her young son in Warren, Ohio.

Vivian Vande Velde has published short stories for adults and children in such diverse magazines as *Cricket* and *Amazing* as well as a number of novels, including *User Unfriendly* and *Dragon's Bait,* a selection of the Junior Library Guild. She lives in Rochester, New York, with her husband and teenage daughter.

Barbara Van Noord has published poems in over eighty journals. In her "other life," she is a full-time psychiatric social worker, running a mental health department for an HMO. She lives in Amherst, Massachusetts.

Thomas Wiloch writes what he calls "prose miniatures and poetry of a cynical/visionary nature." His seven chapbook collections include *Tales of Lord Shantih* and *Narcotic Signature.* He lives in Canton, Michigan, and works for Gale Research, Inc., the reference book publisher.

Terri Windling is an editor, author, and artist, winning awards in all three fields. As editor, she put together the Fairy Tales series and serves as an editorial consultant to Tor Books' fantasy line. Her annual anthology in collaboration with Ellen Datlow, *The Year's Best Fantasy and Horror,* has won the World Fantasy Award three times. She has published short fiction and poetry and has novels forthcoming from Tor and Bantam Books. Her artwork is in private collections worldwide. She lives in Tucson, Arizona, and Devon, England.

t. Winter-Damon has published poetry in innumerable small-press publications, journals, and anthologies. He lives in Tucson, Arizona.

Jane Yolen, called "America's Hans Christian Andersen," is the award-winning author of over 130 books. She has won the Kerlan Award and the Regina Medal for her work in children's books. Her picture book *Owl Moon* won the prestigious Caldecott Medal. And her adult books have won the World Fantasy Award, the Mythopoeic Society Award, and been nominated three times for the Nebula. The editor of the Jane Yolen Books fantasy and SF imprint for Harcourt Brace's childrens book department, she lives with her husband in Hatfield, Massachusetts, and St. Andrews, Scotland.